SCRAMBLED
A TUESDAY NIGHT
BOOK CLUB MYSTERY

What Reviewers Say About Jaime Maddox's Work

Bouncing

"Jaime Maddox, Jaime Maddox. She always seems to start out with these feel good lesbian romances. You're reading along, enjoying the fun and light ride, and then—BAM—you get hit with the twisty and suddenly the light ride turns into a twisty, turney awesome mess."
—Danielle Kimerer, Librarian, Reading Public Library (Reading, MA)

Deadly Medicine

"The tale ran at a good, easy pace. ...It was one of those books that it is hard to put down, so I didn't. ...Very, very well done."—*Prism Book Alliance*

Hooked

"[A] compelling, insightful and passionate romantic thriller."—*Lesfic Tumblr*

[Maddox] did an excellent job of portraying the struggles of addiction, not the entire focus of the story, but informative just the same. ...All the characters are deep, bringing them to life with their complexities. An intricately woven story line adds credibility; life leaps from the pages."—*Lunar Rainbow Reviewz*

By the Author

Agnes

Bouncing

The Common Thread

Deadly Medicine

Hooked

Love Changes Everything

Repatriate

The Scholarship

Paris Rules

Scrambled: A Tuesday Night Book Club Mystery

SCRAMBLED
A TUESDAY NIGHT BOOK CLUB MYSTERY

by

Jaime Maddox

2024

ISBN 13: 978-1-63679-703-8

THIS TRADE PAPERBACK ORIGINAL IS PUBLISHED BY
BOLD STROKES BOOKS, INC.
P.O. BOX 249
VALLEY FALLS, NY 12185

FIRST EDITION: OCTOBER 2024

CREDITS
EDITOR: SHELLEY THRASHER
PRODUCTION DESIGN: SUSAN RAMUNDO
COVER DESIGN BY TAMMY SEIDICK

Acknowledgments

I would like to thank all the great ladies at Bold Strokes Books who made this and all my books possible—Rad, Sandy, Cindy, and my fabulous editor, Shelley Thrasher. You're all much appreciated. Thanks as well to my friends at the Tuesday Night Book Club for your friendship and the inspiration for the characters in this book. I hope for many more TNBC adventures to come. Margaret, thank you for teaching me big words and for your peregrine falcon-like editorial eye. Carolyn, Jamison, Max, Linda, and Carol—you all inspire me to shoot for the stars, and help me to reach them. Finally, thanks to all of you who read my words and learn, or smile, or think. You make it worthwhile.

Dedication

Yankee

If I could say only one more thing to you, after all these
years of talking about every little thing, it would be this:
Thank you. Whenever it is that I draw the last breath
into my lungs, it will be with you in my heart.

XOXO Doc

CHAPTER ONE

September 11, 2001

Curtis Hutchins slipped from beneath the sheets as soon as the alarm sounded. On the other side of the bed, his wife stirred, but if Morgan was awake, she didn't let on. And that was a relief, because talking to her was a strain, even on the best of days, for both of them. So she'd started pretending she didn't hear him as he began his day, and he pretended he didn't notice.

Padding quietly across the dark room, he eased open the door and stepped into the hallway, then turned toward the guest suite. This was his real domain, the place of his desk and his clothes, the recliner from which he could peacefully watch a game or catch up on the news. It was where he found quiet time to think, to dream of what his life might have been like had he made different choices. It was the place he plotted the changes that would set things right again. And after almost a year of scheming and maneuvering, thieving and deceiving, today was the day. It was the last day of his life.

In the bathroom he quickly readied himself, going about his business as normally as possible. His reflection didn't betray him: outwardly, he had the same sandy hair, the same dark eyes, the same smile. It was inside where the chaos revealed itself in a racing heart and rapid breaths, a gurgling stomach that made him appreciate the lavish bathroom. Calm down, he told himself. It's all going to be fine. Just put one foot in front of the other. Repeat.

When he finished in the bathroom, boxers and silk socks came next, and then a tailored suit from the walk-in closet. After dressing quickly, he turned to assess the room. The T-shirt and shorts he'd slept in were folded and put away, and the closet and bathroom doors closed. The papers on his desk—none of them important—were organized and stacked, and would give no hint at the thoughts that had passed through his mind as he sat at that desk planning for this day. The chair was pushed in, the garbage can aligned just so beside it. Sighing, he allowed himself a moment of satisfaction. There was no sign he'd even been here.

In the hallway he turned the handle of a door and peeked into his son's bedroom. Jon was sleeping, his sandy hair a mess on the pillow, the resemblance to Curt undeniable. His looks were the limit of their similarities, though. Jonathon's personality was all Morgan—outgoing, outlandish at times. From infancy, this boy had startled his father with his energy and will, and he continued to do so. Curtis worried what would become of his son, but he also understood he had little control in the matter. The children were Morgan's job, and little he said changed her opinions or the direction in which she steered them.

Across the hall, he opened the door to Avery's room. His daughter, the image of her mom with her Mediterranean skin and hair tones, was the best part of him. Innocent, sweet, intelligent, she loved him best. Avery had been an attempt to fix their marriage, a failed attempt, but the best thing he'd ever done. The one thing that broke his heart, that made him reconsider his plans, was Avery.

He didn't have time for those thoughts now, though. No time to feel. If he'd been inclined to do something typical like getting a divorce and shuttling kids back and forth on weekends, he would have made different plans. This one didn't include his children, and it allowed no room for emotion.

Still, he walked into the room, knelt beside Avery's bed, and kissed her softly. For a moment he closed his eyes, breathed in the scent of whatever soap and shampoo Morgan used to keep her clean, and tears formed in his eyes. *I'll miss you, Avery.*

Beside her bed was a picture she'd drawn and colored, and he smiled as he looked at it. Morgan had brought her to the office a few weeks earlier, and while his wife talked with her dad, who happened to be Curt's boss, Curt had taken Avery to the observation deck in the

South Tower, and they'd enjoyed the view. He loved looking out of his window in the North Tower, and he had binoculars in his desk for just that purpose. Avery delighted in gazing through their lenses and seeing the boats in the river and the tall buildings, but mostly the Statue of Liberty. Morgan was currently at work procuring a Halloween costume of Lady Liberty in size four.

The drawing, colored using every crayon in the box, from the looks of it, showed the two of them, sitting atop the tower, their legs dangling down about twenty floors, looking through their binoculars.

When he'd come home and saw the picture, he immediately took her out and bought binoculars just for her, and they were now sitting beside the drawing on her table.

"Fuck." He sighed as he looked at his daughter. "Fuck, fuck, fuck," he said as he turned and walked from the room, her picture in his hand.

Navigating the hallway and stairs in the dark, he crossed the foyer on the main floor and cut across the kitchen to the mudroom and the garage beyond. This time he didn't hesitate, didn't stop for one more look at his life. As he backed his Mercedes sedan from the garage, it was still dark outside. He glanced at the clock. 5:10 a.m.

Curt cut across the rolling country roads in Livingston, New Jersey and pulled into traffic on I78 toward his office in Manhattan. It amazed him, the traffic. Why did he do it? Why did anyone? But his father-in-law, the founder of MGT Investments, felt the office at the World Trade Center was good for business. Seeing and being seen, whether in the lobby or the elevator or at the restaurant in the sky, put you in the front of people's minds, so when they had financial questions, they thought of you first. That was all wonderful, but it meant that he and fifty other employees of Morgan-Gloria-Tiffany had to suck exhaust fumes twice a day on their commutes to work. He envied the regular guys, the three hundred other employees, who worked in New Jersey and the other boroughs of New York.

Thirty minutes later, Curt exited the interstate and made a series of turns that put him in the driveway of a walk-up in Jersey City Heights. Using his remote, he opened the garage door and entered that way, closing it behind him.

From the stairs he heard the radio, a commercial playing on New York City's Z100. And then he heard a soft humming, and it made him smile. *This is the right thing.*

"Good morning," he called softly. "Is anyone up yet?"

Yvonne took a step from the kitchen into the foyer and blew him a kiss. "I have a quiche for you later. But do you want to go up on the deck? We can do sunrise yoga."

Her long, dark hair was pulled up, and she wore a tight T-shirt and stretchy yoga pants that clung to her every curve. Even without makeup, her flawless skin glowed. She was thirty years old, five years younger than him, but the choices she'd made had been good ones. She could have passed for a college student.

Curt puckered his lips as he took two long strides and pulled her into his arms. "Do you have any idea what my day is going to be like?" he asked with a soft kiss to her lips.

Her eyes opened wide, and she nodded. "I do."

"And you want me to be late for work so we can do yoga?"

She kissed the tip of his nose. "That's precisely why you should do yoga. Your tension is going to be crazy, and you'll need to summon an inner calm."

Curt nuzzled her neck. "You turn me on when you talk like that. Can we just go to bed and meditate there?"

"Soon, we'll be able to go to bed whenever we want. But today, you can have yoga and quiche or coffee and quiche, but no sex and quiche."

He pulled back and frowned before grinning. "I'll see you on the roof," he said, and walked up the stairs to the bedroom he considered his. He'd given Yvonne the money to buy the walk-up two years earlier, and it was clean, with no trace of him on any paperwork. He'd met her when she'd done a corporate yoga clinic at a conference in Boston, and they'd talked about their city—New York—and other mindless things. They'd talked and talked and talked, and since that night, everything Curt had done had built toward where he was now. Ready to move on, out of Morgan's life and into Yvonne's.

Carefully placing his suit over the back of a chair, Curt pulled on shorts and a muscle shirt. He'd always been slim, but with Yvonne's guidance in the gym, he'd bulked up in the past two years. It could have been his age making him thicken a little, but he thought it really was the extra work. Before he met her, he'd spent hours every week in the gym, with little to show for it. Since she started working with him, he liked what he saw in the mirror. His body looked good.

Shoeless, Curt opened the door and walked up another flight of stairs to the roof, where he turned to see the first hint of dawn across the river. The New York City skyline was still dark, but an orange outline was already visible and promised a beautiful day.

Yvonne was already there, resting on her mat. Taking his place on his, he followed her softly spoken commands. Knees to chest, breath out, heels to the heavens. And even though he'd done this same thing hundreds of times, he was still surprised to feel the tension leaving his body. He felt relaxed, and, as was usually the case when he was in Yvonne's company, he was happy.

Twenty minutes later they were done, and he kissed her as he looked out at the magnificent sunrise. It's hard to give this up, he thought, and for a moment his breath caught as he wondered what he was doing. Because what he was doing was insane. Unimaginable. Criminal.

He heard her sigh, and she pulled him close, sensing the change in him. "Have you put all the pieces in place?"

"Yes."

"Is the paperwork in order?"

"Yes."

"Do you want to be with me?"

"Yes," he whispered as he kissed her head.

"Then let's do this."

Following her down the stairs, Curt changed back into his suit and followed the smell of coffee all the way into the kitchen. His mug sat beside hers on the island, and he eased onto the bar stool and took a sip. As usual, she had prepared it perfectly and turned around as he was smiling into his cup.

"What's that smile for?"

His grin broadened. "It's bliss. Good coffee is bliss."

"Even decaf?" she asked as she carefully placed a 4×4 inch-square pastry before him.

"I don't even notice anymore." He didn't tell her that his secretary kept the break-room fridge stocked with Coke, or that he'd often have a cup of coffee when he arrived at the office, and again in the mid-afternoon, when he felt his edge softening.

Cutting the food with his fork, he tasted the first bite and moaned. "Wow."

"Right? I found a new bakery, and this was on the menu."

"That's a keeper."

"You're a keeper. Maybe I'll open a coffee shop in Garden and bring things like this from the city."

They'd purchased their escape property just a hundred miles away, so her suggestion was possible. He could see her doing that, serving healthy food in the front under the notes of harps and flutes and guitars. Beyond, on wall-to-wall mats framed by mirrors, people in stretchy clothes would tone their bodies and spirits.

What would he do, though? Yvonne could simply be herself, in a new place. His days as a fund manager were over, and the only other jobs he'd had involved serving alcohol and fast food. Not that he'd have to work—he wouldn't need the money. But he'd need something to keep him busy. Maybe he'd take up golf, he thought with a laugh. He could join his father-in-law's country club.

The thought made him smile. "Tomorrow, after yoga, we're going back to bed."

Smiling, she walked a few steps and turned to him. "How about tonight?" She opened a cupboard door. From within, she pulled out a package, about the size of a mini-football, wrapped in bubble wrap. "Catch," she commanded as she mocked throwing it.

He laughed. "Talk about safe and secure."

Smiling, she pulled two more identical packages from the cupboard, closed the door, and came around the island. Kissing him softly on the lips, she placed the packages in his hands. "The safe at the Garden house will withstand a nuclear blast. I didn't think it was a worry here."

Curt made the motions of weighing them. "Hard to believe, isn't it? Something so small…"

"Human beings are idiots," she said. Unlike his wife, who treasured status and possessions, Yvonne treasured the simple things. His future with her was still taking shape in his mind, but he knew it would be so much less complicated than the one he lived now. He'd need money, of course, and thanks to his illegal activities, he had plenty. After today, he'd have even more. He looked at the spheres in bubble wrap in his hands. Plenty more. What he'd need most was anonymity, and the money could really help with that. He'd already shelled out more than a million in cash on the Pocono property and renovations to the house there, but it was a vast estate, which ensured the level of privacy they needed.

"One more thing," Yvonne said as she walked to the closet and opened it, pulling a new briefcase out before closing it again. She was as fastidious as he was. It was just one more thing he loved about her.

"This is it, huh?" he asked as he inspected it. It didn't look like much, but he knew it cost a fortune. He would never have chosen it, but it was just a small detail that they'd had to take care of to ensure today went as planned. "A genuine Ferragamo," he said softly. Morgan probably had a dozen of them in her walk-in dressing room, but it had been a long time since he'd noticed such things about her.

Yvonne smiled. "Brown leather with brown leather trim."

"It looks sort of casual," he said as he placed the packages on the counter and took the bag from her. As he opened and inspected the two compartments inside, she offered more details.

"It's a messenger bag, so it *is* a bit casual, but it'll fit our little treasures."

"Lynn will probably notice, and she'll mention it to Jonathon. But by then, it'll be over." He handed her the bag, and she rested it on the counter, then held out her hand.

He gave her the first package. After she nestled it into the bag, he handed her the others, and she placed them beside the first, then fastened the flap and the snap and shook it. "Safe and secure."

Standing, he draped the strap over his shoulder. "How do I look?"

"Rich and successful."

Curt shrugged. He probably did. His suit had been made for him, and the shoes cost more than his first car. The bag, he knew, had a four-figure price tag. Yet he looked at Yvonne, in her yoga clothes and no makeup, glowing with the light of life, and he knew he wouldn't miss such shoes and bags.

She seemed to sense his thoughts. "You can still change your mind."

He shook his head. "Nope. My days are numbered. I could walk in today and have a problem, if someone was nosy or astute enough to check their account closely. It's time."

"You're right. It is. Now go. And good luck," she said as she pulled away.

"My Aunt Kathy once told me good luck is all you need. Because with bad luck, you're not getting very far."

"Well, good luck, and planning, and cunning, and a few other things, too. Whew. When will I see you tonight?"

Curt screwed up his mouth as he pondered the question. After today, he had no reason to stay at work, but leaving too early might arouse suspicions. To buy himself a few days, he'd told Morgan and her father that he had some business meetings starting tomorrow. They wouldn't question his absence until at least Friday. As long as no one inquired about missing funds from their account, they wouldn't pay any attention.

"I'll leave at the normal time. Sixish."

Staring into his eyes, she nodded, and her shoulders dropped an inch as she took a deep breath and exhaled. "I wish I could tell you nothing will go wrong. But I can't. You've done everything you can to protect yourself, and this will be fine."

He pulled her closer. "Yes, it's going to be fine. And it'll all be worth it." He said it again under his breath, a dozen times, willing his words to come true.

CHAPTER TWO

The Holland Tunnel was predictably backed up at seven when Curt entered the queue to cross beneath the Hudson River and into Manhattan. Once through, he headed downtown toward the tip of the island, then followed the traffic already pouring into the underground garage at the World Trade Center. From the West Street entrance, he circled down to his reserved space on level B3, then took the elevator to the concourse and walked across to the next one. The World Trade Center was the first complex in the world to use both express and local elevators, and Curt couldn't even imagine what it would be like if he had to wait while people got off at various floors on the way to his office near the top.

As he navigated the opulent lobby, he passed multiple security officers. Their presence had never bothered him before. Today, he swallowed as one approached, then sighed as he walked by. After the elevator door dinged, Curt happily climbed aboard the car. He glanced at his watch. 7:33. He was late.

He shouldn't have done yoga. Instead of being relaxed, he was stressed about being tardy. And now he felt rushed. More potential witnesses were arriving at the North Tower every minute. Although he knew his father-in-law golfed on Tuesday mornings, others there might see him, wonder what he was doing coming out of Jonathon's office. They might say something to Jonathon. This was, without question, the biggest moment of his life, and he was more anxious than he could ever remember being.

I need an excuse, a reason for going into Jonathon's office, just in case someone notices. A minute later, he exited the elevator to the sky lobby on the 78th floor, walked thirty feet, and waited with twenty other people for the elevator to his floor, thinking as he walked along.

He had few excuses to enter Jonathon's office. The only thing they had in common other than their work was their family. And there it was—the reason. Avery's picture. He'd stop in the admin's office and make a color copy, and he'd leave it for Jonathon.

Since MGT occupied much of the floor, he exited the elevator when the door opened and strolled only a few feet into the massive lobby. The receptionist wasn't at her desk, and he veered to the left, around the counter space, and into the executive suites.

He made it to the private corridor near his office without seeing anyone. A half-dozen lights were on, though, which was typical. He reached the private-executive lobby and found that empty as well. Officially, the support staff was supposed to be at their desks at seven thirty, but Curt rarely found them anywhere other than the break room until the first meeting of the day began, when their bosses began assigning them jobs to complete. Sherry, the personal assistant he shared with the other VPs, operated in much the same fashion. He was sure she was already there, preparing coffee or depositing her lunch in the break room, but for now, her desk in the small sitting area guarding the administrative offices was empty. He sighed with relief.

Like Sherry's, most offices in the MGT suite were on the interior of the massive building, with no windows. Such was the hallway he navigated. Near the end, he keyed the lock and walked into a 20×20-foot space, the office he'd occupied for the ten years he'd worked here. It was a vice-president's office, one of three identical setups, but he was married to the president's daughter, so his door was located across from the largest office on the floor.

After placing his bag on his desk, he took a moment, as he always did, to marvel at the view. Even though the windows were narrow, they ran from floor to ceiling, and he could see north along both rivers, from New Jersey to Queens and Brooklyn, and the entire island of Manhattan. The sight was mesmerizing—the sheer mass of buildings, one taller than the next, their proximity to each other, and the millions of people who called New York home. From this height he couldn't see them, those people, but he could see their cars on the streets and bridges, the buses that shuttled them all over the city, moving in mostly straight lines, marching like soldiers.

Curt sighed. He wouldn't miss much about his job at MGT, but he'd miss this view.

Turning away from the skyline, he deposited the messenger bag on the desk and pulled Avery's drawing from the inside pocket of his suit. Back in the lobby, he quickly copied it, then returned the original to its place and headed back to his office. Still no sign of Sherry.

Moving quickly, he went to work. Opening the messenger bag, he removed the bubble-wrapped packages. With great care, he teased away the edge of plastic and unraveled the layers, one by one. And then, there it was, a five-inch bejeweled orb and its golden pedestal, a copy of one of Fabergé's eggs, the key to his future.

Though this was not his first time to inspect this copy of the Imperial Palaces egg, Curt marveled at it. With its bright blue-sky enamel and tiny stones of every color, the egg sparkled. He was told the stones alone were worth millions. But it wasn't just the stones that made this piece valuable. It was a masterpiece of design, a creation of Peter Carl Fabergé or one of his assistants, and it was as unique as a Picasso or a Renoir. It was one of a kind, and Curt knew it was worth every bit of the money he'd get for it.

He chuckled to himself. The real one would be, anyway. The piece in his hand, complete with a four-car train carrying tiny replicas of the Russian royal family from their Winter Palace in St. Petersburg to the Alexander Palace in Tsarskoe Selo, had cost only about a thousand dollars.

He put the egg down and unrolled the second package. Moving just as carefully, he uncovered the shining, golden replica of the Turn of the Century egg. This one was also encrusted with carvings and jewels, each depicting Russia's great advances in the nineteenth century. Pavel Shilling's telegraph, as well as a ballerina, a miniature of *Last Day of Pompeii* by Karl Bryullov, and others. Curt knew all this, not because he was a student of fine art, but because his father-in-law had bragged about these eggs since purchasing them a dozen years earlier. One for each of his girls—a wife and two daughters. What would Morgan think when, one day, she discovered they were fakes?

Curt only hoped that day was a long time off, that no one suspected he had taken the eggs as well as all that money on his way out the door.

Just as cautiously he unwrapped the final egg, this one a replica of the Victoria egg, made by Fabergé for the last tsar to impress Britain's great monarch, his wife's grandmother, Queen Victoria. Victoria's birth name was Alexandrina, and the Tsarina of Russia, born in Germany, had been named for her. The egg, a replica of the globe representing Britain's vast empire, was gold and enamel and jewels, and inside was a miniature portrait of the queen and her namesake.

A glance at the clock on his desk told him Sherry would be back soon. He cocked his head and listened, yet heard nothing but his own breathing. As usual, the office was quiet.

He took a moment to breathe. From now on, he had to remain calm and do what he'd been rehearsing for months. He exhaled and went to work.

First, he loosely draped each egg in its bubble wrap and put them back into the messenger bag. Next, he removed the key to Jonathon's office from his ring. It would be easier to pocket it off the ring, and after this moment, he'd no longer need to worry about losing the copy he'd made one night when his father-in-law had too much to drink. Finally, he glanced out the door and down the hallway. Finding it clear, he crossed the space between the two doors and slid the key into the lock. This was the only door in the suite that didn't have a combination, a security measure Jonathon had taken to protect his secrets. Curt smiled at the thought, and after the knob turned in his hand, he pushed the door open an inch before returning to his own office. There, he picked up the messenger bag and hustled across the hallway again.

Once inside Jonathon's spacious suite, he closed the door and leaned against it. It was the corner office, with two walls of windows, and for a second the bright morning light blinded him. Blinking, he walked to his right, past the custom glass cabinet displaying three eggs. Like the ones in his bag, they were fake. The real eggs were just a few feet away, in the large safe tucked into the closet at the back of the room.

Pausing in front of Jonathon's huge antique desk, he glanced at the photo that sat prominently to one side. Three smiling women stared back at him, the women for whom this firm was named. Morgan on the left, the first-born, a beauty on the outside but rotten inside, spoiled by the wealth of her family. She looked like a Greek goddess, all bronzed and curvy, her dark hair cascading over one shoulder and with a phony mega-watt smile for the camera. Gloria in the middle, the glue that held them all together, a beauty herself, a forecast of what Morgan would look like in thirty years. But Gloria was a wonderful human being and a genuinely kind woman, and it showed. Her smile looked joyful. And on the right was Tiffany, who didn't have the looks of her mother and sister, but more brains and heart than most of the people working in this building filled with financial wizards. Her smile seemed to suggest amusement. He'd miss Tiffany, just a little.

He'd gazed at that photo hundreds of times over the years, and it always struck him. Once, when he'd been in love with Morgan, he'd thought of asking Jonathon for a copy of it. But it had been the only photo on the desk then, and something told him it was a private treasure he wouldn't want to share. So Curt peppered his desk with his own photos, some of Morgan, and then baby Jon, and eventually Avery.

Glancing at the photos opposite the three Giles women, Curt looked at the smiling faces of his children, images captured by the school photographer. Tiffany's two kids were sandwiched between his, and so Jonathon and Gloria had four grandchildren in the same number of years. He couldn't believe how much they'd all changed since last fall, when all these photos were taken. How much would they change before he saw them again? Would he ever see them again?

For a second, he questioned his sanity. What was he doing? But too much was already done, and he saw no way out but forward.

He turned, and a few more steps carried him to the closet door. This time a combination lock stood in his way. He punched the code and the door buzzed, and in a second he'd closed it safely behind him. Next came the eggs, one by one from the bag and into a nest on top of the large safe that covered much of the back wall of the closet.

He went to work on the lock.

Who would have thought a man with a mind for money like Jonathon Giles wouldn't be able to remember the combination to his safe? Years ago, Curt could hardly believe his luck when he saw it—a pink sticky note, plastered on the door to the safe. Jonathon had sent Curt into the closet to retrieve a clean shirt after he'd soiled one, and there it was. Neon pink, practically blinding him. The paper was blank, except for three numbers scrawled in black ink. They could have meant anything, but considering their location, he knew their significance.

At his first opportunity, Curt went back to the office and tried the combination he'd committed to memory, amazed at what he'd learned about his father-in-law.

Now as he twisted the dial, he felt a surge of confidence. He was a clever man, and he'd planned his moves carefully. He was going to have the life he wanted, and the means to finance it was on the other side of the thick steel door. He held his breath, as he always did when he was snooping in the safe, and slowly released it as the handle glided across neutral and the door sprang open.

The eggs were on the top shelf in the safe, all in wooden boxes Jonathon had made for them. The first one he pulled contained the Palaces egg, and Curt easily switched the copy for the original and wrapped it, then placed it in his messenger bag before returning the box to the safe. He repeated the process with the second egg. As he was switching the Turn of the Century egg, Curt heard a muffled voice, then another that he recognized as his father-in-law's.

Fuck, he thought. What happened to golf? He never missed golf, not for bad weather or illness and especially not for work. Even on the day his playing partner had suffered a massive heart attack and died, Jonathon had still gotten in eighteen holes. The office joke was he'd called the man's widow to offer condolences when he'd had a minute on the long ride from the front nine to the back.

Curt looked around, then began moving. As quietly as he could, he returned the box to the shelf, closed the safe door and locked it, then looked around for a place to hide. The closet was a little bigger than a typical walk-in, but laid out just the same, with a shoe carousel and rack holding suits and coats and ties and shirts, even a pair of tuxedos, identical except for their color, one in black, the other in white. But there was no sub-closet of large drawers, no boxes of junk to use as cover. If Jonathon noticed a light leaking from beneath the closet door, Curt was fucked.

After hitting the light switch, he positioned himself in the corner on the opposite side of the door, beside the safe. Pulling some clothing toward him, he did the best he could to camouflage himself, but in the darkness, it was hard to measure the success of his efforts. If Jonathon did more than glance into the closet, he would likely be discovered, and his mind raced with plausible explanations for his presence there.

He strained to hear but missed some of what Jonathon said to his secretary. It was as if he were moving, and when he turned away from the closet door, his words lost the power to penetrate the thick wood. What Curt did learn was shocking, though. "Never at his desk…

Incompetent...Morgan could have...unhappy...Never liked him... Strike first...New guy from...Breakfast at Windows..."

Holy fuck! Curt tried to process what he'd heard. If his interpretation was correct, he couldn't have timed his exit more perfectly. His father-in-law was heading to Windows on the World for a breakfast meeting with a man who might be Curt's replacement. Was Morgan planning to divorce him? Was Jonathon firing him first, so Curt couldn't damage the firm on his way out? Or maybe Morgan was dating this guy, and he'd move into Curt's bedroom as well as his office.

If Jonathon only knew what Curt had done! It was a small theft, as far as these things went, approximately ten million dollars. He'd done it at the beginning of the month, by tacking on a bogus fee to one of their union accounts. The account was huge, about two billion in assets, so to their managers, the dip could easily have represented a change in the market. It wasn't until their auditors saw the charge that they'd act, and by then, Curt and the money would be gone, and most likely no one outside of MGT would know about his crime. The money was nothing to Jonathon, and it would be worth the ten million to keep his reputation intact. Who'd do business with him if his house was in such disorder? So, Jonathon would pay the money himself and perhaps quietly try to find Curt and get his revenge.

Good luck with that, Dad.

Curt bit his fist to keep from laughing. They were fucking each other, but neither one knew about it. Well, he did, and it did ease his guilt to some degree, knowing that this was war, and all was fair.

Maybe it was an omen that he'd heard him, a sign that today should indeed be Curt Hutchins's last day on earth. He glanced at his watch. 7:53 a.m.

When the voices faded, Curt eased from his hiding space and opened the door a crack. Jonathon had shut off the lights, but the fake eggs still glowed under the spotlights in their custom cabinet. The bright day's light shone on his desk, on the faces of his wife and her family.

He quickly switched the last egg and didn't look back as he hurried from the room and to his own office across the hall.

CHAPTER THREE

Once sheltered by the large, wood-paneled door to his office, Curt leaned against it and took another breath before securing the lock. Then he eased the eggs from the bag and unwrapped each of them, placing them side by side on his desk.

The day was bright and the overhead lights on, and beneath them, the eggs sparkled. Wow. They were magnificent, so much more so than his copies. Obviously, he knew they would be, but he hadn't thought the difference would be so blatant.

Damn! If Jonathon checked on the eggs in his safe, he might not be fooled by the copies. Curt hadn't really taken the time to compare the fakes with the real ones in the closet, but Jonathon would have plenty of time, and he had his own fakes in the display cabinet to take his measure.

Sighing deeply, he got back to work. He could do absolutely nothing about it now, and a bigger problem was sitting just a few floors above his head: Jonathon was at Windows on the World, the same place Curt was scheduled to meet the buyer for the eggs.

Focus! This time he took great care to wrap each egg securely, using packaging tape from his desk to hold the protective layer in place, and a red marker to label each one. After he completed his task, he replaced the first two eggs in the messenger bag and snapped the magnetic closure into place. The third egg went into his inside jacket pocket. It was the Imperial Palaces egg, the most precious of the lot, much too valuable to leave here in his office, not when he was on the verge of losing his job. For all he knew, he could come back from breakfast and find his office empty, the egg on display on Jonathon's desk.

Nope. He couldn't chance it. He wedged the bulky package into his pocket and hoped no one would notice. Maybe he could even exchange all three eggs today. The deal was for all three—three eggs for fifteen million dollars in diamonds. It was a steal. The eggs were probably worth twice that. He planned to exchange two eggs today—two-thirds of the merchandise for only half the fee. After both parties verified the authenticity of the goods they received, they'd meet again and complete the deal.

This complication with Jonathon tempted him to change his plans, finish the deal now. But he couldn't risk giving up all three eggs, could he? First, the buyer might give him fake diamonds. He'd get away with that, too, because how could Curt ever force him to hand over the money unless he revealed his own hand in the crime? Second, the buyer had only half the diamonds today. And even if they were real, why would he ever turn over the final payment if he already had everything he wanted?

Self-consciously, Curt patted his jacket, knowing it was bulging, and shook his head. It was just too obvious. The ten pounds he'd put on in the gym were making themselves known. Then he unbuttoned it, letting it hang open, and that was better. Not perfect, but it'd work.

Picking up his bag, he glanced at this watch. 8:04 a.m.

His first challenge of the day was behind him, but the bigger one was just ahead. In forty-one minutes, he was supposed to trade briefcases with someone named Nick, in the restaurant on the top floor of the building, where his father-in-law was having breakfast with his potential replacement.

Curt had realized that meeting in the tower was risky—he'd worked in the building for ten years, so of course people recognized him—but that was the beauty of the plan. He'd sit and eat, read the financial papers, and casually place his briefcase near his chair. Nick, a stranger like hundreds of businessmen visiting the restaurant every day, would sit at the next table and place his briefcase nearby. When they left, separately, it would be with the other's bag, and no one would ever suspect anything unlawful had taken place. Months, or perhaps years from now, when the discovery was made, no one would find it peculiar that he'd had breakfast at Windows on the World on his last morning at work.

But…how could he go into that restaurant with his father-in-law there? When his disappearance was noted in a few days, Jonathon would mention that Curt had been at breakfast. It wasn't unheard of for him to eat at Windows, but it wasn't typical, either. Someone might review security footage from the restaurant and see the entire transaction with Nick. They'd not only see his face, but they'd see Nick's as well. A savvy police detective wouldn't have much trouble putting the pieces of this puzzle together, finding this Nick, and striking some sort of deal that would put Curt in jail for a long time. Jonathan might cover up the theft from the managed account, because it would protect his reputation. The theft of the eggs was different. More personal. Jonathan would want revenge. There would be a major insurance investigation, and with that much money on the line, he was sure the people trying to find him wouldn't be easily deterred.

He leaned against his desk and looked out the window. He should abort the meeting with Nick, reschedule somewhere else, perhaps even on another day. But they didn't have an emergency plan, no backup strategy, and he had no phone number to call to simply cancel. The meeting had been set up by someone unknown, a man who'd reached out to Curt after he'd inquired discreetly about selling the eggs. That same man had worked out details such as the date and time and the Ferragamo messenger bag, and no one had asked Curt his opinion. He had only requested this exchange be on a Tuesday, when Jonathon was golfing. So much for that.

Curt put his hand to his forehead, rubbing away the beginnings of a headache. Aborting the meeting wasn't an option, not if he wanted to ever sell the eggs. This deal had not been easy to arrange. He wasn't a criminal and didn't know any criminals other than the guy in the diamond district who'd recently sold him ten million dollars' worth of precious gems in exchange for the money he'd looted from the retirement fund. Nick was his only option, and if Curt walked out now, his chances of ever meeting up with him again were slim.

As he saw it, he had two choices. He could try to intercept Nick in the massive lobby on the main floor, or in the elevator lobby on the 107th, near Windows on the World. In the ground-floor lobby his chances of being seen with Nick were much greater than in the restaurant area, simply because of the sheer volume of people navigating the main concourse. Not only that, but security guards were there, tons of them, ever since the bombing in 1993. There were cameras as well, and if he lingered too long, he'd draw attention.

As far as his father-in-law went, his being at breakfast meant a change of plans, but it didn't necessarily mean they had to abandon them. Jonathon would probably hold a meeting of this caliber in the private dining area, and Curt wouldn't even see him. A vestibule near the elevators opened into the lobby, and Curtis could hang out there. Certainly, Jonathon's meeting would last much longer than his. Really, you can't just hire a new VP over Eggs Benedict and a single Bloody Mary. No, this breakfast would take two hours, minimum. Curt had time to make the exchange. Someone like the hostess or others from the building might see him, but he had to take a chance. This could work. He only had to time it correctly.

The express elevator from the concourse lobby to the 107th floor made the journey in less than a minute. Would Nick know that and time his entrance to avoid being in the building longer than necessary? Or would he arrive fifteen minutes early, prepared for a delay? In the first case, Curt could get there just a few minutes before their 8:45 meeting time, but in the other scenario, he'd have to ascend to the restaurant level early and hope he didn't run into anyone. The elevator lobby on the 107th floor was much smaller than the one on the main concourse, so fewer people would be there. Also, he wouldn't have anywhere to hide. Everyone who exited any of those lifts would walk right past him. Yet it seemed the better of his two options, because once Nick got to the restaurant and sat down for breakfast, Curt would have no choice but to meet him there. And then another thought came to mind—what if Nick arrived early, just to scout the environment? He might already be seated, enjoying the view and a cup of coffee while Curt was twenty floors below, pulling his hair out.

After all his planning, he simply didn't know what to do. He couldn't go upstairs, though. Not yet. He could hang out in the restaurant elevator lobby for a few minutes, but not for half an hour.

He sat, turned on his computer, and logged in, so if anyone checked on him, it would appear he'd just stepped away for a moment. He checked his watch. 8:10 am.

"Fuck," he whispered. He was going to drive himself crazy in the next thirty minutes. He should go to the morning briefing, or at least pretend this was any other day. Or maybe not going to the meeting would be more normal, since he often skipped it, preferring yoga and sex with Yvonne to boring financial reports. Maybe coffee would help. Real coffee, packed with caffeine, not that fake stuff Yvonne served.

He looked at the messenger bag. Could he leave it? Surely if Jonathon was firing him today, security would let him take his personal items. It beat carrying the bag through the entire MGT suite. After securing it behind the closet door, he locked his office, then zigzagged to the break room. It was the smallest room on the floor, with a refrigerator, a microwave, and a coffee pot, the requisite water cooler, and a counter with a sink, but only a tiny bistro table and two chairs. Top investment advisors ate at their desks. They didn't waste time socializing, and this room certainly reflected that fact.

Even so, Curt saw a half dozen of his colleagues on their way out of the room, and another four stood huddled inside, all of them waiting for the pot to finish brewing. One of them was talking about a lackluster date the night before. None appeared to be concerned about the clock.

"*The Music Man*, huh?" another guy asked. "Maybe you should try *Phantom* next time. I think that'll improve your chances of getting laid."

The remark elicited the expected chuckle, and the jokester then poured a round of coffee for the group, including Curt. The guy who'd struck out on his date pulled a flask from inside his suit pocket and added a splash of something amber to the mugs.

Curt raised his glass. "To better luck with the ladies."

They all laughed, but one of them had a retort that stung more than Curt would ever let on. "From the guy who had the ultimate luck with the ladies."

Curt shrugged. "Maybe if he had a few ugly daughters, you apes would have a chance."

"Well, it had to be your looks because it wasn't your brains," one of them said. *Ouch.* That one hit its mark, too, but Curt smiled anyway. It didn't matter anymore that he wasn't as good at this job as they all were. He had a golden parachute they could only dream of.

"On that note, I'm going to go make some money." He smiled and winked, hoping that one day they'd know why, know how, in the end, he'd been smarter than all of them. Curt strode from the room and back to his office, then sat with his coffee.

He couldn't wait for this day to end. Not just because of the eggs and the changes he was planning in his life, but because of people like the guys in the break room. The office was filled with them, and the largest of them was the man in the big office across the hall. Before MGT, Curt had done okay and fit in well in the small firm where he'd started his career. But his career, his life, his entire existence had changed because of his decision to marry Morgan. He'd been wooed by her and her family money, but he'd lost his own identity along the way. Yvonne helped him find himself again.

Those jerks at the water cooler were right. He didn't belong here.

When he'd met Morgan, they'd both been studying finance at NYU, and after graduation, she'd gone to work for MGT, while he accepted a job with a small firm in New Jersey. He'd liked it there. He was raised in the Trenton area and actually took the train into the city for his classes because he couldn't afford to live in Manhattan. After graduation, he got a job and bought a small condo. He worked hard and saw Morgan occasionally. They were friends, working in the same field. Then he saw her more often. But then they became serious, and his life went sideways, as it became clear he'd need to work for her father and make a seven-figure salary to keep her happy.

It might have seemed great to the guys in the break room, but working for your wife's father is emasculating. He should have just frozen his sperm and cut off his balls and given them to Jonathon, because they didn't seem to work when his father-in-law was within a five-mile radius. They'd stopped functioning when Morgan was around, too.

Curt continued to look out at the city. What would his life have been like if he'd stayed in Trenton? His parents were alive then, as was his Aunt Kathy. He'd had friends. Guys from school and sports, girls he'd ridden with on the bus, hung out with, and worked with at the bar where he made spending money during college. They were good people, real people, but he hadn't seen them in ten years. They didn't move in Morgan's circle, the circle he'd migrated to.

What would life be like if he'd married the nursing student at Rutgers he'd dated back then? He'd be a part of a big, warm, loving Italian-American family who shared Sunday dinners and a week at the Jersey shore in the summers. Hell, he'd been doing well. They probably would have purchased a condo at the beach, an investment property they could rent during the summer and enjoy during the off-season. He'd have coached their kids in sports, and she'd be in the PTA. They'd talk and do yard work together, and he'd be happy.

Maybe he had a shot at something like that with Yvonne, a chance to hit the reset button but without the kids. Without in-laws. The mountains instead of the beach. He could be happy with Yvonne. He *was* happy.

Whoa. The whiskey hadn't seemed like much at the time, but to him, who didn't imbibe often, a few sips seemed to be making his head spin. He looked at his watch. 8:25.

Head spinning or not, he downed the rest of the coffee, then opened his closet and removed the messenger bag. It was time. Though the express elevator from the lobby took only a minute, he'd have to descend to the 78th floor sky lobby, then board another elevator to the top floor. If he wanted to be there when Nick arrived, he needed to go.

He moved at the normal MGT pace, walking quickly as if he had somewhere to be. Sherry sat at her desk, on the phone. He saluted her as he went by. No one stopped him, no one questioned him, because they all had somewhere to be, too.

The elevator came in seconds, and the ride down to the sky lobby took only a few more, as did the ascent to Windows on the World. Although both cars could hold dozens of people, thankfully only a few were in each, and no one he recognized.

When he exited at the top, he paused to let the other passengers walk by, then pretended to tie his shoe near the express elevator. Ahead, he saw the reception desk was unmanned, and he breathed a sigh of relief. No prying eyes to report back later. Not yet anyway.

He glanced at his watch. 8:35 a.m.

A dinging sound caught his attention, and he stood and picked up his bag, ready to move with the people from the elevator. Seven men exited the car, all of them talking in the hurried tones typical of the workers at the World Trade Center. In their rush, they hardly noticed him, though standing there, surrounded by mirrors and marble, he felt absurdly conspicuous.

He'd come too early. Maybe he should ride the elevator down to the main concourse just to get out of sight. He might miss Nick, though, since two elevators came from the ground to the top floor. Just then the bell dinged, the doors opened, and another group exited. No one had a Ferragamo messenger bag, but one nodded to Curt, so he decided to act as normal as possible. He boarded the elevator. Once inside, though, he held his finger on the button to keep the doors open, and after a few seconds of debate, he got out again.

"Fuck," he whispered as the door closed behind him. "This is crazy."

If only he had someplace to hide, an alcove to sit in and read his *Wall Street Journal* or make a phone call. But the lounges where he could do so were ahead, near the restaurant and all the prying eyes he was hoping to avoid. So he leaned against the wall and pulled his flip phone from his pocket, pretending to talk on it. With one eye on the elevator door and the other on his watch, he paced, hoping to appear busy. If he looked just like everyone else in the building, no one would notice him.

He agonized in this manner until 8:42, when the elevator from the ground floor opened, and a dozen people emerged. The last was a tall, dark-haired man, dressed in a tailored suit that accented his muscular build. Over his left shoulder, he carried a Ferragamo messenger bag identical to the one in Curt's hand. He turned toward the reception desk but paused when Curt cleared his throat and softly called his name.

"The plan is to meet in the restaurant." Curt detected a faint accent. This wasn't the man he'd spoken to when he arranged this meeting.

Nick slowly turned and caught him with a penetrating glare of his icy blue eyes. He took a step in Curt's direction.

If Curt had been nervous before, this man sent him spinning, and he squeezed his fingers shut, reassured by the pinch of his nails against the tender flesh of his palm. He was in charge here. He was the one with the eggs, valuable merchandise this man wanted. He would set the tone. "The plan has changed," Curt said, standing a little taller, holding his ground.

"I don't like changes," Nick hissed, though he stopped moving.

Curt swallowed. "The man who owns the eggs is in that restaurant right now, and something tells me it wouldn't be smart for him to see us together."

Nick turned and pressed the button to call the closest elevator car, then dropped his bag to the floor. The doors opened immediately. "Get in the car, and leave the bag. Then get out."

So much for making the rules here. Curt followed the instructions, keeping a close eye on Nick. The last thing he needed was for him to make off with both bags. But when Nick stepped toward the elevator car, his bag was still sitting on the marble floor.

"If we wish to purchase the other egg, we will contact you. If there are problems with the merchandise, we will contact you."

Curt swallowed at the subtle warning, but then he reassured himself that all would be fine. The eggs were perfect.

"The diamonds?" he asked.

Nick nodded toward the floor. "All there."

Curt smiled. "Thank you," he said, relieved to be done with this business. Picking up Nick's bag, he watched as the doors closed, and when they had, he laughed, a quiet little sigh of relief and disbelief and a bundle of other good emotions.

He stepped back and glanced at the edge of the lobby, to the windows that looked out at the city, and smiled. He'd done it! Of course he'd have to authenticate the diamonds. The guy in the diamond district who'd helped him with his recent payout from the union would do that for him. Maybe he should just do it now and get it over with. It beat carrying a bag full of diamonds around, especially if Jonathon was thinking of firing him. He had no way of predicting when that would happen, but it might not be easy to get the diamonds out later. It would deviate from the plan, and if he knew anything, he knew the plan was good. He'd wait and finish his workday, acting as if this was like any other day at MGT.

But why? What if he got tossed today? What if Jonathon discovered he'd switched the eggs? He might lock down the floor, search everyone. The express elevator arrived, and he debated for a second as a group emerged. Why not take a cab up to the diamond district and get an appraisal right now, rather than waiting and worrying? And he could stash the third egg as well, get it out of the MGT space. Maybe his friend in the diamond district would hold it in his safe. Maybe he'd even buy it, and Curt wouldn't have to see Nick again. With traffic he'd be up and back in an hour, ninety minutes tops, not much longer than if he'd gone to breakfast.

His mind made up, he hopped in and pressed the single button to take him to the lobby, then glanced at his watch. It was 8:45.

CHAPTER FOUR

Present Day

Imma Bruno smiled as she opened the front door of the old farmhouse, happy to see her friends, Jess and Mac. "Good morning." Imma greeted them with open arms. Mac's hug was short, like their relationship, but Jess's reflected the love of a lifetime. Imma and her partner Jo weren't those women who'd been confused about their sexuality and married a man or had children first. They'd met in college and fallen in love, and were still together nearly fifty years later. Jessica, the daughter of one of Imma's oldest friends, was as close to a child of their own as they'd come.

"It's good to see you," Imma said as she ushered them through a hallway and into the kitchen, where her wife Jo sat at the table nursing a cup of something that smelled like coffee.

Jo looked up, her eyes bright to match her smile, and Imma knew this would be a good day. Jo recognized them.

She stood and hugged them, then offered coffee. Before either of the younger women could answer, Imma did. "I don't think we should push it. We have a long drive, and you never know about traffic when you're heading into New York City. We don't want to be late."

"I was kind of hoping we'd go out for breakfast." Mac nodded toward Jo. "Then maybe do a little fishin'."

Jo nodded. "Trout'll bite in the afternoon."

Imma watched closely as Mac and Jess smiled. "It sounds like a plan," Jess said.

Imma felt tears at the corners of her eyes, and she brought her hand to her mouth. Even though they were a generation apart, Mac and Jo had a special friendship, for which Imma was so grateful. Especially on days like this, when the Tuesday Night Book Club was heading out for the day, and she needed someone to keep an eye on Jo. Mac was a million times better than the woman who came in on Tuesdays when Imma was at book club, and having her here meant Imma could truly enjoy her day out with friends.

"Maybe if you have time, you two can straighten out the shepherd's hook," Imma suggested.

"What's wrong with it?" Jess asked.

"I keep the bird feed there, and a bear seems to have tangled with it."

Mac laughed. "That sounds like a fool's errand, Imma."

Jo nodded and pointed at Mac. "That's what I said. We'll fix it today, and he'll bend it again tomorrow."

Imma held her hand to her heart. "It brings me joy to watch the birds."

"You can always hang it from a tree branch. You have quite an oak in the yard."

"And how would these old knees climb up there to add seed?" Imma asked, shaking her head. "The shepherd's hook is perfect."

"Forty-nine years it's been like this," Jo said with a smile.

Imma walked a few steps and kissed the top of her head. "Yes. It's been full of excitement. Never boring."

Jo looked at her affectionately. "Never."

"And how are you newlyweds?" Imma asked. Mac and Jess had been together for quite a few years, but had married just a year ago.

A blush crept up Mac's face, telling her all she needed to know. They were happy. "It's all good," Jess said. "But we should head out. If we keep the ladies of the Tuesday Night Book Club waiting, they may leave without us."

"Wait," Mac said. "Aren't you driving, Jess?"

She nodded. "Yes, but trust me, that won't matter. They're a feisty bunch."

They shared a laugh, and both women hugged their partners, then set off in Jess's Jeep Grand Cherokee, a vehicle that seated seven. She'd purchased it just for these book-club outings. Since she was the youngest member, and the one most comfortable behind the wheel for long distances, they'd been asking her to drive for years. Often, they'd borrow someone's car, or rent a van, so when it was time to trade in her old car, Jess had purchased this one with her friends in mind. It was just one of the many reasons everyone in the book club loved her. And she loved them enough to spend the extra money on the larger vehicle.

"Would you like me to turn the air on?" Jess asked.

Imma sank into the seat. Since she was here first, and had known Jess the longest, she always got the front seat when Jess was driving. Which was always.

"No. It's pleasant out." Though it was the end of July and might be sweltering later, it was still morning in the mountains and just perfect.

"It'll probably be a scorcher in New York."

"Then you can turn the air on when we get there."

Jess laughed, and they were quiet for a moment. "So, Jo looks great."

"Hmm," Imma said, tired of everyone telling her how great Jo looked. She'd been with her since they met at East Stroudsburg State College, and *that's* when Jo had looked great. She'd been pretty hot right up into her fifties, in fact. But then Imma's cooking had started to catch up with her, and she'd put on a few pounds. But still, she'd been attractive. Now, though, Jo looked like she was fading away.

Because Jess was a doctor, she was the first one Imma had gone to about Jo's troubling little memory lapses. After asking Jo a few questions, Jess was worried enough to set her up with a specialist. As Jess had suspected, Jo was in the early stages of Alzheimer's. That had been two years ago, and fortunately, Jo had responded to treatment. Imma knew the disease wasn't curable, but her neurologist had written Jo a prescription for medication, and the regimen was slowing the rate at which she worsened. Most of the time, Jo was still very much her normal self. It was just the rest of the time that was the problem, and her near-total disinterest in food.

"Is there something you're not telling me?" Jess asked as she reached out and rubbed Imma's elbow.

"She doesn't eat. And you know it's not my cooking. I'm a great cook. She used to beg me for lasagna, or my linguine, and she'd eat my meatballs right out of the pan."

Jess sighed. "It's probably a side effect of the medication. Does she complain about nausea?"

Imma thought for a moment. Mostly Jo didn't say anything. She just pushed her food around until it grew cold and rubbery, giving her an excuse to throw it out.

"It may not be her fault, Im."

Suspecting Jess was correct in her speculation, Imma turned and looked at her. Her mother, Patsy, had been Imma's dearest friend, a friend from childhood, a true friend who'd only hugged her and given her unwavering support when Imma came out in the 70s. Everyone was in the closet then, but Imma couldn't keep that secret from Pat—they were just too close. And after she told her, they grew closer still, because for many years, Imma dared tell no one else.

She'd been there at Pat's wedding, standing beside her as maid of honor, and next to her at the church as Jess was baptized, and for most of the other important events in Jess's life. And so had Jo. And now, Pat and her husband Zeke, Jess's dad, were both gone, and Jess had no one but Mac.

And Mac was wonderful, she truly was. But as Imma understood well, the people who knew your people mattered a great deal, and she was one of the few people left who knew Jess's people. She was fond of bringing them into the conversation, and she thought Jess liked when she did that, too.

"How strange that your dad and my Jo should both suffer from the same dreadful disease," Imma said.

"Makes you wonder about the water, huh?"

"Everyone should be so lucky as we are. The poor people drinking rusty city water. Eck!"

Jess laughed. "Nothing wrong with you, Imma. You're still spunky. So the water must be just fine."

"It's my Italian genes. We live forever."

"I think it's the wine and olive oil, not the genes."

Imma redirected. "These new drugs...my Jo's lucky. Nothing seemed to help your dad."

"Oh, I'm not sure that's true. I think he had a few good years, even after his symptoms started."

"I'm glad you moved home, Jess. The last years of his life were happy ones, because of you and Mac."

Jess nodded. "It was a good move. I don't know how I would have survived if I hadn't come back. I could be dead now."

Imma knew Jess had struggled with addiction, and she'd educated herself about the disease, volunteered with Jess on a community effort to provide Narcan to at-risk people. Pills that used to be cut with harmless fillers and allergy medicine were now laced with fentanyl, and people were dying. Jess was right. Everyone using drugs was at risk, and if Jess hadn't gotten herself into recovery, she might have become a statistic.

"You were very brave," Imma said.

"I just did what I had to do."

"If it was that easy, no one would be addicted."

Jess laughed. "You have a point."

"It's funny how life works out, isn't it? I chose to teach. I had three choices, really—nursing, teaching, or working in an underwear factory. If I had chosen differently, I never would have met Jo. And if you hadn't gotten turned around with pills, you would have stayed in Philly and never would have met Mac."

Jess nodded. "It does seem to work out the way it's supposed to."

"Your Mac is a gem. Everyone loves her. Especially your father."

"She was great with him."

"And she's great with my Jo." Imma patted Jess's arm. "That's why I can escape for a whole day, because I know she'll be in good hands."

"And what an escape it'll be."

Imma rubbed her hands. "I went to the library yesterday and printed out a list of restaurants within walking distance of the museum. We can vote when we pick up the girls. And I also printed a little information about Fabergé eggs. From what I've read about this new museum, this exhibit will be one of a kind."

They turned into the library parking lot, and Jess smiled at her. "Your energy amazes me. I didn't even shower today."

"I thought it was the new leather."

Jess cracked up as she pulled in next to three other cars near the rear of the lot, where five women waited for them.

Imma hopped out before they even stopped. "This is going to be one of the best field trips ever! Now let's get going. You never know about traffic."

Jess waved toward the group, then opened her rear door and flipped down the seat to gain access to the rear seats. Annie, a retired federal judge, was the most petite, so she usually ended up back there. Imma thought it fortunate that she didn't get carsick. Her usual companion, Dominica, crawled into the back beside her.

Into the middle seat went the other three members of the group—Blanche, an accountant; Rio, a realtor; and Gigi, the postmistress. Missing was Denise, a Garden police officer, who was closer in age to Jess and Mac than the rest of them, but a welcome addition to the group.

It seemed one of them was always missing, which worked out great with the seating in the car. If they all showed up, Jess would have to strap one of her friends to the roof.

As usual, the chatter was nonstop, and Imma hated that she couldn't turn her seat around to face them. Instead, she gave them a few minutes to catch up before she brought up the topic of the book they'd chosen. When they all worked full time, the book club had met monthly, though they would get together on Tuesdays to celebrate all the holidays, and they gathered for everyone's birthday on the day that was closest. When they began to retire, they changed their schedule to every other week, and now they met every single Tuesday, except when they planned a special trip. That could be any day, depending on where they were going. And they'd gone to some interesting places, from the coal-mine tour in Scranton to musicals on Broadway, to Penn State football games, to craft shows. They'd learned to paint pysanki at the Ukrainian church, filled baskets at the baby pantry, and baked cookies for the homeless shelter. Their adventures were diverse, and Imma loved every new one, even the ones she hated. Today's trip, to the Manhattan Museum of Alternative Art, was one she thought she'd really enjoy.

"Okay. Let's talk about the book. Did anyone read it?" She knew the nice weather drew her friends outside, and they often got busy with gardens and visiting and sometimes didn't have time to finish their reading.

A bunch of affirmations came from the rear of the Jeep.

"Who's the moderator today?"

"I am," said Ann from the rear seat, and Imma listened as her friends answered questions and gave their opinion about the book Ann had chosen. With her background in the law, she tended to choose works that focused on that field, and this one had been a doozy. The debate lasted well into their two-hour trip, and only when the Manhattan skyline came into view did they turn their conversation toward the exhibit they'd see.

"I tried to get a book on Fabergé eggs from the library, but Jenn said they were already on loan," Blanche complained.

Imma reached into her bag, pulled out a small book, and passed it back. "All yours," she said. She too had been unable to get the book until just the day before. She felt terribly unprepared for this trip and hoped her friends didn't notice. She prided herself on researching their destinations and knowing all the trivia, and she thought they appreciated the effort. Hopefully, the exhibit spoke for itself.

"Before we get started, I have a tidbit of gossip," Ann said.

Everyone grew silent. Ann was the quiet one in the group, and when she spoke, she usually said something worth hearing.

Imma turned in her seat to look at her. "Were you ladies aware that the Giles family owned three Fabergé eggs?"

"No!"

"Get out!"

"Really?"

Imma was silent as she wondered how that bit of information had eluded her. The Giles family had owned property on the outskirts of Garden for hundreds of years, and though the most recent generation didn't spend much time in the Poconos, the Brunos knew the Gileses and had socialized back in the day. Imma had worked with one of them at a summer camp during her teens, and Imma's older sister had briefly dated a Giles. But even people who didn't personally know a Giles knew the family—they were one of the old, monied Pocono families who had given much to the community, and their name was everywhere.

"I mentioned the exhibit to my mother's sitter, and she told me about the connection. I looked it up, and she was right. Jonathon paid ten million for three eggs back in the eighties. That's probably about fifty million today."

"At least," Jess retorted.

"Does the family still have the eggs?" Dominica asked.

"No. Unfortunately, they were lost on 9/11."

A chorus of sympathies echoed through the car, and they were quiet for a few seconds before Gigi spoke.

"It's no wonder the people revolted, right? The tsar was spending a fortune on Easter eggs while the commoners starved," Gigi said.

"They are beautiful, though," Blanche added. "And they've been a great investment for the people who bought them at the right time."

"That's the problem with art, though, isn't it? It's an investment now."

"Oh, I think it always was. But like everything else in the world, the prices are crazy," Blanche said.

"I agree, Blanche." Gigi sighed. "As you all know, we held on to Terry's mom's condo in Florida after she passed. Today it's worth ten times what her parents paid for it. Terry thinks we should sell."

As they passed the book around, they commented on the eggs they liked best, all wondering which of the existing ones would be displayed. Collectors from around the world owned them, and they speculated how the Russian-owned eggs had been procured during the war with Ukraine. Personally, Imma thought the eggs were safer in Manhattan than Russia, but she didn't voice her sentiments.

Soon Jess was handing over the keys to the parking attendant in Manhattan, and they navigated the pedestrian traffic in Midtown. The day was warm, but not as hot as Imma had thought it might be, with clear skies overhead and a soft breeze that perked up at the cross streets. They wandered and window-shopped before deciding on a place for lunch. They were all adventurous in the food department, and they chose a Balinese restaurant not too far from the museum. After a traditional meal of flavorful pork and rice, they made the short walk to their destination.

The Manhattan Museum of Alternative Arts resembled no museum Imma had ever seen. It wasn't far from the Hudson River, on a street otherwise full of apartment buildings and restaurants. The two-story facade was made of hammered copper, into which images had been etched—a waterfall, nude lovers in an embrace, animal forms, the sun. Ten-foot-tall double doors, also copper-plated, guarded the entrance. Above this, a three-story banner depicted the current exhibit of Fabergé eggs. It was a stunning entrance and would certainly catch the eye of pedestrians wandering past.

With Imma in the lead, they entered the queue, and, beside her, Dominica gasped. "Look. It's Max Montgomery!"

Imma looked and saw the handsome British actor and a striking woman beside him exiting the building through a door twenty feet from where they waited.

"I read about him! He owns one of the eggs on display."

Imma had read that, too. She'd been lucky to get the tickets for today, the opening day of the exhibit, considering the number of dignitaries on hand for the ribbon-cutting. She watched as a few people left the queue and snapped pictures, some of them of a bodyguard's hand keeping them at bay. Max waved to the crowd, and then a man at the curb opened a car door, and Max and his model slipped into a limousine, another pulling into its place.

All eyes turned to the exit doors a moment later as a stunning couple emerged. The man wore an immaculately tailored tan suit that matched his fair hair, with a purple tie, and she had on a business suit in dark blue, one that also complemented her dark hair and skin. She reached into her bag and pulled out a pair of sunglasses, big ones that nearly covered her face.

"Who are they?" someone asked as people began snapping pictures. While she seemed to shy away from the cameras, hiding behind those glasses, he sported a huge smile and waved to them as they walked around the crowd, onto the street, and back toward Broadway.

"There are a lot of different contributors to the exhibit," someone said. "They could represent any of the owners."

"Maybe they're tech billionaires, and they own their own egg."

Imma refrained from commenting but strained her neck as the exit door opened and an elderly couple exited the building and, without acknowledging the crowd, entered a waiting car.

Another car immediately took its place, and a man at the curb spoke with the driver, and another couple exited. Imma wasn't sure how, but he was somehow signaling someone inside to let them know whose car had arrived. It was all very orderly, and actually fun, watching to see who might emerge through that door.

Then, a tall, dark man sporting a goatee walked out. He was shockingly handsome in a tailored suit cut to fit his broad shoulders, and a shiny black tie. Imma followed him with her gaze as he approached the waiting car, then gasped as another man approached from the opposite direction.

The second man, who'd been loitering in the adjoining building's entrance, touched the first on his shoulder. This second man was a doppelganger for her neighbor, Chris Henry.

At Imma's gasp, Dominica and Rio, who stood closest to her, followed her gaze. "Is that Henry?" Rio asked, referring to him by his surname, as Imma typically did.

"It sure looks like him," Dominica added. Then she called out, and the doppelganger looked at them, his eyes flying open wide. Goatee turned in their direction for a fraction of a second, then pushed the other man into his car. Imma and her group turned and watched it pull away from the curb and disappear.

"Was it him?" Rio asked.

"Did you see that look on his face when he saw us?" Dominica asked. "That was classic *deer-in-the-headlights*. It was Henry!"

Imma couldn't fathom it. Henry and his wife had purchased the farm next to theirs twenty years ago, and Imma knew the purchase price was well over a million dollars. But they'd never displayed the sort of wealth she associated with VIPs at a Fabergé egg exhibit. The Henrys drove Toyotas and Jeeps, never went out to dinner, and, as far as she knew, they rarely traveled.

But how could Imma really tell? The wife had taught yoga until her illness, so she interacted with people, but Henry was the definition of anti-social. He grunted in response to greetings and walked the other way to avoid people. He preferred solitary activities like jogging and kayaking, and he spent most of his time on his large estate near the game lands. If you looked up the word antisocial in your Webster's Dictionary, Henry's face would surely be there.

Mysterious would also be a good descriptor. All any of them knew—thanks to Rio, who'd handled their real-estate purchase—was that they'd bought their property, a hundred or so acres of mostly forested mountainside, for cash, shortly before September 11. After the terrorist attacks, they'd left New York permanently and had lived in the Poconos since then. They all speculated, as people in small towns do, that the Henrys were quite wealthy. So, perhaps Goatee, obviously a man of means, had known Henry before, when Henry was part of this world instead of a part of theirs.

As Imma stood there brooding, another thought occurred to her. Or perhaps it was an image that came to mind, of the attractive young couple who'd left the exhibit just before she'd spotted Henry.

The handsome young man, the one in the tan suit, bore a striking resemblance to Henry. Not the current version with the graying beard, but the young man who'd moved to the Poconos almost twenty-five years ago.

It was so very fascinating. Who would have thought that someone who'd lived in such circles, connected to such obvious wealth, would disappear into the mountains like that? Hmm, hmm, hmm. Fascinating, indeed.

CHAPTER FIVE

D r. Avery Hutchins observed the chaos on the street from the window seat at her favorite mid-town restaurant. On a Friday at lunchtime, the city was crazy busy, and she enjoyed the show as cars jockeyed for position on the roadway, and pedestrians did the same, spilling from the sidewalks to the pavement well before the lights signaled them to move. Plus, the new bike lanes only added to the excitement, as cyclists tried to navigate all that other traffic. It was a beautiful, sunny day in New York City, which made it even better, because in addition to the locals, plenty of tourists joined the mix.

As a second-year pathology resident at Bellevue Hospital, she didn't usually have a day off on Friday, but today was an important one, and her supervising doctor had given his blessing along with his signature on the time-off request form. Knowing she might not have this opportunity again for months, she enjoyed the people-watching.

Avery took stock of her emotions, a habit she'd formed since her psychiatry rotation as a medical student. Today, she really felt all over the place. It was nice to be off from work, and in that regard she felt excited. She'd been immersed in hematology and coagulation pathways in the classroom and lab, and the experience was intense. A three-day weekend, after months of difficult, long days, was a welcome respite.

At the same time, her morning field trip had reopened old wounds. Some of those wounds would never heal, and she'd learned to deal with the pain of a very public loss. It was part of her life that she accepted, like having brown hair and eyes, or an allergy to shellfish. So, all in all, being in what had been a potentially difficult situation really didn't turn out badly at all. In fact, she'd really enjoyed herself at the MMAA's Fabergé-egg exhibit.

And she was thrilled to see her brother. The demands of her schedule over the past months hadn't allowed them much time together, and sacrificing Jonathon was painful. Their calendars needed to sync so they could do more lunches like this one.

If only he'd actually join her. Jon was chatting up someone at the bar, an attractive woman who seemed to find him interesting, judging by the attention she paid him. What a heartbreaker he was.

Jon had agreed to join her today under duress—she'd threatened to never speak to him again unless he went to the exhibit—and she wondered if the buildup to the show had been as stressful for him as it had been for her. The eggs would be traveling to multiple cities around the country, but the exhibit opened here, and her family's eggs were among the ones featured. At one time, her grandfather, Jonathan Giles, had owned three of the Fabergé masterpieces. Like him, they were all lost when the North tower of the World Trade Center collapsed.

Avery had been young then, too young to remember her grandfather or the eggs, but while growing up, she'd heard their story many times. The eggs were part of her heritage, and even though they were gone, Avery still considered them a part of her family. When the organizers of the exhibit reached out to her grandmother to ask about including them, Avery had persuaded her to participate. Her grandmother owned replicas of the eggs, as well as numerous photos, and paperwork, including the insurance policies and provenance of their three pieces. Even though her grandmother had collected more than twenty million dollars in insurance for them, Avery was sure she would have preferred the eggs, and the husband who had vanished with them.

Since the exhibit was starting here, in the city where they met their fate, Avery considered it a fabulous way to pay tribute to her family's treasures. Unfortunately, her eighty-year-old grandmother wasn't up for the ceremony, and her mother couldn't come home from Florida, and her Aunt Tiffany couldn't be bothered, so she and Jon simply had to represent them.

That was fine by Avery. Even though Jon was four years older, the two of them were especially close. Avery didn't know if that was because they were both gay, or because they'd lost their father and their grandfather on September 11, or that their mom had so quickly remarried. Avery had no definitive answers, and all that mattered was that her brother had been there for her through it all, and she loved him beyond words.

As her stomach growled, Avery glanced at her watch. It was actually her father's, an antique Vacheron Constantin, worth more than her car. It was getting late, and she planned to drive to the Pocono Mountains later, if only her brother would hurry along.

As if her thoughts had summoned him, he turned from the woman at the bar and began to walk back to their table. He was handsome and graceful, with a slim build, and people stared as he strolled by in his tan tailored suit and purple tie. He looked like a successful New Yorker, but if you bothered to look closely, you'd think he really didn't belong with the rest of them at all. He was just too perfect.

Seeming to sense Avery's thoughts, he met her eyes and blew her a kiss that she caught and placed on her cheek.

"Since you've made me wait, you're buying lunch."

"You're richer than I am."

"Only because you spend too much money on clothes."

"Yes, I suppose I do. But since I've given up drinking and cocaine, I have to indulge in something."

Avery sucked in a breath at the mention of his former drug use, which had stressed them both for a few years. He had it together now, though, and had a nice boyfriend and a cute apartment. He even seemed to have settled into his job.

Although MGT had collapsed with their grandfather's death, Jon now worked for the company's successor, founded by all the company leaders who'd survived the attacks because they were out of the office or working in the MGT satellites. He was most comfortable in the world of money, making deals and schmoozing people, and she knew he was where he belonged.

"When I have my own money, I'm not letting you manage it."

"You do have your own money. Boatloads of it."

Avery shrugged. She and Jon had been the beneficiaries of their father's life-insurance policy, and it had all been carefully invested for them over the years, but she didn't consider that *her* money. They'd also received a check from the World Trade Center Victims' Fund, and that was also put away for her future. Maybe one day she would use it to buy a house or put her own children through college, but for now it was more like her legacy, the only thing she had left of the father she knew only through pictures. Kind of like the eggs, her father was a lost treasure.

Avery thought a change of subject was in order. "Wow. How about that exhibit?"

She'd met Jon outside the MMAA two hours before it opened to the public and joined the VIP line. After a guard checked their names from a list, another escorted them inside. Avery had dressed in a dark suit, the skirt cut to a respectable level just above her knee. Well aware that she and Jon looked nothing alike, and had often been told they made a striking couple, she smiled to herself as she imagined those queuing for the exhibit wondering just who they were.

No one important, she thought. Or, at least, important for the wrong reasons.

In the grand, three-story foyer, a sculpture of metal and glass hung above them, and as they walked beneath it, a woman called their names.

This was Adrienne, the administrative assistant who'd gathered their information for the exhibit. Although they'd never met in person, they'd exchanged dozens of emails, and she opened her arms to hug them.

"I'm so happy you two made it," she said sweetly. "And I'm going to let you start your preview, but first I'd like to show you what we've done to remember the Giles eggs."

In all her years, Avery had never heard them called that. They'd simply been *the eggs*. She wondered how her Gram and her mom, and even her Aunt Tiffany, would have felt about that name. Happy, she'd guess, because all three bore it.

Avery and Jon followed her to a rounded archway of stone and glass, above it a ribbon of shiny orange metal, inlaid with large, colorful, faux jewels proclaiming it to be St. Peter's Gate.

"This was once the entrance to the Peter and Paul fortress in St. Petersburg, at the eastern entrance to the city."

After admiring the gate a moment, they followed her through it. A few steps in, they stopped and stared in wonder. Avery had been expecting a series of glass cases, each holding an egg, with a tasteful description of the work, its provenance, and little else.

Instead, she was transported into another world. And the tribute to the Giles eggs had been spectacular. Sitting back, Jon smiled slowly as he met her gaze. "It was one of the most extraordinary things I've ever seen. Like entering a fantasy world."

They agreed they'd loved the exhibit but that one detail puzzled them. No authentic Fabergé eggs were displayed. Instead of the sterile glass cases Avery had anticipated, each egg had been represented by a room, telling a story of coronations and births and unfathomable wealth.

"How much would our eggs be worth today?" Jon asked.

Avery shrugged. "Fifty million, maybe. Perhaps more." But no doubt, if her grandfather had left the eggs to her mother and aunt as intended, they would have sold them. Both lived the high life, and it cost money. For the millionth time, Avery was thankful for her grandmother. Her egg would have sat on the vanity in her dressing room, where the replica now replaced it.

After the server took their order, they talked about her work, a subject that fascinated him. She'd chosen medicine, pathology in particular, for one reason only—to help find closure for the 1,100 families like hers whose loved one's remains were still unidentified after the towers collapsed and burned. Technology was always advancing and the ability to extract DNA from small fragments of bone improving. Avery hoped that, in her lifetime, kids like her, who'd lost a parent in the attacks, would at last be able to bury *something.*

"I get a little respect because of my situation, but I'll never be able to do any real work until I finish my residency."

"But I thought…"

Avery sighed in defeat. She'd hoped she'd jump right in, analyzing DNA segments, but that was a real specialty in her field. She had to do a ton of lab work in clinical pathology before her chance would come. "Yeah, me too. But in some cases, if there's just this one little shard of bone, they don't want someone inexperienced like me screwing with it and destroying all chances of ever making an ID. So I get it."

"But you're still disappointed."

She nodded, and he reached across the table and squeezed her hand. "It's probably never going to happen for Gram," she said, referring to her still-missing husband, "but for us…maybe. And I plan to keep plugging along, doing the things I have to do. Then one day I'll be a board-certified pathologist, and I'll spend my entire career in that lab, trying to bring closure to all those families."

Jon smiled at her. "You'll do it. You'll find Pop-pop. And you'll find Dad."

Avery felt her throat closing and looked away. Of course that's what it was all about. She was sure everyone knew it, though only Jon had the courage to say it. Clearing her throat, she changed the subject. "I'm going to the Pocs tonight," she said. "Wanna come?"

He shook his head. "No internet, no cable. How do you stand it?"

"You know, they actually do have internet in the Poconos. Just not on our property. It's only a fifteen-minute drive to that wonderful bakery I told you about."

"Is Lauren going with you?" he asked.

Avery's heart skipped a beat at the mention of her wife's name. They'd been together three years, after meeting on their emergency-medicine rotation in medical school. Avery had been completely overwhelmed by all the chaos of the ER, but Lauren had thrived there, and she took Avery by the hand and walked her through four terrifying weeks. They'd been together since, and married four months ago, when they both had a break in their residency schedules. "She's working. Trauma call, so I won't see her anyway. She'll get home tonight around six, then go in tomorrow morning at five. I'll leave tonight when she goes to bed and avoid the traffic."

"It makes me nervous when you're up there alone."

Avery rolled her eyes.

Jon sighed. "I know the place has its charms, but it's just so...vast. The perfect place for a serial killer to hide out. And you know they prey on beautiful young women."

"Jon, the people there are kind. The cars stop to let you cross the street. The guy at the market leaves the cash register to help you find something in the aisle. They hold Bingo benefits for sick neighbors."

Jon's eyes flew open in shock. "Wait. You go to Bingo?"

"Not personally, but I see other people going. It's nice."

Jon sighed and seemed to reset his attitude. "I'm glad it's your happy place. And maybe one day...but for me, the best part of the Poconos was spending time with Dad. He was relaxed there, you know? Swimming in the lake and playing tennis with me, teaching me to ride a bike. They were great times."

Avery smiled, happy for him that he had some memories, unlike her, who had absolutely none. She'd been not quite four when he died, and all she knew of him was from pictures and other people's stories. He squeezed her hand. "I wish you could remember him, too. He adored you. Everything he did with me, you tagged along. I remember the summer before he died, you diving off his shoulders into the lake, coming up and spitting out water and squealing with laughter. "Again, Daddy, again."

Avery bit her lip to keep the tears in check and changed the subject yet again. Today was supposed to be a happy day, a triumphant celebration, a time to honor her family and spend time with her brother. She refused to let the sadness in.

She spoke of another memory of the lake. "Remember that babysitter who almost let me drown?" she asked with a chuckle. In med school, during her psychiatry training, they'd asked about first memories with their indelible impact. That day at the lake, when she was under the water, surrounded by darkness, was her first memory. It was a wonder she'd turned out fairly normal.

"Yes. I do. Hard one to forget. Sarah. She was a piece of work."

"Thank goodness someone called Gram about her, and she had us watched. We might not have survived childhood."

"That was crazy, right? It was like special forces breaking into the house."

"I thought it was totally normal to play video games while the babysitter and her boyfriend were playing hide-and-seek. The detective guy at the door scared me more than Sarah ever did."

"Yeah, but if you remember, we were baking cookies when he knocked. So there's that, you know, burning the house down, and the fact that we answered the door and let a total stranger in while she was upstairs boffing her boyfriend."

Avery shook her head. It was almost surreal. "Who do you think called Gram?"

He shrugged. "Nosy neighbors. Or maybe concerned neighbors. People looked out for us afterward."

Avery had always felt that, too. Sometimes she stopped in the street and turned around, feeling as if someone was following her. It had happened dozens of times near their New Jersey home, and a few times in Manhattan, but most frequently at their vacation home in the Poconos. In truth, it was one of the reasons Avery loved the place so much. It was strange, because the Pocono property was in her mother's family, not her father's, but she felt her father in the mountains.

She shared her thoughts with Jon. "I feel like he's here sometimes. Do you ever get that feeling?"

He smiled. "I used to, in the Poconos. And at the New Jersey house. But not since I moved to New York."

"It's strongest in the mountains, I agree."

"Is that why you go?" he asked.

"Sometimes. But this weekend, I'm going because Gram sent me on an errand. She wants me to inventory the china and crystal and all that shit. She's finally writing a will, I guess. And I have to start Pop-pop's convertible and take it for a spin. It's one of my jobs when I go."

He laughed. "I forgot about that car. He used to let me sit in the front seat."

"That sounds safe on country roads, hundred of miles from the nearest trauma center."

"Ooh, you're such a doctor. But he did, I remember. I don't think we went far, just for ice cream or to the market. What kind of car is it? I remember it being pretty big."

"It's a Toyota. Gram says he bought it just so he could take us out for a ride. It has a pretty big backseat."

Jonathon smiled. "Tiffany says he was a real prick, but I just remember him being fun. I felt like I was a little prince when I was with them. The whole world stopped, and they just catered to me. And you, too. I know you love Gram, and she's great, but she changed so much after he died. I think she really loved him. I don't think he was just her husband. I think he was her love. Ya know?"

Avery studied him. It was a profound observation from someone who tended to keep things on the lighter side. Yet she was happy he'd shared it with her. As always, she was happy to learn about the family she never had a chance to know. And she thought for a moment about her own interactions with her grandmother. When Jon was a teenager and doing more of his own thing, Avery had accompanied her grandmother to the Poconos. Avery had spent her days at tennis camp and theater camp and golf camp and dance camp, but the evenings had been filled with her grandmother. They'd take walks on the vast estate, through the forests and along streams. They'd also look at family photo albums and check books out of the library and read them on the screened porch, staying out until the cool night air forced them into the house.

It wasn't what most of her friends would describe as exciting, but Avery didn't need excitement. Her mother and the many men in her company provided that. They traveled extensively, and Avery and

Jonathon were always forced to tag along so Morgan wouldn't look like a bad mother. They'd moved a few times, and although they stayed in the same private school, they'd lost friends from their neighborhoods. And, of course, the men themselves were always a new experience. One had a yacht, and they were forced to stay on it for weeks at a time, disembarking for only a few hours every other day or so. Another had a ranch in Oklahoma, and they spent the entire summer of her ninth year in the middle of nowhere while the adults were doing adult things. The worst was the one who'd fantasized about RVing across the continent with his family, only his own family wasn't interested, so he dragged Avery's. Six weeks in a recreational vehicle is a long time by any standards, but when confined with two adults who communicated primarily by screaming at each other, it was interminable.

That was the life Avery and Jonathon had lived with their mother, so when given the choice, they spent time with their grandmother. And when Jonathon was old enough to stay home alone, Avery was happy to have the one-on-one time with her. It was quiet time, but quality time, and it was time she treasured, and, Avery suspected, it was what she needed most during adolescence, when so many kids went off the rails. Jonathon did lose his way for a while, but Avery, tucked into the quiet woods of her family's Pocono estate, was buffered from most of the troubles and temptations that affected her brother.

"I think you're right. He was only sixty when he died. She was attractive and intelligent. She certainly could have dated if she was interested. I think she was devoted to Pop-pop. Still is, I guess, if you think about the car."

The server came and they placed their orders.

"We've lived a really fucked-up life, A," Jonathon said as he sipped the water the server had just poured. "It's amazing we've survived."

On so many occasions, Avery wished she could remember more. She wished she'd known her father and her grandfather, and the Giles eggs. Then other times, she was happy she didn't remember—not just her father and her grandfather, but the grief and the chaos that followed their tragic deaths. Having known them might have made the loss even worse.

Avery looked at her brother, grateful for him, for his sobriety, and for his unconditional love. She knew he felt the same way. Picking up her water glass, she offered a toast. "We made it."

CHAPTER SIX

Curt took a moment to catch his breath and realized he was still afraid of dying. He feared prison, and pain, and, as he watched Nick across the seat from him, he knew he feared death. Since starting this business all those years ago, Curt had realized it could end that way, but he'd been lucky. He was lucky twice on September 11— once when Nick took the eggs and left a fortune in diamonds, without harming him, and again when he exited the elevator mere seconds before the plane hit the North Tower.

Perhaps doing business with this man and living were conflicting ideals, but Curt was desperate. So here he was, trapped in a limousine, staring down a hulking bodyguard who certainly could dispose of him and be out of the country before anyone discovered his body. And no one would ever even miss him.

"So, Curtis Hutchins, you're alive," Nick said, breaking a tense silence.

Curt nodded, shocked to hear his name after so many years. Shocked that Nick knew his real identity. "You know who I am."

"Of course. Do you think I'd risk that kind of money on an unknown? I followed you for weeks, hanging out in the parking garage in the morning and following you home at night, watching soccer games and trips to the grocery store. What a boring life. No wonder you left. I always wondered about your plan. You didn't seem too happy with your wife. I figured you were thinking about a divorce. This was better. Amazing!"

Not really, but Curt didn't plan to debate with him.

"I thought you were killed," Nick said. "But you can hardly blame me for my faulty assumption, can you? The rest of the world also thinks you're dead."

"As you can see, I'm alive, Nick."

"Yes, you are. And it makes me wonder. I always thought I was incredibly lucky to have survived. If you hadn't canceled breakfast, if I'd taken a few seconds longer in the restroom…"

"It wasn't our time, Nick."

"I don't believe in that crap. Fate or destiny, whatever you call it. But luck. What a stroke of luck that Jonathon Giles was at Windows on the World. And the building was destroyed. No trace of your crime!"

Nick showed no hint of remorse that thousands had died in the towers. Instead, he seemed gleeful about Curt's deceit. What a psychopath.

Curt offered a thin smile. It was luck that he'd survived, but what had happened after that had been a matter of choice. And instead of choosing to go back to his family and seek a quiet divorce, he'd elected to disappear with Yvonne. He'd sentenced himself to a life of isolation and fear, and the past years were not at all what he'd imagined as he'd quietly crossed the Hudson River on a ferry on September 11, clutching the railing as he watched the smoke obliterate the lower Manhattan skyline. On the three-mile walk to Yvonne's condo, he'd formulated his plan as he stopped in one shop after the next, watching the television coverage of the attack. The towers had collapsed, and it was likely thousands had died. If he didn't check in with Morgan, wouldn't she assume he was one of them? This was his chance! He'd been planning to disappear anyway. His "death" would make it so much easier.

Curt had been so in love then and couldn't fathom how foolish his plan really was, because all he really thought about was Yvonne.

What an idiot I was, he told himself once again.

"I was still in the lobby," Nick said, "when the plane hit. It shook the whole building. But I didn't know how bad it was. I just wanted to get out of there without security checking my bag. I never imagined you escaped. Or that you had the balls to disappear." Nick laughed. "But I guess with all that money, disappearing wasn't too hard, was it?"

"I managed."

Nick nodded, and Curt could tell by the way he squinted that he was thinking. Sure enough, just a second later he spoke again. "And now, you must be out of diamonds. You want to unload the third egg."

"I'm considering my options."

Nick laughed. "They must be limited. The pool of buyers for such a piece is small. And even smaller for someone like you."

Curt suspected he knew what Nick was talking about. On the surface he seemed like a law-abiding citizen, who moved in circles with similar people. Then a thought occurred to him. What had Nick said about luck? Curt had thought for a moment he planned to insinuate Curt knew the attack was going to happen. And of course Curt would have denied that, because how could he? But if Nick had even entertained the idea, perhaps it held some merit. Maybe Curt could use that to his advantage, let Nick think the Saudis were interested in the egg, too.

"You weren't the only bidder, Nick. Just the highest. That other party is deciding on an offer now. However, you and I had a successful transaction before, so I trust you."

Nick studied him, and Curt concentrated all his effort on holding Nick's gaze. He was successful.

"How much are you asking?"

"Seven point five million. Plus the balance you owe me on the last transaction."

Nick laughed, but Curt held his ground. At that price, the egg was a bargain, and they both knew it.

"I'll have to speak to my..." Nick hesitated a second before continuing, "the buyer."

"I know all about Mikhail Bichefsky," Curt said. "I'm the one who reached out to him, remember?" He looked for a reaction, but Nick didn't flinch at the mention of the former ambassador's name. "Let me know. Soon."

Nick held up both hands in a defensive gesture. "Surely you can understand things are different now, Mr. Hutchins. Bringing that much money into your country isn't as simple a matter as it was when we last did business."

Curt wanted to scream. He was well aware how difficult it was to make cash transactions, to sell diamonds, to buy anything of value in the post-9/11 world. Still, he cut Nick no slack. "He was the ambassador, Nick. He'll figure it out."

The car had been traveling across town, from the museum near Tenth Avenue toward the East River. Curt looked out the window and saw a street sign for Lexington. He reached into his coat pocket, found the note he'd written, and handed it to Nick.

"I'll have that phone on me for the next two hours."

Curt knocked on the glass partition to alert the driver, and when the car stopped, he opened the door and stepped out. Before the limousine could move, he began walking back the way they'd come. Fifty-sixth street was a one-way, and unless Nick hopped out of the car and chased him on foot, the car couldn't follow him.

Still, Curt looked over his shoulder and watched as the limo began moving with traffic, through the intersection and toward Third Avenue. He stood there until it disappeared, then doubled back to Lexington and began walking south, heading toward his ultimate destination at the Port Authority Bus Terminal, contemplating his next move.

He stopped near a pharmacy on 53rd Street, casually squatting to tie his shoe, and looked around. Nick probably wasn't following him, but it wasn't impossible. He didn't notice anyone suspicious, but what did he know about such matters?

Suddenly, he felt anxious and fought to steady his nerves. What had he been thinking in coming here, to New York? It was the first time he'd been back in the city since September 11, which was stressful enough, but then—oh, wow.

Never did he imagine his children would be at the exhibit. He was there hoping to run into Nick. He hadn't known Nick's identity when they first met that fateful morning, but he'd done his due diligence since and found a picture on the internet, to put a name to the face. And he'd followed that name and that face for years, waiting for the right moment. He hadn't been sure Nick would even be at the MMAA, but he'd taken the chance, and sure enough, he'd arrived in the same shiny limo that whisked him away ninety minutes later.

Curt had arrived early, to watch the entrance. There was too much activity there, though, to try to intercept Nick when he arrived. An attendant had opened the door to Nick's car and ushered him along a red carpet, where two others surrounded him and escorted him inside. Curt had paced the street on the opposite side, knowing Nick wouldn't keep him waiting too long, and then he'd spotted his children.

When Avery and Jonathon had walked down that street, Curt had nearly fainted. It was so tempting to run to them, to confess everything and beg their forgiveness. Yet he'd frozen in place and could only watch as they presented themselves to the attendant at the door and disappeared behind the copper facade.

His mind raced the entire time they were inside, wondering what had brought them to the exhibit. Their family eggs were lost, so were they just curious about Fabergé eggs in general? And how had they scored VIP tickets to the ribbon-cutting? Curt had called, pretending to be a member of the press, inquiring about obtaining credentials for the event. He'd learned the preview for owners and dignitaries was scheduled for ten o'clock, two hours before the doors opened to the public, but no more tickets or press passes were available. Space was limited. Yet his kids were there. Unbelievable.

His panic level rose again. Was the man in the black T-shirt and jeans following him?

Curt had taken a bus into the city and planned to return home the same way, but now he wondered if it might be smarter to take a train somewhere, then double back. He hadn't been on a train in years, but he was sure he could figure it out. He could go out to Trenton, maybe see his old condo, or the house where he'd lived as a child. Visit the cemetery where his Aunt Kathy and his parents were buried. Then he could get a train back and pick up his bus. Or he could get the train all the way to Philly and pick up a bus there. Yes. That was a better idea.

He paused and looked in a window, then casually turned, looking for the man. His head was buried in his phone, and he walked hurriedly past Curt and on through the intersection without pausing, without looking back.

So, not him. But he honestly didn't know what a person following him would look like. The older couple, posing as tourists? The college girl, wearing a Fordham sweatshirt, heading toward the campus? It could have been anyone. And there were so many people! But would Nick have been able to set up surveillance so quickly? If Curt was sure of anything, it was that Nick had been surprised to see him that morning.

His head spinning, he stopped again. He had to think, to try losing anyone who might follow him. Walking through a revolving door, he entered a hotel lobby. He spotted a gift shop and ducked inside, keeping an eye on the door. No one came through it. After a minute, he wandered through the shop and picked up two items: a Yankees cap and shirt. Telling the attendant he was heading to the game, he pulled off his golf shirt and pulled on the T-shirt, then donned the cap. The attendant said nothing but shook his head and threw Curt's golf shirt in the trash.

From the gift shop, he once again perused the lobby before moving, then hurried across it, exiting into the restaurant. From there he went back to the street and continued his journey. After a block, he popped into a souvenir shop and watched the pedestrian traffic, willing himself to be calm.

Finally, his heart began to settle, and his breathing eased. What a day.

After seeing nothing suspicious, Curt walked from the store, then stopped for lunch, continuing to watch for a tail. But he was more relaxed now, certain it would have been logistically impossible for Nick to arrange surveillance so quickly. It took him two hours of eating and shopping and evading to finally accept it was safe to get on the damn bus and head back to Garden.

It was well past the two-hour time limit for Nick to call.

Fuck! If he had another way to sell the egg, Curt wasn't sure what that might be. Who had that kind of money? And the desire so strong they didn't care that the merchandise was stolen? No one he knew. In spite of his proclamation to the contrary, the ambassador had been the only one he'd contacted about the first eggs.

Well, he told himself. You're going to have to rethink your plan. Find out who owns a collection and might want one more egg. He'd gambled the first time, walking into the United Nations and handing someone a business card, asking to speak to the Russian ambassador, telling them he'd met the man at a Lincoln Center gala. Someone else, probably an assistant to an assistant, had politely spoken to Curt, giving him nothing more than a promise to pass along the information. Curt had a piece of art to sell. Was the ambassador interested?

One day had passed, then two. After a week, Curt had accepted his failure and was thinking of his next move. Then his phone rang. It was a company phone, untraceable to him. The voice at the other end took the details about the eggs and made him wait another week. He'd been in the Poconos with his family when it rang again, and Curt had scrambled to find a pen so he could write down the specifics. That had been Labor Day. Eight days later, Curt met Nick on the 107th floor of the North Tower.   '

He'd figured it all out once. He could do it again. And really, what did he have but time? Time to research, time to wait for a response, time to schedule another fateful meeting.

Then an idea occurred to him. He'd done business on his first illegal deal with a man in the diamond district. And Yvonne had been back several times after, to sell the diamonds Nick had given him for the first two eggs. The kind of man who did that would probably know someone who'd be interested in a Fabergé egg.

Now with a purpose, Curt walked more briskly, turning on 47th Street and heading west toward the Diamond District. When he reached 5th Avenue, he began window-shopping, moving slowly, watching the people going by, knowing a dozen eyes in the sky were watching him. He reached the store in question, saw a few customers inside, people buying engagement rings or anniversary earrings, with no clue that the real business happened upstairs, where diamonds were bought and sold by the truckload.

Curt saw the man, and as if sensing him, the man looked up. He met Curt's gaze and didn't seem surprised. Curt was sure he'd seen more exciting things in his lifetime than a dead man looking back at him through the window of his store. He gave an almost imperceptible nod and turned back to his customers.

So, he was still here. It had been a few years since Yvonne's last trip to New York. The man was old—he certainly could have retired. Or worse. But the fact that he was still in his shop gave Curt hope. If the man didn't want to buy the egg, he could probably arrange a meeting with someone who would.

Curt continued walking along 47th Street, still pausing to look in windows, a show for the cameras. He even decided to stop in a shop a few blocks away. He inquired about the length of time for a custom engagement ring, made a show of looking around, and then exited. He stopped in one more store before deciding he'd looked innocent enough to anyone watching.

It was time to head for home. Nick hadn't called, but he had another option, now. Today wasn't the day, but he was going to pay the diamond guy another visit. This would be okay.

He was a block from the bus station when the phone rang.

Only one person had his number. Nick had made him wait again.

CHAPTER SEVEN

Imma's was the only car in the visitor lot as she pulled in and parked. Turning in her seat to face Jo, she wondered if her wife recognized the library. To her delight, Jo smiled.

"I want to pick up a spy novel," she said.

"Sounds great to me. Pick one out for me, too."

Indeed, the library was empty on Saturday morning, and as they walked in, the new librarian waved and greeted them by name. Jo went off toward the fiction section, and Imma sat at a cubicle to use the computer. They had internet at home, but it was spotty, so Imma often printed things here, and as long as she didn't get crazy, the new librarian didn't charge for that service. Besides, she needed to get Jo out of the house, to keep her stimulated. A morning trip to the library, followed by breakfast and a stroll through town, would be a great start to their day.

Taking a seat that gave her a view of both the door and the stack of shelves where Jo was headed, Imma used her same old ID and password, and she was online in seconds. She'd absolutely loved the Fabergé exhibit, and she wanted to know more. But, first things first. She wanted to see if she could figure out who the guy was who'd practically abducted Henry. And how about that attractive young couple? The people who had VIP access to events like this could often be found online.

"Who was the man in the limo?" Imma asked aloud, with no real idea about how to start looking for him. Unless…she searched for the VIPs who'd attended the exhibit. She might never know any more about Henry, but she could possibly answer her last two questions by simply searching the list of people who'd attended the exhibit's opening ceremonies.

When Imma looked for the information, she found a dozen results. After glancing over to see Jo studying titles in the stacks, she began scrolling through the articles.

Clicking on the piece from the *New York Times*, Imma began to read, fascinated to learn things that hadn't been obvious to her a day ago. A New York company that makes trains for amusement parks had designed and built a train that transported them through the last of the exhibit, a play on the Imperial Palaces egg, which featured an actual tiny train that traveled along the shell of the egg from one palace to the other. Several rooms of the exhibit that featured real snow were transformed walk-in freezers. The skating rink in one exhibit was covered in sequins to make it sparkle. And Imma's favorite exhibit, which featured the lost Giles Victoria egg, was cast as four pieces of acrylic, fit together to resemble a revolving ball, which represented the globe. Inside the twenty-foot structure, Victoria sat on a throne, a young Alexandra resting on her knee as they surveyed the vast British Empire.

The Giles eggs were her favorite, and not just because she had known Jonathon Giles. The creativity was jaw-dropping, and Imma marveled as she remembered where she'd been the day before. It was sad to think they'd been destroyed in the World Trade Center, but what a great tribute the MMAA had given them. And the other eggs as well.

Thinking about the various eggs made her smile. The real ones were scattered around the globe, and none was on display at the museum, but the tribute to Fabergé and his work was better than any exhibit she'd ever seen. She'd never forget it. And for so many people around the world, this exhibit would bring the eggs, and history, to life. Unlike a sterile exhibit of the real eggs, this artistic rendering would be loved by people of all ages, art lovers or not.

As she contemplated this idea, another thought crept in, and she shook her head. She was irked that she hadn't known about Jonathon Giles's collection and was determined to learn everything she could now. They were such a prominent Garden family, and her sister had actually dated one of theirs! The Giles estate wasn't far from the sportsman's club where she'd learned to shoot and fish, and she passed their road whenever she took her dog to the vet. How could she have not known about those eggs?

Pressing a button, she printed a long article about the exhibit, then scanned another. Most were heavy on details about the exhibit, but light on information about the attendees. Of course they mentioned the really big VIPs, such as the mayor and the celebrities, but didn't give a full list of dignitaries. It took her half an hour to scan all the articles, and still she was no closer to learning the identities of those people than she was before. She learned a ton of other interesting facts, though.

Leaning forward and to the side, she spotted Jo, a book open on her crossed knee, head resting on her palm. She sat relaxed in a big, cozy chair, obviously oblivious to the world.

Seeing Jo brightened her mood a little, and Imma indulged in a minute of unobserved gawking, thinking of the first time she'd seen her, back in college. As Imma looked at her now, she didn't see the graying, wrinkled septuagenarian, but the coed she'd fallen in love with all those years ago. Apparently sensing her stare once again, Jo looked up and waved, and Imma looked around before ducking to the side of her cubicle and blowing a covert kiss. Playing along, Jo looked around before catching it, and instead of putting the kiss on her lips, or even her cheek, she held her open palm to her heart, as she gazed at Imma.

This was how it had always been between them, and how it still was. On Jo's good days, anyway. Imma had learned to treasure those.

Sitting back, Imma thought again about her fruitless internet search. She closed her eyes and took a deep breath. Simply feeling the flow of air through her nasal passages, down her throat, and into her chest miraculously relaxed her. After several repeats, she opened her eyes, and a new idea came to her.

Typing in a fresh search, she found something she was looking for. Then she entered a number into her phone, glanced once again at Jo, and stepped out to the vestibule before hitting *Send.*

After several rings, her call was answered. "Good morning," she said pleasantly. "My name is Imma Bruno. I'm with the *Garden Gazette.*" A true statement, because she'd been doing a weekly book review for the newspaper for thirty years. "I had the good fortune to attend the exhibit yesterday and am writing a review on it for my newspaper. I wonder who I might talk to in order to get some details about your museum in general and this show in particular."

Imma listened as the man on the other end told her that the assistant to the producer of the exhibit, a woman named Adrienne, could help her. Unfortunately, though, since this was only the second day of the show, and it was sold out, Adrienne was quite busy, and he was sure she couldn't come to the phone. Imma had to settle for the woman's e-mail address, which she entered into her phone in real time before heading back into the library.

Jo was in the same place, seemingly still engrossed in her book.

Imma walked back to the vestibule and dictated her correspondence, congratulating Adrienne on the exhibit before asking a dozen questions about it, including a request for a copy of the VIP list. Pressing *Send*, she sighed. Now she couldn't do anything but wait.

Back inside, she walked over to check on Jo. The book that held her attention was a classic spy novel, one they'd both read years ago. Gently, she squeezed her shoulder. "How's the book?"

"The first twenty pages are very good," she whispered.

Imma laughed quietly. "Okay. I'm going back to my research."

"My stomach's growling," Jo said. "Maybe we should head to breakfast."

They'd both had yogurt cups before leaving the house, but Imma supposed it was time. Glancing at her watch, she smiled. "We can get an early lunch if we want. Just give me ten minutes."

The trip to the library had been a complete failure. She knew no more about the people at the exhibit than she had before, and she'd done nothing to expand her knowledge of Fabergé eggs.

"Ten minutes," she whispered. "You've got ten minutes."

Searching for *Fabergé eggs*, Imma found hundreds of hits. Perhaps more. "Whoa," she said quietly, then randomly clicked on one of the results. The article talked about the first Fabergé egg, and she skimmed the story about Tsar Alexander III and his wife, Maria Feodorovna, to whom it was given. It was the Jeweled Hen egg, the very first one showcased at the exhibit.

Imma loved how they portrayed that one. At the entry to the exhibit, half of an eggshell the size of a small car blocked the path, forcing the patrons to walk around it, observing the fine details of the hen nesting inside on a bed of golden straw. A motion detector or a timer caused the hen to stir, and it blinked and rotated in the bed. The other half of the shell lay on its side, and visitors had to walk through its golden interior to exit the exhibit.

Not every egg created for the Russian royal family by the House of Fabergé was celebrated, but the ones they'd chosen to represent were amazing. Each "room" of the MMAA exhibit was different, a huge showcase dedicated to a particular egg, using an array of artistic mediums. Glass and metal, jewels and fabric, animation, mechanics, water, and light all created an alternate universe in which the egg was the star.

Imma's favorite had been the Imperial Palaces egg, and she read next about that one. It had been one of the last eggs created, celebrating the railway that connected the Alexander Palace in St. Tsarskoe Selo to the Winter Palace in St. Petersburg. At the exhibit, visitors boarded a miniature train car that shuttled them through a tunnel in a large egg, around the exterior of the Alexander Palace, and through to the next exhibit.

Her article briefly mentioned the VIPs who'd been present at the event: heads of all the New York museums, the mayor, and multiple collectors of eggs from around the globe, as well as some New York celebrities of stage and television. It mentioned that the former Russian ambassador to the UN, Mikhail Bichefsky, couldn't make it to New York, but his representative, Nick Orlov, had been there, as had the grandchildren of Jonathon Giles, who'd perished with three eggs in the North Tower of the World Trade Center. Imma printed the article to read later.

Imma glanced up from her computer, saw Jo still flipping pages of her hardcover, and returned to her own task. She typed the ambassador's name into the search engine, and the computer whirled with responses. Amending her search to include Fabergé eggs yielded instant results. She clicked on one from an art magazine and skimmed through it. The article seemed to be more about the man than his eggs, but she decided to print it so she could read it in full later. She found several pictures, including one of him posing in his office, his collection of art behind him. Imma printed this article, too.

Another headline caught her eye, and she skimmed an article about an egg that had sat in someone's house for years before it was discovered to be an authentic Fabergé. It was sold for tens of millions of dollars. Next, she read the story of a scrap dealer who bought an egg at a flea market planning to melt it down, only to realize he had a masterpiece on his hands. Again, that egg sold for millions of dollars.

Next, Imma searched for information on the Giles eggs, as she'd learned they were called. The first hit was about all the more than $100,000,000 in art lost by the various companies whose businesses were housed in the World Trade Center complexes, including a company called MGT. It was an investment firm founded by Jonathon Giles. Although the article looked interesting, only a few sentences mentioned the Giles eggs.

After scrolling farther, Imma found an article about Jonathon Giles's widow, Gloria, and her fight with the insurance company over the lost eggs. It took more than three years to settle the claim, according to a follow-up story. Imma printed the article and paused to check on Jo, who was walking in her direction.

"Time to go," she said aloud. After logging off the computer, Imma stood and smiled. "Ready?" she asked.

"I found you a good one," Jo said, handing Imma a brand-new title from one of her favorite authors.

"How'd you get this? It's a new release."

"I asked Jenn for a recommendation, and this is what she gave me."

"When was that?"

"When you were outside," Jo said matter-of-factly.

So much for being the unconfused partner, Imma thought. "Thank you."

They approached the checkout desk, and Imma handed over the new release, and then Jo put hers on top. Jenn gave them a big smile. "I think you'll like this book, Imma. It has a great twist at the end."

Imma could see her eyes dancing and laughed. She liked Jenn. She was friendly and energetic, extremely well read, and knew authors from Hemingway to Radclyffe.

"Thanks so much. I need a good book to keep me busy between book-club titles."

"I heard the book club went to New York," she said.

"That's right. We saw an amazing exhibit at the MMAA. Try to go if you have a chance."

"I read the review, and I'd love to. So that's why you wanted the books on Fabergé eggs."

Imma suddenly remembered the book she'd borrowed. Pulling it from her bag, she handed it to Jenn and thanked her.

"Those eggs are amazing," she said. "I had a chance to visit St. Petersburg in college and saw about a dozen of them at the Hermitage."

Imma had read about the Hermitage collection, and it was actually nine eggs, but she didn't correct Jenn. Perhaps they'd had more when Jenn was there. "Really? That must have been amazing. I haven't seen any, but I feel like I know all about them now."

"Well, if you want to learn more, that other book is here. It was in the night drop when I opened up this morning."

When Imma had searched the library system for books, she had seen two on the topic of Fabergé eggs. One had been unavailable, and the other she'd just returned. But the unavailable book had been in the Philadelphia area, not Garden. She mentioned that fact to Jenn.

"I know, right? The library there sent it here. What a coincidence that two different people from Garden borrowed both books on Fabergé eggs."

Imma had a funny feeling about who that other person was and longed for the days when the name was written on a card on the inside cover of the book. Before she could ask, though, Jenn volunteered it.

"I can understand you reading about the eggs, Imma. You're quite the intellectual. But Chris Henry?" Jenn shook her head. "It just goes to show, you never really know people."

As they left the library, Imma's head was spinning, though she wasn't really surprised it was Henry who'd borrowed the book. After all, he'd been at the exhibit—he was obviously interested in Fabergé eggs. Imma just couldn't fathom why.

Henry and his former wife, Yvonne, had led quite the simple life. Once a year (according to Gigi) their mail accumulated at the post office while they were vacationing, but other than that, they were rather reclusive. If they bothered to attend any of the many local craft fairs and fund-raisers, they smiled politely but kept their distance. They didn't attend church. They rarely ate at restaurants, and they weren't involved in the community.

When they first moved to Garden, Yvonne had opened a fitness studio. Not only did she do personal training for half the citizens in town, but she taught yoga and tai chi as well. She'd purchased the old fire station at the end of Main Street and used the existing brickwork in her decor. The place had been a huge success until Yvonne became ill about five years ago. One day she closed the doors, and a year later

Henry shuttered the building. It was rumored that Yvonne had left him, but why he hadn't sold the building, or at least the business, mystified everyone in town.

Not quite the mystery that Henry was, though. Googling his name was useless—she found far too many Chris Henrys. He had no presence on social media. He didn't seem to work, and he had no known hobbies other than running. On the rare occasions he left his house these days—whether to shop for groceries or pick up his mail—the locals acted like they'd seen a celebrity. It was mentioned in conversation and passed along as gossip. "Henry was at Shop Rite today. Looks like he's stocking up on canned goods for the winter." Or, "I saw Henry at the post office. He got quite a few packages from Amazon." Or, "Looks like Henry has a cold. He picked up a bottle of cough medicine at the pharmacy."

While Imma couldn't be quite certain no one was talking the same way about her comings and goings, she was sure they didn't talk about other Garden residents in the same manner. By being so scarce, Henry had made himself popular.

Through her work in the library, Imma knew him better than most. Henry might have had an aversion to humans, but he had an intimate relationship with books and read voraciously. Before e-readers, he'd take home a book or two a week, often engaging Imma to borrow them from other libraries. His tastes were eclectic, from what she liked to refer to as "the Holy Trinity of men's fiction"—history, mystery, and science fiction—to self-improvement and home-improvement. When Henry came to her counter, Imma tried to engage him in conversation, but other than enthusiasm about what he'd just finished or was about to begin reading, he didn't speak much. He usually met a "hi" from her with a nod and a half-smile, and she knew from conversations with friends, such as Gigi, that her experience was the norm.

As she buckled her seat belt, Imma bit her lip, wondering once again about her mysterious neighbor and his interest in Fabergé eggs. Then she pushed her thoughts aside as she realized she desperately needed a cup of coffee.

"Tori's?" Imma asked as she buckled her seat belt. "Or would you like to take a ride to the lake?"

"Tori's," Jo said. "It's closer."

"You got it," she replied, shifting the car into gear. Imma could only hope Jo ate once she had food in front of her. But just showing an interest in food was a victory. Jo had been slim when they met, but Imma wouldn't have been surprised if her old college bell-bottoms slid right off her hips now. She was frighteningly thin.

Garden's library was located on one of downtown's side streets, allowing the generous parking lot most of the businesses on Main Street lacked. Imma was tempted to leave the car at the library and walk, because Tori's Coffee Bar didn't have its own lot. In fact, on a Saturday morning, Imma wasn't optimistic she'd find a spot anywhere near the place. But she tried anyway.

They found a metered spot three blocks past it and enjoyed the morning sunshine. It was just after eleven o'clock, and already the heat was evident as she exited the car. By early afternoon, it would be a scorcher. Hopefully, a little rain in the forecast would cool it off. Either way, she and Jo would be fine, with new books to enjoy. They'd sit in their sunroom, reading and bird-watching from the windows, sipping homemade lemonade, and, more than likely, fall asleep in their chairs.

And with all those articles Imma had printed, she hoped she'd be able to find out a little more about who'd been at the MMAA yesterday.

CHAPTER EIGHT

A very placed her order with Tori, the fifty-something owner of the great coffee shop on Main Street in Garden, then took her buzzer to a table in the corner and had a seat. She'd started coming to Tori's a few years ago, after reading about it in the local paper, and hadn't been disappointed. At least once a month, when she escaped to her grandmother's estate in the mountains, she'd visit the shop, log into the Wi-Fi, and spend a mindless hour checking emails and downloading things to read later at the house.

After she finished her coffee, she'd stroll along the street, concentrating on her breathing, allowing all her stresses to float away on the breeze. She window-shopped but occasionally walked inside the stores and made purchases. Since she'd started visiting Main Street as a teen, many of the businesses had changed hands or folded, but in just as many, the same familiar faces greeted her. Avery loved Garden and supported its economy, and those small shop owners, who greeted her by name, sold her everything from ski equipment to cosmetics to flip-flops and gourmet cheese.

She hated to consider what would happen to her family's home here when her grandmother died. Even though she was a strong-willed woman, she had long passed eighty, and Avery knew she wouldn't live forever. Her job constantly taught her how short life could be, and at her grandmother's age, each day was a gift. Avery brought her to the mountains whenever she would come, but lately she made the trip less often, citing any number of ailments as her reason. The rest of the family had stopped coming here after September 11. It was as though the memories were too painful, and they simply walked away.

Avery had been thinking of the property's future for a while now. Was it time for her to walk away, too? As a pathologist, she could probably live in Garden and work here. Yet it would be difficult to follow her calling to identify remains from Ground Zero. To do that, she had to live somewhere within a reasonable train ride to Manhattan. But she could keep coming here as she did, enjoying a weekend in the mountains after her work-week in the city. Even if she bought her own home here, something small, she could visit this peaceful place whenever she wanted to. Or maybe her grandmother would sell her some of the land, the parcel by the lake, and she could build her own little home.

Both ideas gave her joy, a feeling interrupted by a woman's voice.

"Good morning, Tori," someone called cheerfully.

Avery looked up to see two women walking toward the counter, their elbows locked in solidarity. It wasn't unusual to see lesbian couples in Garden, and Avery studied them as they approached the counter.

The one who called out was shorter but seemed to gently guide the other, pointing out items under the bakery glass and reaching for her wallet when it was time to pay. Yep, definitely a couple, Avery thought as she heard her name called for her order.

As she picked up the tray containing her toasted apple muffin and iced caramel coffee, Avery smiled at the women. The shorter one looked at her and stared for a second before returning the smile. It seemed the woman recognized her, and she seemed vaguely familiar, but Avery couldn't place her face.

"Good morning," she said before turning with her tray and heading back to the window.

Imma's job as a librarian brought her into contact with many of the local residents. At least the literate ones, she thought with a smile. But the woman who'd just picked up her order from Tori wasn't from the library. Imma had seen her somewhere else, and recently.

As she and Jo split the newspaper and settled into comfy chairs to read, she looked around the edge of the world news and stared at the woman again.

Her dark hair was pulled up, but tendrils escaped all around, framing her face in waves. She wore no makeup, but her flawless skin didn't need it. She was tanned or Italian, hard to tell, but based on her hair color, both could be true.

"Jo," Imma said. "Be discreet. Look at that woman over there. The one at twelve o'clock. Who is she?" Even though Jo's short-term memory was failing, she was still good with faces.

Jo abruptly turned her entire body toward the front of the shop and very obviously checked out the object of their conversation.

"Never saw her before," Jo said loudly enough for the entire store to hear. "But if you want to know who she is, go ask her."

Imma looked at Jo and was reminded why she'd fallen in love with her all those years ago. Jo made things seem so simple.

"I think I will."

The woman's attention was divided between her muffin and her phone as Imma approached her, but she seemed to sense her presence and looked up with a smile.

"Hi," she said, and Imma's brain focused back just twenty-four hours, to the street in New York just outside the museum, and she made the connection.

"You're the girl from the museum. The Fabergé egg exhibit in New York City yesterday."

She must have sounded like a stalker, because the woman appeared cautious as her smile slowly faded to neutral.

Imma shook her head and brought both hands to her heart. "I'm sorry. I didn't mean to startle you. I'm Imma, and I live here in Garden. My friends and I were in New York yesterday to see the exhibit at the Manhattan Museum of Alternative Arts, and I could swear I saw you there. With a very handsome young man, I might add."

The smile slowly re-formed on the woman's face as she wiped her fingers and reached a hand to Imma. "I'm Avery Hutchins. And yes, that was me. And my brother."

Imma recalled the woman leaving the exhibit before the public entered, during the VIP opening celebration. She wondered what sort of VIP Avery was, but her sense of decorum prevailed, and she didn't ask. Instead, she inquired about the exhibit.

"What did you think?"

Avery sat back in her chair and met Imma's gaze. "I thought it was really amazing."

Imma felt an adrenaline rush as she remembered it. "Me too," she said as she felt a gentle touch on her elbow.

Turning, she saw Jo beside her.

"Have you figured out how you know this young lady?" Jo asked.

Imma nodded and introduced them, then explained the chance sighting the day before. "It was hard not to notice them—they're a striking couple."

"Imma." Tori's voice boomed behind her.

"That's our food, Avery. I won't keep you any longer."

"Would you care to join us?" Jo asked. "I'm sure Imma would love your take on the exhibit."

Avery didn't hesitate. "I'd love to."

Avery gathered her things while Imma collected her food, and they met back at the table.

"So you ladies live here?" Avery asked.

Jo nodded. "I grew up in Philly, but I came to college in the Poconos and fell in love."

Avery nodded. "The mountains are very appealing."

"Yes," Jo said. "But it's Imma I fell in love with. And she's from Garden, so here we are."

Avery smiled warmly, and Imma felt a connection to her. She was a beautiful young woman, but she was also a beautiful person. Imma could sense it. And she was dying to know more about her. Why was she at the exhibit in New York City, with the VIP crowd? What was she doing alone at Tori's coffee shop in Garden less than twenty-four hours later? The two places couldn't have been more divergent.

"How about you, Avery? Are you a native or a transplant?" Imma asked with a smile, well aware of the population shift post September 11. Once, she'd known most people in town, but now with e-readers and new arrivals, not so much. From the looks of her, Avery was the right age to have come after the tragedy that caused so many people to seek the relative safety of the mountains.

"A little of both, actually. My mother's family has lived here since before the civil war. One of my ancestors fought in that conflict, and he has a huge marker on his grave from the Union Army. But after World War II, my great-grandfather moved his family to New Jersey, and that's where I grew up. The lake house in Garden is still in the family, though, so I've been coming here since I was born."

"What's your family name?" Imma asked.

"My last name is Hutchins, but my grandfather was a Giles."

Now Imma understood. "Oh, Avery. I'm so sorry. I can't imagine how bitter-sweet the exhibit must have been for you."

"What?" Jo asked. "What did I miss?"

Imma didn't take her eyes off Avery as she spoke. "Avery's grandfather was Jonathon Giles. His family owned the candle factory out on the old highway. He was killed in the World Trade Center."

Jo reached a hand across the table and squeezed Avery's. "Oh, honey. I'm so sorry. How awful that was."

Avery gave them a sad smile. "Thank you," she said softly. "What's really awful is that I don't remember him. My father, either. I like the Poconos because I feel close to them here."

Her words stunned Imma. "So, it wasn't just your grandfather? Your father, too?"

Avery nodded. "My dad worked for my grandfather. They were in the North Tower, the first tower that was hit. They were above the impact area and couldn't get out."

Imma left unsaid the horror of that experience and instead jumped up and rounded the table to hug Avery. Her own grief and anger and fear from that time returned, but she fought her tears. What right did she have to cry when the events of that day had impacted this young woman so tragically?

"Thank you," Avery said as she hugged Imma back.

Avery wiped away a tear.

"It's good that you come here, Avery. To the mountains. The Giles family helped build this area. They were part of the foundation that started the hospital, they have been involved in land conservation, and there's a business school at the college your grandfather sponsored. Even though the family moved out of town, they're very much a part of the fabric of our community."

"You sound like the local historian."

"Close enough. Former librarian."

Avery nodded and studied her for a moment. "The Garden Library?" she asked, and Imma nodded.

"You seemed familiar to me when I first saw you, but I couldn't place your face. Now I think it's from the library. My grandmother used to take me there when I was little."

"I've put on a few pounds since you were a child, and added a few strands of gray to my hair, so I can understand why you wouldn't recognize me. But I remember your grandmother coming in with you. She brought you to story time."

All three of them laughed as they shared their memories of those days. Avery was always excited to hear the story at the library, but disappointed because it didn't have enough copies of the featured book for her to take one home with her.

"That was always a big concern. Plenty of tears when the children learned they couldn't borrow the book. We actually made a policy that we wouldn't loan the book out the same day as the reading because it caused too many problems."

Avery nodded. "I imagine the parents were the real issue."

"It took a little time to adjust, but eventually I trained them."

They shared a laugh and then grew quiet. Imma realized they'd finished their food as they'd talked and were nearing the bottom of their coffee cups.

"I'm so happy we ran into each other today. You mentioned you're from New Jersey, but how much time do you spend in Garden?"

Avery smiled. "As much as I can."

"Do you work?" Imma knew the Giles fortune had been enormous at one time, but who could tell how people squandered money, or made bad business decisions, or were victims of progress, like typewriter salespeople.

"I do. I'm a doctor. A resident, actually, in Manhattan. So when I'm off for a few days, I like to come out here."

"By yourself?" Jo asked.

Avery laughed. "Yes. All by myself. My grandmother has a cleaning woman who comes in every week, and she makes sure all the repairs and maintenance are done, so I just bring some food and my hiking shoes and a good book, and I'm set for the weekend."

"Do you have a gun? For protection?" Imma asked.

Avery stared at her. "Do you have one, for protection?"

"Several."

"I have an alarm system, so I'm fine. I'm safer here than in New York, I'm sure."

"I did read that the homicide rate is on the decline," Jo murmured.

Avery laughed. "You two are adorable."

"I'd love to see you again, Avery. Do you want to share your contact information, and you can let me know when you're in town?"

The beam of Avery's smile gave Imma her answer, and they exchanged phone numbers.

"Are you free tomorrow?" Imma asked, eager to spend time with her. "I usually make brunch on Sunday mornings. You're welcome to join in. Sometimes a friend or two stops by, but it's not usually a big crowd. Members of the Tuesday Night Book Club."

"I'd love to stop by." Lauren would come home in the morning and sleep for half the day, so Avery planned to leave Garden around lunchtime. Brunch would be perfect.

They said their good-byes and shared a group hug, and as she and Jo walked from the coffee shop, Imma had a little bounce in her step.

• 85 •

CHAPTER NINE

Curt, dressed casually in athletic shorts and a T-shirt, looked like any other typical citizen who had finished running and rewarded himself with a coffee. As he sat on the bench directly across from Tori's Coffee Bar, watching Avery and reading his phone, he felt certain he blended in with the rest of the citizens of Garden.

He might have followed her there, but her schedule was so predictable that he'd simply gotten up early and waited for her. Since he'd planted the tracing device on her car, he always knew when she was visiting the Poconos, and he'd been alerted the night before that she was close by. This morning he'd enjoyed a leisurely five-mile run to town, inspected the firehouse, stopped at the hardware store and placed an order, and then gotten his coffee and waited.

The run had done him good. Since he'd decided to sell the third egg, he'd been plotting and scheming and worrying. He could no longer simply walk uptown to the UN and contact Bichefsky, who'd long since resigned his position. After considering other buyers, he'd returned to the former ambassador. Better the devil he knew, Curt rationalized. But how to contact a man in Russia, during an ongoing war when travel was restricted? Even if he didn't have worries about his passport, Americans traveling to Russia had to draw a little attention.

Discretion was the key. He hadn't had any idea how he would sell the egg, but he began his planning process, and six months ago he'd read an article about the upcoming exhibit at the MMAA. This approach had required patience, but Curt considered it the safest strategy. So, he waited and was rewarded by a meeting with Nick yesterday. Now, he had only another week, and this twenty-something-year-old affair would finally end.

Just thinking about it made his tension palpable, and he forced himself to relax. *Breathe in, breathe out.*

Just then Avery pulled up in her old Camry. As he watched he saw the three-year-old he once knew—carefully assessing the traffic before exiting the car, dutifully inserting quarters into the meter, shyly nodding and smiling at the people passing by. His heart swelled, and he felt that familiar connection. Suddenly, she stopped and turned her head, as if she felt his presence. His mouth grew dry as he buried his head in his phone, watching from the corner of his eye as she moved on.

He'd had that thing with her since the first time he saw her, when he held her close to him and she settled in and fell asleep in his arms. He'd been too afraid to move, to startle her or wake her. Now he was afraid to move, afraid she'd see him. But why? What did he have to lose, really? It was all gone. His family, his money, Yvonne. Why keep pretending?

Then he remembered the fear he'd felt yesterday when Nick pushed him into the car. He hadn't wanted to die. And he didn't want to go to jail, either, even for a few hours while his lawyer determined how to bail him out.

He had this, these little moments of pleasure when he got to see her. It had to be enough. For now, anyway.

When he and Yvonne had begun plotting his escape, they'd chosen the Poconos over other destinations such as Florida and the Southwest because he'd hoped his proximity would allow him some time with his daughter. Morgan's family had been there for years, and she'd spent her summers there, and Curt figured the children would, too. Of course, when he'd been formulating those plans, he'd thought he'd be divorced, sharing custody. After his plan to steal the money and the eggs evolved, he realized the Poconos was the perfect place to disappear. It offered vast stretches of undeveloped land, millions of acres of forest and state parks to hide in. He'd thought Garden was the perfect small town, a place where no one knew him and he could blend in. Little did he know that he and Yvonne would be instantly famous here, simply for being new.

He'd managed to maintain his distance, and though he knew the people of Garden considered him an oddity, he'd become *their* oddity, and they'd accepted his presence like a mismatched piece of furniture inherited from the in-laws. Not their first choice, but tolerable.

Sipping his coffee, he watched as Avery ordered hers. On occasions when he felt daring, Curt would drive to Tori's and hide in the corner behind his laptop, eavesdropping as she ordered. He loved the sound of her voice, startlingly deep for such a young, thin woman. He was considering doing that today, slipping in and hiding behind the newspaper, when he spotted Imma Bruno walking toward Tori's.

What was up with her? It seemed she was following him, yet how was that possible? It wasn't. It was just his paranoia again. But of all the people in Garden to show up at the MMAA, why did it have to be her? And why did she have to be at Tori's now, when he wanted to get closer to Avery?

Fuck! Curt thought and sipped his coffee, practicing the things Yvonne had taught him all those years ago. *Breathe in. Breathe out. Relax. Don't stress over the things you can't control.*

He forgot about Imma and instead focused on his daughter. Like today, Avery was typically alone, but in the past three years or so, she'd brought a woman with her a few times. It hadn't taken much detective work on his part to determine who she was, and that his daughter was gay. One of his many regrets about the choices he'd made was that he couldn't tell her he loved her. His favorite aunt had been an "old maid," though she was only a few years older than his dad. She had a "roommate," and Curt was never allowed to stay overnight at her house, except in emergency cases when there was no one to watch him.

It was her, his Aunt Kathy, and her friend Maureen, who taught him to throw a ball, and took him to Phillies games, and bought him his first baseball cards. Of his vast collection, many of the treasures, the older and rare cards, were Maureen's. She'd been a sports fan as a child and treated those cards as if they were paintings at a museum, so they were in mint condition. When she died of cancer at forty-five, she left her collection to him. Never once, no matter how poor he'd been in college or when he needed a down payment for his first condo, did he consider selling those cards. Before he disappeared, he'd drawn up paperwork that bequeathed them to his children, leaving the paperwork and the collection with his lawyer because he didn't trust Morgan to follow his wishes.

Few people in his life had loved him, but Curt knew Kathy and Maureen did, and what he saw in their eyes was a deep love and respect for each other. He didn't understand gay or straight as a child, but he understood that. Theirs was the best relationship he'd ever known, and if his daughter could have something similar with her girlfriend, he was happy for her.

He caught himself. She was Avery's wife now, and he'd been shocked when he saw their wedding photos posted on her social-media account. He hadn't even known she was engaged. How he wished he could have been there, to walk her down the aisle and dance with her. Did she even do that? He had no idea. Wedding details were limited, but he saw the pictures, saw how beautiful and happy they both looked.

He only hoped Morgan had been supportive, that Avery had a parent to talk to and trust, who loved her unconditionally.

It was easy to look at a thing retrospectively and find the mistakes that shouldn't have been made, but at the time he decided to leave, Curt had no way to know September 11 would happen. He was supposed to leave his wife abandoned and angry, with her family to support her and the children. Instead, he left a widow who'd lost her father, dealing with tremendous grief and a frightened community of friends, in an uncertain world. Morgan had remarried within a year, and the children suffered yet again, losing their surviving parent to her new husband. As far as he could tell, Gloria was their rock, and Curt was so grateful the kids had her.

Why hadn't she been at the museum yesterday? Hopefully her health was still good. She was at least eighty, and though she'd lived a charmed life, eighty wasn't young. Obviously, she'd sent his kids to represent the Giles family, and he was happy with that decision. He'd seen Jonathon, who seemed to despise the Pocono Mountains and rarely visited. Because Curt feared who might recognize him in Manhattan, he didn't want to risk spying on his son there.

A few years earlier, he'd created a Garden page on Facebook. He was too afraid of the IRS to earn income, but he needed things to keep him busy, especially in the winter, so he played around on computers. Web design was a hobby, and he volunteered his services to non-profits and tried to promote them. By creating the Garden page, he controlled it, and after leaving fliers at Tori's, he waited patiently for Avery to respond. He was rewarded a few weeks later when she joined the group, and surprisingly, Jonathon soon followed. Since they'd friended him, he was able to covertly watch them. Sadly, neither posted much, but he did get to see some of what happened in their lives.

His son should have been a model, because all his postings involved showing off new clothes. His daughter loved to travel, was a Phillies fan like him, and seemed willing to try almost any type of food. Her postings made him smile, especially pictures of herself in exotic locations. That was another thing he hadn't anticipated when he'd walked away on September 11: the security screenings involved in air travel had made it too risky for him to go anywhere. He wasn't willing to chance his fake passport being discovered, and so he'd let it expire. Christopher Henry had a Pennsylvania driver's license and a Social Security number, but no passport.

As he watched, Avery stood and retrieved her food from the counter. He knew from the times he'd followed her that she always tried something different, and he wondered what her breakfast was today.

Why was she alone? He knew Lauren was a physician as well. Was it a work issue? Surely they weren't having relationship problems. They'd just tied the knot. But of course, he knew from his own marriages—the legal one to Morgan and the fake one to Yvonne—things aren't always what they seem. He hoped for his daughter's sake she was happy with her new wife.

Curt thought of the early days of his relationships. With Morgan, it had been just a big show. Money everywhere, spent lavishly on food and clothing and jewelry, on travel and houses. Morgan was making a statement, all day, every day. Curt was no angel, but he found himself exhausted by that game and quickly grew bored with it. Not that he didn't like having money or enjoying nice things—he did. He just didn't want life to be so much of a competition.

He thought he'd hit the jackpot with Yvonne. Her spirit had seemed so pure, and she enjoyed things so diverse from what he'd known his entire life that everything about her enchanted him. The Poconos had seemed like an ideal place for them, where they could enjoy nature and all four seasons. They had a beautiful home, a greenhouse where they grew their own plants, a stream for fishing, and their own mountain for hiking. But she'd grown bored with the cultural isolation she experienced in Garden, and she missed her family and friends in New Jersey. At first, she simply visited them, but after a year or two, she began spending more and more time away. Then her parents died, and she seemed to sense life's limitations for the first time. After a breast-cancer scare, she decided she'd had enough. She wanted to start a new life, which was okay, he supposed. But she took most of the money with her.

He should have seen that coming. But who could think straight on September 12? He'd thought she loved him and that would be enough. That by faking his death he got away with the theft from the pension fund, and the theft of the eggs, and from the legal battles with Morgan. They had a fortune in diamonds that they'd used to buy the old firehouse for Yvonne's yoga studio, and they had a beautiful house and property, but it was like caging a beautiful bird. She was unhappy and longed to be free. She missed her friends in the city. She missed traveling and living a normal life. Why would a thirty-year-old, beautiful, single woman want to go into hiding forever? All that money they'd had was useless, because they couldn't spend it, given the lifestyle they were forced to live.

Faking his death had seemed like a brilliant idea at the time but was the stupidest thing he'd ever done. He'd gotten no interest on any of the money he'd stolen, so his account was drained with every purchase, every tax, every home improvement. He was too afraid to travel far, afraid of all kinds of things. What if there was a fire while he was gone, or a burglary, and someone learned things he didn't want them to know? Or if someone discovered his fake identity if he got pulled over for a traffic stop? They had no visitors to their home because he was afraid Yvonne's friends and family would be curious about his past and investigate him.

And how much time could you spend with just one person? It had been inevitable that she'd leave.

If only she hadn't gotten greedy.

Curt watched in shock as Imma Bruno approached Avery, and, a moment later, her friend joined them. Then Avery picked up her food and walked with the two women, away from the window.

"What the fuck?" he asked aloud. Why would Imma be talking to Avery? How could they possibly know each other? The library, perhaps? Gloria had taken Avery there many times when she was young. Was it possible they remembered each other? Or had they met somewhere else? Curt had no idea where, or how. Avery was a creature of habit. She'd arrive late Friday, spend a relaxing Saturday, and head back home early Sunday afternoon. Other than her typical Saturday-morning venture to Main Street, Avery stayed on the Giles property, hiking, sometimes gardening, occasionally—to his dismay—kayaking or swimming in the lake. He couldn't think of any occasion that she'd run into Imma, unless it was as simple as it seemed—they recognized each other from the library.

Curt knew he had nothing to worry about. Why would Avery speaking to Imma cause him any issues? It couldn't. It wouldn't. They could never make the connection between Chris Henry and Curtis Hutchins. They'd never connect Curtis to the Fabergé eggs. As far as the world knew, those eggs were gone, burned to ashes in the North Tower. Still, he wished Imma Bruno would mind her own business. He hoped he wouldn't have to teach her a lesson.

CHAPTER TEN

The weather had turned while they were in the coffee shop, and the rain that had been forecast was falling gently as they reached the car.

"Groceries or not?" Imma asked Jo as she started her car.

"How about the farmers' market, and we can pick up some fresh vegetables and figure out dinner."

"Perfect," Imma replied as she headed in that direction, all the while thinking about Avery Hutchins. I must be getting old, she thought. *It never occurred to me that those young kids at the exhibit were the Giles grandchildren.* Not even when she'd seen Avery in the coffee shop. *I would have figured it out eventually.* And that much was true. Sometimes things took a little longer, even thoughts, but given enough time, she figured it all out.

Fortunately, the farmers' market was covered, so even though the rear of each booth was open, and trucks backed up to the stalls, the central walkway was protected from rain. They wandered through it, window-shopping and-people watching, and picked up what they needed to sustain them for a few days, then headed home.

One of Imma's favorite places in the world was her sunroom, and even though this was a cloudy day, it was a perfect place to spend time. They had ample light for reading, and the pat-pat-pat of raindrops against the roof and windows made good company. Only the birds were missing. As Jo cozied up with her book, Imma pulled out the articles she'd printed and began reading.

Mikhail Bichefsky, the former ambassador, seemed like an interesting man. He'd made a fortune importing cars after the collapse of the former Soviet Union and was named ambassador based on the economic ties he'd formed while growing a successful business.

The article in *Vanity Fair* showed him in his ornately paneled office, surrounded by priceless pieces of artwork created by the world's most famous painters, craftsmen, and sculptors. His fortune was estimated to be over a billion dollars, and he was mentioned as a possible future leader of his country.

Imma pulled out her magnifying glass and examined the artwork on his walls. A painting that appeared to be from Renoir, a dark portrait, hung behind him. The edge of another one, this one reminiscent of Van Gogh, hung behind his desk. On the desk—a massive piece of carved wood—sat several Fabergé eggs.

On the left, behind Bichefsky in the picture, the eggs were small, their detail too blurred by the distance and technique of the photo to distinguish their identities. But on the right, in the foreground, Imma could clearly see two eggs. Both had been featured in the Giles section of the exhibit at the MMAA. The first, The Turn of the Century egg, was easily identified by the tiny painting, *The Last Days of Pompeii.* Orange fire lit the background as black smoke filled the sky and colossal statues toppled from their columns. The second egg was The Victoria, as remarkable and memorable as the first, with the queen on her throne, surrounded by her empire.

Putting down her magnifying glass, Imma continued reading and learned more about Bichefsky and his life. He was married to a movie star thirty years his junior. His first wife was assumed drowned when she fell off their yacht on the Black Sea near Sochi, but her body was never recovered. Their three children were now grown and worked in his portfolio of companies. Like many successful Russian oligarchs, he'd once been part of the KGB, a topic he didn't often discuss. In fact, he didn't discuss much, and his assistant, Nikolai Orlov, had provided most of the information in the article.

Imma put down the pages and turned on her iPad. Good! She had internet service, which wasn't always guaranteed in her little farmhouse in the shadow of a mountain. Typing in his name, she read more about the former ambassador. He wasn't a particularly handsome man, but he dressed well and had a nice smile. He'd served at the UN for five years, from the late nineties to the early two-thousands.

Imma sat back and did some mental calculations. The Berlin wall had fallen just after the Reagan administration (she remembered the late president's famous directive to Mikhail Gorbachev), and the Soviet Union fell apart not long after. That was in the late eighties. It hadn't taken Bichefsky long to amass his fortune if he was named ambassador just a decade later.

"Whatcha reading?" Jo asked.

Imma told her about Mikhail Bichefsky, his eggs, and his missing first wife.

Jo sighed. "Sounds suspicious."

"Just a little."

"You don't seem convinced."

Imma looked up. Jo was studying her. "It's not that. Something else seems off with this guy. I just can't put my finger on it. I'm reading all this information and trying to process it, and it's strange."

"What's strange?"

"I'm not sure. Maybe it's just the timing of everything." Imma told her about how he'd risen from a public servant to ambassador in such a short time.

"Was his wife alive then?"

"Yes. He bought his first Fabergé egg as a gift for her. That was Easter of 2000."

"He's a traditionalist, giving Easter eggs."

"Yes. Then he got another soon after. It doesn't mention much about the rest of his collection. It seems he developed a sudden need for privacy."

"I would imagine there's a big security risk with all that art."

"Maybe. But who would be stupid enough to steal from a former KGB guy?"

Jo screwed her mouth up. "Good point."

"So, something's bugging me. But I don't know what."

"Can I ask you a question?"

"Shoot," Imma said, swiveling her chair to face Jo.

"Why are you so interested in this subject?"

Imma paused. She was curious by nature. Some would say nosy. But it wasn't really that. She just loved to know things, to understand how a bomb exploded or cancer destroyed a human body. It was why she'd chosen her profession—access to information, all the time. These days, you could learn almost anything you wanted to know by typing in a few words on the phone. But Imma still found something satisfying about opening a book or newspaper, turning the pages of a magazine. Yet her interest in this instance was beyond curiosity. Chris Henry had been a source of frustration to her since he came to Garden, and asking her to ignore what she'd seen at the MMAA yesterday would be like asking an oyster to ignore that grain of sand. It was impossible.

She explained the notion to Jo, who smiled indulgently before turning back to her book.

Even though Jo had signaled the topic was closed, Imma still thought about it. It was so crazy how the egg exhibit had so many connections to Garden—from the Giles eggs to Henry to Avery Hutchins. She found it all so interesting, and other people might think so, too.

On impulse, she picked up the phone and dialed. She'd told a little fib on the phone this morning, when she'd used her position at the *Garden Gazette* to gain information about the exhibit. Maybe she should make good on her promise to write an article. The phone was answered on the first ring.

"Hi, Imma."

The friendly voice on the other end of the phone made Imma smile. "Hello, my dear friend." For a few moments, Imma caught up with Johnny Burns, the editor of the newspaper, better known as Gigi's younger brother. She'd been acquainted with him since childhood.

"Gigi told me you guys saw a fabulous exhibit in New York, but she didn't give me any details. She had to work today, you know."

Imma told him a little about the exhibit before sharing her thoughts about writing an article. She peppered the details with the interesting trivia about the ties to Garden, hoping to sell him on the local interest.

"I've never seen you write anything boring, Imma. You even made the high school newspaper exciting with that story about the mascot."

"Well, Johnny, you know as well as I do that a girl can be just as spirited as a boy. I didn't see any reason to restrict the mascot role to male members of the student body." Imma chuckled when she realized her voice was rising, and Johnny did, too.

"I hope you never lose that spirit."

"I can have something ready by Wednesday evening."

They discussed the word count and necessary photos, but Johnny thought he could pick up some pictures from the internet.

"And you don't usually need much editing."

"Thank you, Johnny," she said, and she realized how excited she was about the article. Already, she thought of the first person she'd interview—Avery Hutchins.

"Maybe this could be the start of something regular. I know the Tuesday Night Book Club is always doing something interesting."

Imma loved the idea. Since she'd retired, she had way too much energy, not to mention that curiosity to satisfy. She played hard to get, though.

"Let's see how this one goes before I sign a long-term contract."

Imma disconnected the call to the sound of Johnny's laughter.

"I guess I'll be cooking dinner," Jo said. "So you can work on your article."

Imma smiled and rubbed her palms together enthusiastically. "I'm so excited."

"I'm sure you had the whole thing written in your head before you even dialed the phone. So what are you going to write about?"

Imma explained her idea for tying in the local connection to the eggs, and Jo supported her. "What do you think about interviewing Avery? Would it be too forward of me to ask, since I've only just met her?"

Jo pursed her lips. "She did get a little emotional when she talked about the eggs." They were silent for a moment. "Not to mention, she might think you set her up by inviting her to brunch."

Imma bit her lip. Jo was right. This would look like a setup.

"I better straighten this out right away."

Imma scrolled through her contacts and called Avery. When the call went to voice mail, Imma left a message. She gave her no information but asked Avery to call her.

For the next few hours, Imma outlined and referenced details and came up with the general body of her article. She looked up the Fabergé workshop and learned it had opened in St. Petersburg in 1842. She thought of names for her article: "From St. Petersburg to Garden: the Journey of the Giles Eggs." But she didn't know if the eggs had ever actually been in Garden. If Avery responded to the interview request in a positive manner, Imma would have to ask her.

"Hmm," she said aloud, suddenly questioning the wisdom of this article and the time constraint she'd given herself to write it.

Reading her mind, Jo asked softly, "Second thoughts?"

Imma laughed. "No, but I may have to take you up on that offer of dinner."

"Which offer was that?"

Imma's pulse raced as she studied Jo's face. Was she teasing, or had she forgotten?

Then Jo smiled, and Imma relaxed. "What would you like? I have a whole bushel of vegetables."

Imma laughed. "Know what?"

"What?"

"You're a keeper."

CHAPTER ELEVEN

Imma woke with a start and fought to hear over the pounding of her heart. Frightened, she reached for Jo, comforted by her warm body beside her, and relaxed just a bit. What had startled her? The house was quiet, with the rain long since stopped and no neighbors or roads close enough to hear.

Occasionally, an animal in the trash startled them in the night, but as Imma listened closely, her heartbeat was the only thing she could hear now.

Glancing at the clock, Imma was disgusted to see it was just three o'clock. It had taken hours to quiet her mind, and it seemed she'd fallen asleep only an hour before. Visions of Fabergé eggs had danced in her mind, and she felt like she could name every egg, describe its details, and give the provenance of each if she had to. If she were taking a final exam on the House of Fabergé, she would ace it.

She'd become somewhat of an expert on Mikhail Bichefsky as well. The man was fascinating, from the KGB to a collector of fine arts...

"That's it," Imma whispered. "I know what's been bugging me!"

Slipping from the bed, she eased her arms into a hoodie and zipped it up, then slipped from the room. Retrieving all the materials she'd printed at the library, she took them from the sunroom to the kitchen, where the light was better, and set to work.

First, she read the article about the Giles eggs. Using a highlighter, she underlined thirteen words. The Imperial Palaces egg, The Turn of the Century egg, The Victoria egg.

Next, she went to the internet and looked up each one. On a blank notebook page, she made notes, detailing each of them. Then, using a trick Jessica had taught her, she took screenshots of each.

An hour later, satisfied she had the information she needed, she pulled out the article about Mikhail Bichefsky. Referencing her notes and her screenshots, she went over the pictures of Bichefsky with her magnifying glass.

"Hmm," she said aloud.

Back and forth she went, from the article to her notes to the screenshots. Finally satisfied, she picked up her phone and sent a group text. For the first time in history, she called an emergency meeting of the Tuesday Night Book Club.

When Imma woke the next morning, half the ladies of the Tuesday Night Book Club had responded to her text. She assumed the others were still asleep. Of course they were all concerned, but after assuring everyone that she and Jo were both still breathing of their own accord and still possessed the same body parts they'd had the day before, she promised to fill them all in at brunch. By the time their group text was quiet, all seven members of the group had responded.

As they had been for most of her life, her friends would be there for her.

Imma went to work. After all, she still had brunch to prepare, and instead of the normal four or five people, she'd have three times that many. While they prepped, Imma told Jo the news about their guests and begged Jo's patience. She didn't want to have to tell her tale twice.

After pulling a pie crust from the freezer, she turned on the oven and went to work on a quiche, dicing vegetables and turning them into an egg mixture. She poured the whole thing into the pie crust and then prepped a small ham. Jo had already put champagne on ice and mixed a batch of Bloody Marys, in addition to slicing fruit and mixing a sweet-potato casserole. In an hour's time, their feast was ready for the oven, and just in time, too. As Imma was cleaning up the mess, the doorbell rang. Their first guest had arrived.

Jo was hugging Ann when Imma walked into the living room. Ann, a regular at brunch, handed Jo a bottle of champagne to replace the one they had chilling. "I thought I'd pop by early and see if I can help. It looks to be a bigger crowd than usual."

"Thanks for the offer, but I think we've got it all covered. Maybe you can pop the cork, though. I'm due for a mimosa."

Ann went to work, retrieving glasses from the cart Imma's grandmother had brought from Italy. After pouring an inch of orange juice into each one, she topped them with champagne and passed them around. Then she raised her own. "To the first ever emergency meeting of the TNBC. I can't wait to hear what you're up to now, Imma."

Imma raised her glass, hoping her friends didn't think she was being ridiculous. But if you can't be crazy in front of your friends, when can you?

The doorbell rang again, and Imma ushered in Gigi and her partner, Terry, who hadn't attended their recent trip to the museum. After a long hug, Gigi looked at Imma inquisitively. "You're sure everything is all right? That text worried me. I didn't sleep all night."

"I'm sorry. I didn't realize the text would wake you."

Gigi patted Imma's back. "This better be good."

The doorbell rang again, and within a few minutes, the entire book club was there, sipping mimosas and Bloody Marys and looking expectantly at Imma.

"As I told many of you on Friday, I planned to learn more about Fabergé eggs."

The doorbell interrupted Imma's declaration, and everyone looked at each other before turning toward the door, where Jo opened it and welcomed Avery.

Imma slapped her forehead. When she'd called the emergency meeting, she'd totally forgotten about the invitation to brunch she'd issued her new friend.

As Imma hugged her, she realized this might be a little overwhelming for Avery. Imma had said a few people, but the basketball team had turned into a football team, complete with subs. "C'mon in, dear. No one bites."

"A new member?" Blanche asked.

"Of course not," Imma replied defensively. New members had to be vetted and agreed upon unanimously before an invitation was issued. "I met Avery yesterday at Tori's and invited her to brunch. That was before I called this meeting, of course." Imma paused. "Avery is Jonathon Giles's granddaughter. We saw her at the exhibit."

"Oh. Welcome," Dominica said, and everyone else echoed her sentiment.

"I'm going to throw some food into the oven, and then we can start this meeting. Avery, I'm sure you'll be interested in what I have to say."

Imma retreated to the kitchen, then ushered the ladies to the sunroom before speaking.

"Thank you all for coming today. I know this was an unusual request, but something is bugging me, and I need your input."

Imma went on to explain how she'd spent time at the library and on her iPad reading about Fabergé eggs, and why something was bothering her. "I couldn't put my finger on it, but I awakened with a start in the middle of the night, and it came to me."

Imma handed them her iPad and instructed them to scroll through the pictures. "These are the Giles eggs. There were three of them, all destroyed in the World Trade Center. They include The Turn of the Century egg, The Imperial Palaces egg, and The Victoria egg. They were the subject of the last three rooms of the exhibit yesterday, as I'm sure you remember."

A chorus of murmurs indicated her friends did remember those particular rooms of the exhibit.

"When I was reading about Fabergé eggs, I found an article about the former Russian ambassador to the UN. His name is Mikhail Bichefsky. Has anyone ever heard of him?"

Everyone shook their heads as Imma handed them the first page of the Bichefsky article, the one that showed him posed in his wood-paneled office, with paintings on the walls behind him and eggs on his desk.

"This guy is a billionaire. He owns rare art, valuable art. In 2000, he purchased his first Fabergé egg, the Baltic Sea one. He bought it from a Middle Eastern prince for eight million dollars. It was an Easter gift for his first wife, who loved the water. It's made of dark blue enamel and decorated with diamonds and sapphires, in a pattern representing the ocean's waves. Inside is a boat made of solid gold that floats on a wave of sapphire."

Imma glanced up. "If you look closely at the egg on the edge of the desk, it appears to be the Baltic Sea egg."

"Imma, how can you see that?" Blanche asked. "It's just a little blob."

"Oh. I forgot something." She handed Blanche the magnifying glass, and she tried again, while her friends huddled around her. Ann pulled up a picture of the egg on her phone to compare. "It's hard to see the sapphires because of the blue-on-blue, but I could imagine those clear stones are waves."

"It says the egg is five inches tall," Dominica said as she read from her phone. "That looks about right. Check out the letter opener on his desk. That's probably about six inches, right?"

"Duh," Gigi said. "Why are we looking at this black-and-white copy? We can all pull it up on our phones."

Grateful the wonky internet was functional this morning, Imma waited patiently for her friends to search the internet, then watched as they pinched their fingers on the screens and blew up the images before them. After they'd all had a chance to look at the egg, she asked their opinion. They all agreed that it could be the same egg, but none of them could be sure.

"Okay. Now look at the ones on the other side of the desk. They're much closer, so you can see them better. There are two of them. Do they look familiar?"

Everyone turned to their phones again. "These are the Giles eggs!" Rio said.

Imma nodded. That's what she thought, as well. Their position made it easier to see small details, such as the burning sky on the Brulyv painting, and Queen Victoria sitting on her throne, visible through the clear glass globe surrounding her.

"I agree," Blanche said.

"Me, too," said Ann.

"Does anyone see a problem with this?" Imma asked.

All eyes were focused on her, everyone clearly wondering what she was getting at. Yet all was quiet as they seemed to wonder what was irking Imma so much she'd sent a three a.m. text to summon them to brunch.

Finally, Avery spoke. "I think I do, Imma."

"Go on," Imma said.

"Why does a guy with all this money and an eight-million-dollar egg on one side of his desk have two replicas on the other side?"

A chorus of murmurs erupted, and Imma let everyone talk at once, knowing they'd quiet down eventually. When they did, she spoke again.

"That's exactly what I'm wondering."

"So you think this guy, Mikhail Bichefsky, somehow stole my family's eggs?" Avery asked. "Without us knowing about it?"

"I know it sounds pretty far-fetched," Imma said.

Stepping forward, Avery looked around the room, making eye contact with most of the women there. "Let me share something with you—something that few people know. The eggs my grandfather displayed in his office were fakes. Why would he put such precious treasures at risk, in reach of a crooked security guard or a disgruntled employee?" When no one answered, she continued. "He wouldn't. The real eggs were in a safe. A supersonic safe about five feet tall, hidden in a locked closet in his office. No one had access to those eggs. So they weren't stolen. And if you're implying my grandfather sold them to this Bichefsky guy, you're wrong about that, too. They weren't his eggs. He bought them as gifts, for my mom and my grandmother and my aunt. So they weren't his to sell. Who knows why this guy has copies on his desk? Maybe he's just sentimental and feels bad the eggs were destroyed. Maybe they were his favorites. It doesn't really matter why he has them. This is a ridiculous idea, and I can't believe you would even bring it up."

Imma felt awful at the obvious anguish she'd caused Avery, and she apologized.

"Thank you for the apology. I'm going to leave now. I'll grab something to eat on the road."

Imma closed the gap between them, aware of the silence in the room as everyone stared at them. "Avery, please don't. There's plenty of food, and we'd love to get to know you better."

Despite the sincerity of Imma's plea, it appeared Avery had made up her mind. "Perhaps another time," she said. "I can see myself out."

Rarely in all her seventy-plus years had Imma felt so humiliated. What had she been thinking? A retired librarian from a small town turning a little coincidence like the eggs in the photo into an international crisis. Or at least a crisis that was a big-enough deal to cause Avery pain. She'd never anticipated that outcome, and she felt just awful.

All at once, everyone began talking.

"Can you believe Jonathon Giles didn't display the real eggs?"

"If the real eggs were in the safe, what happened to them?"

"She seemed really upset. I hope she's okay to drive."

Then Mac, the retired state police officer, spoke, and they all fell silent. "I think Imma makes a very strong point."

Imma still felt awful about Avery storming out, but if Mac agreed with her, at least the wounds to her pride would be less painful at the end of the day.

"Think about everything Imma said about this ambassador. For one, he's ex-KGB, so not likely a sentimental guy."

"Yeah." Jess interrupted Mac. "But he bought the egg for his wife because she was fond of the ocean."

"Didn't you tell me there are only a handful of these eggs left in the world? He probably didn't have a lot of options. He bought the one that was for sale."

"Makes sense," Imma said. She sat, and Mac slowly moved toward the room's entrance, where she could face them all.

"Maybe Imma's theory is wrong, and these aren't the Giles eggs. But let's assume she's right. How would the ambassador have gotten them?"

"Jonathon must have sold them to him," Rio said.

"But what about what Avery said? The eggs didn't belong to him."

Blanche laughed. "I know you ladies love to pick on me because I'm a money person, and sometimes I do deserve the harassment. But let me ask you this—if those eggs belonged to his wife and his daughters, why were they on display in his office?"

"So he could show them off," Gigi said.

"Perhaps, but also so he could protect them. They were safer in the office," Rio suggested.

Blanche jumped in again. "Or they were an investment. And maybe they were only *intended* for the women. As in, when I'm pushing up daisies, if I still have the eggs, Mom gets one egg, and Suzy gets one egg, and Janey gets one egg, and don't fight over who gets which one."

Mac laughed. "You're brutal, Blanche, but I see your point. They were his eggs, so his eggs to sell."

Blanche pointed a finger at Mac. "Precisely. And if he bought those eggs as a collector, he might never have sold them. They would have gone to his family, just as Avery said they would. But this is a man who ran an investment firm. They bought and sold stocks and bonds to make money. Why not buy and sell art, or Fabergé eggs? If someone offered him enough money…"

Jess spoke up. "So he held onto the eggs for a few years, doubled or tripled his money, and sold."

"I see some problems with this idea," Dominica said. They all turned to look at her, and she continued. "First, why wouldn't the family know he'd sold the eggs? Two—why would he sell them? He didn't appear to need money. His company was successful. Three—if he did sell, why were they still insured? The article over there mentioned it took three years for Mrs. Giles to get payment from the insurance company, but she did get it in the end."

"So the insurance company believed Jonathon Giles still owned the eggs."

"It seems like a long time to wait for insurance money," Ann said.

Blanche shrugged. "I'm sure there was a lot to sort out in that time. Something like thirty billion in losses for the whole thing. They had claims for property, art, building contents, cars in the underground garage. And, of course, the human loss. The insurance companies were busy after September 11."

The faint beeping of the kitchen timer suddenly chimed into the conversation, and the ladies headed to the kitchen. Imma was happy for the distraction. Her emergency meeting had been a colossal failure. What had she been trying to prove? Even if Bichefsky had the Giles eggs, how could she prove it? And why did it matter? She told herself to let it go, and after she pulled the hot food from the oven, she slid out of the kitchen and poured herself another mimosa. Gigi followed her.

"You really got carried away with this, Im."

Imma poured more wine for her friend, and Gigi added the orange juice. They both took a few sips before Imma spoke again.

"I don't know why I got so obsessed with this idea. I guess there's just so much mystery. The eggs destroyed in the World Trade Center. Henry showing up there Friday and getting abducted by the guy in the limo. Seeing Avery yesterday at the coffee shop. This is all so fantastic, it's hard to believe."

"It is. And maybe you're right about this guy and the eggs. This meeting might have turned out completely differently if Avery weren't here."

"I'm not sure I'd want to hear this stuff if it was me. What was I thinking?"

Gigi hugged her. "You're always thinking something, Im. That's what makes you so amazing. Give it a day, apologize to Avery, and move on to the next thing."

"I told your brother I'd write a story about the eggs. Throw in the Giles connection, the connection to Garden."

Gigi's face brightened. "That's great!"

"I'm going to stop causing trouble and write a good article."

Gigi poured them both more alcohol and winked. "I'm going to make yours a double."

CHAPTER TWELVE

A very wished she felt something other than numb as she cruised the country roads that took her to the interstate and back toward New York. But before she went home, before she could possibly relax with her wife, she needed to speak to her grandmother. Because, what if Imma's hunch was true?

The memory was a strong one. It was one of her first. Her entire family—Grandmother, Aunt Tiffany, her husband, and their two kids, she and Jonathon, and Morgan and her boyfriend. Or maybe by that time he was husband number two.

They were at the Pocono house. It was the summer of 2002, and Avery was distraught that she couldn't go to school. Since her birthday was late, she wouldn't be five before the kindergarten deadline. Morgan was complaining about the cost of sending her children to private school, and each time she mentioned money, her grandmother redirected the conversation. Gram didn't like to discuss money at all, but since her husband had left her in control of quite a bit of it, she was trying to learn.

Even at her young age, Avery could sense the tension in the room, and when the other kids ran off to play, she stayed close by, listening. She was worried, and she wanted to help her mommy and her gram and her Aunt Tiffany feel happy again.

When the men left and it was just the Giles women, her grandmother admonished her mom for speaking of money in front of the men. Morgan might marry him, but he would never be the children's father. He would never have control of or access to any of the family money. Morgan should not discuss it with him.

Then her mother explained that she needed money. Curtis's life insurance had all gone in trust for the children, and she'd gotten nothing. The children were collecting Social Security, but Morgan was expected to work and support herself. Why wasn't the insurance company paying for the eggs? Morgan demanded her mother pressure them.

"I can't prove they were destroyed," her grandmother said.

"That's ridiculous. Everyone knows the eggs were at the office. He never took them out of the building. Of course they were destroyed."

"Apparently some eggs have turned up in Europe that are similar to ours."

"What?" Morgan had been agitated, practically screaming at her mother, but now she spoke in a near whisper.

"Mom, is that possible? Would Dad have sold the eggs without telling us? They were ours!"

Avery watched her grandmother hug her mom, watched all three of the Giles women hold each other and cry. Then she ran from the place she'd been hiding and hugged them all. "You can have all my money, Mommy," Avery said. "I don't need any."

"Your mommy is fine, Avery. Don't you worry. Grandma has enough money to take care of everyone." Her grandmother hugged her and shooed her out of the room. Her mother never again spoke of money, and Avery had never thought of that day again.

Until today. The memory had come back to her in a flash when Imma suggested the eggs had been sold, and Avery felt as if she'd just overheard the conversation yesterday. She only hoped her grandmother's memory was as good. She was heading there now to talk about the eggs.

Even though it was early, traffic on Interstate 80 heading toward points east was heavy. All the little mountain roads crisscrossing the Poconos emptied into three giant corridors heading east and west— Interstate 84, the northernmost, was a good choice if she was going to her apartment. Interstate 80 was in the middle and would take her on the most direct route. Avery traveled south, past both roads, and picked up Interstate 78 just east of Allentown. From there it was only an hour's drive to the suburbs where she'd lived most of her life. Her grandmother's house was in the same neighborhood.

Avery wasn't sure what Imma's strategy was when she invited her to brunch. What would drive her to think about the Giles eggs in the first place? It was odd and made Avery a little paranoid. Was something crazy going on, like in an episode of *The Twilight Zone*? It sure seemed that way. She was attending an event with her brother, and a woman claimed to see her there. The woman (somehow) follows her to lunch, then to her apartment, then to her home in the mountains. The woman and another agent befriend her, then lure her to their home to find out what she knows about stolen eggs.

Avery laughed at the idea, then stopped. What if Imma was really a detective? Perhaps she'd been undercover at the museum, studying the people there. Or maybe just studying Avery and Jonathon. She'd befriended Avery only so she could learn more about the Giles eggs. But for what purpose? The eggs had been gone for more than two decades. The only interest anyone had shown in years was for this exhibit, and the real eggs weren't even on display.

Avery instructed her phone to play spa music, and she took some deep breaths to reset her personal balance. She relaxed into the worn leather of the car seat and blew out a deep breath.

Neither of those scenarios make sense, she thought. The ladies from the book club were just bored old ladies, trying to find some excitement in their lives. They meant her no harm. Avery was sure of it.

Yet their questions about the ambassador's eggs certainly stirred up something in her own mind. The questions, along with the long-buried memory of the conversation between the Giles matriarch and her daughters, had really set Avery off.

Even with traffic, her drive was an easy one. She'd decided to forego breakfast and lunch, and when she arrived, her grandmother was preparing her own food.

After wiping her hands, she opened her arms, and they shared a hug. Gloria pulled back. "I think it's time for a new car, Avery."

Avery had heard this line before, but she really liked her old Toyota. Seeming to sense her hesitation, Gloria continued. "For me. And then you can have my car."

Avery nodded. "I see."

Gloria gently touched her hand. "Avery, please. You travel to the mountains by yourself. These days…" Gloria shrugged, and Avery saw the genuine concern in her face.

Seeming to sense she'd hit her mark, her grandmother continued. "Leave your car with me today, and take mine. I'll trade yours in, and we'll both be in better shape."

Avery could hardly argue with the offer of a five-year old Lexus SUV, and she supposed her grandmother was right. A newer car was less likely to have trouble on the highways she so often traveled on her way to the mountains. Or, worse yet, in the mountains, where she might not have cellular reception.

"Okay," she said. "If it makes you happy." Then she smiled broadly, and Gloria laughed.

Avery offered her a big hug and asked if she could help with dinner. Effortlessly, as they had done all those years ago in the Poconos, and here in this kitchen, Avery fell in step beside her grandmother as they worked to prepare their meal. Avery chopped vegetables, her grandmother cut up a chicken breast, and they threw it all together in a casserole dish with some marinara sauce.

Her grandmother instructed Alexa to set a timer for the food, and they moved to her sitting room. The house was as ostentatious as a stranger might envision, with a huge room with high ceilings and sparse, expensive furniture and tasteful works of art in the corners and on the shelves and walls. A bistro table was set for tea, with two chairs facing long windows that looked out over the garden. The fact that the table and chairs were priceless antiques, that the lamp was an authentic Tiffany, only added to the overall theme of extravagance.

But to Avery, it was normal. For as long as she could remember, this room had been set up this way, with her grandmother's elegant Chippendale writing desk at one end, sitting regally before bookshelves lined with volumes of poetry and fiction, and an impressive collection of children's tales. The carpet below their feet might be valuable to a collector, but to Avery it was the racetrack on which she'd pushed cars and the wrestling mat where she'd grappled with Jonathon.

Even though a tea service sat nearby, her grandmother instead pulled a pitcher of water from the dorm-sized refrigerator and sat beside Avery, looking out at the woods beyond. She had a surprising amount of privacy, given the population density of North Jersey.

"How's the old house?" her grandmother asked after Avery sipped her water.

"Perfect. No leaks or sparks or mouse droppings. The car started on the first turn, and I drove it around the property. None of the warning lights came on. I have a list of everything you asked for, and I took pictures of things in case you don't remember it all."

"Avery, what do you think? Is it time to sell the place? Get rid of all those dust collectors?"

"Well, when was the last time you used real silver here when you hosted dinner?"

Avery searched her grandmother's face as she responded. "It was before Pop-pop died, I'm sure. I can't imagine a gathering in the Poconos where you'd use it."

"Do you think the cousins want it? I know Jon and I don't."

Her grandmother shook her head. "No. I just don't know what to do with the stuff. No one entertains like that anymore. Some of the artwork is valuable. Not egg-valuable, but maybe enough-to-buy-a-new-car valuable. I just can't bear to sell the car. He loved it. He could have bought anything he wanted, and he chose a Toyota. Your grandfather was a complicated man, Avery."

Avery wished she could debate the point, but she only knew the stories. "Don't you think most people are? Especially the successful ones. They're on the move all the time, making decisions, planning. That gets complicated."

Gloria laughed. "When did my little girl get so wise?"

"I miss this," Avery said as it suddenly hit her. Avery had unofficially lived with her grandmother since her teens. She'd resided on campus for the first year of college, then decided she'd rather commute. So for the last part of her undergraduate education, and all through medical school, her grandmother's house in Short Hills had been home. In the year she'd been a resident, she'd been back only half a dozen times.

"If you get tired of the city, your bedroom is always open. And, of course, you can bring Lauren."

Avery patted her grandmother's hand. Her grandmother didn't understand why her grandchildren were gay, but she loved them anyway.

They were quiet for a few moments as Avery tried to decide how to bring up the subject that was bothering her. She decided to be as honest as possible. "Gram, some people believe the eggs weren't destroyed on September 11."

"Of course they do. There are more conspiracy theories about 9/11 than the JFK assassination."

"So you don't believe them?"

"Of course not."

"Remember that time when we were in the Pocs, the summer after. When Mom was crying about money because the insurance company wouldn't pay the claim on the eggs?"

Her grandmother met her gaze with piercing brown eyes that mirrored Avery's. Those eyes still took everything in and betrayed little, but Avery had no doubt her grandmother knew just what she was talking about. "I do remember that. I'm sorry you had to hear it. That's no sort of worry for a little girl."

"Why wouldn't the insurance company pay?"

Gloria shrugged. "It was a large claim. I'm sure that was the primary reason."

"Were there secondary reasons?"

"Yes. There were."

Avery laughed. "But you don't want to share them with me?"

"I'm not sure why you're interested because, in the end, your mom and your aunt and I all got the money we were owed. But if you really want to know, I'll share what I remember. And you can look through all the documents. There are probably a hundred letters and e-mails from the adjuster and the investigator who followed up on the claim."

Avery was shocked. "There was an investigator?"

"Oh, yes. It's not like a car crash where you see the ruined car. We had only our word, and the statements of various people who knew about the eggs. His personal secretary, for instance. He sent her on an errand, so she was out of the building while he went to breakfast. Otherwise, she would have been gone, too. But she testified to the investigators that he'd been at Windows on the World, and that the eggs were kept in the safe in his office."

"So why did they doubt her?"

"Apparently, right after the attacks, some eggs were for sale by unscrupulous art dealers. The insurance companies track that sort of thing, I suppose, so they can recover stolen pieces. When they heard about those eggs, they put a hold on our claim so they could investigate."

Avery was intrigued. It was amazing that she'd never heard this story before. "So what happened?"

"They looked at all of your grandfather's finances to see if he'd made a deposit that suggested he'd sold the eggs. And truthfully, I think they were just looking to see if he had a reason to sell."

"And he didn't?"

"No. His business was very strong in the years leading up to the attack, and they found nothing out of order with his personal finances. No large deposits or withdrawals, just steady growth over time, like the brochures promise."

Avery saw the twinkle in her grandmother's eyes, and it made her smile. "I guess he was very good at what he did."

"I guess he was."

If her grandfather hadn't sold the eggs, was it possible someone else had, without his knowledge? Avery asked her grandmother. "I don't see how they could. The office had a security system, so no one could get in after hours, except for the VIPs—your father and grandfather, and a few others. The cleaning people were watched by security. His office was locked, the closet was locked, and the safe was—well, it was a safe."

Avery had a thought about her grandmother's home safe. "Gram, do you think Pop-pop left the combination to the safe on a Sticky Note, the way he did at home?"

Gloria laughed. "I did once find a Sticky Note on the office safe. I made him remove it, and he put it in the inside pocket of the black tuxedo he kept in his closet for special events. Who knows how long it was there?"

"So someone could have gotten the safe combination?"

"Oh, Avery, I suppose so. But who would be in his closet? The only one in the office was his secretary, and the only people in the executive suite were the vice-presidents. They were people he trusted, who certainly wouldn't have risked their careers by stealing from the boss."

"So not likely, but possible."

Gloria shook her head. "You're persistent. Yes. It's possible. I'd say the suspects would be limited to the executive suite—Sherry, the administrative assistant; Lynn, the secretary; your father; a man named Dermot Rafferty, who died in the attack; and J. Reynolds, who was lucky enough to be on vacation that day."

"Did the investigator check out all those people?"

Gloria shrugged. "He asked the same questions you're asking. I don't suppose it was hard to investigate the group since it was so small. Why all this interest? Because of the exhibit?"

Avery nodded. "Yes, sort of. A woman from Garden, the former librarian, saw us there. Then I ran into her in the coffee shop, and we spoke. She remembered you taking me to story time."

Gloria smiled. "Those were wonderful times. But how does the librarian figure into the whole conspiracy about stolen eggs?"

Avery explained what had happened, and her grandmother listened, nodding but not interrupting.

"It's an interesting theory," Gloria said. "I didn't realize the ambassador owned an egg when I met him. I would have asked about it."

"You met him?"

"Yes. At the Met, for some black-tie fund-raiser or another."

This situation was suddenly more intriguing. If her grandfather had a connection to the ambassador, maybe there was something to the theory that he'd sold the eggs. She tried to keep the excitement from her voice. "So Pop-pop met him too?"

Gloria shook her head. "He had a schedule conflict. I attended the gala with your parents, and Pop-pop did his own thing that night."

"Gram, why do you think Mikhail Bichefsky would have our eggs on his desk? Copies of our eggs, I mean. Did he have some connection to us, to our family?"

Gloria brought her hand to her chin. "Not that I know of. As I said, I only met him the one time and didn't even know he owned an egg."

Avery reached out and touched her grandmother's arm, smiling deeply. "Did you have any idea our eggs are known around the world as the Giles eggs?"

Gloria smiled as well. "I guess we're sort of infamous, huh?"

They sat in comfortable silence for a moment, lost in their own thoughts. Avery knew her family's eggs were famous just for being lost on 9/11, and she thought it ironic. Their destruction meant their immortality.

After a moment, her grandmother interrupted their silence. "It smells good. Shall we?"

"Absolutely."

While her grandmother plated their food, Avery used the combination written on a Sticky Note, opened her grandmother's safe, and pulled out the documents they'd discussed. Then she sat down and enjoyed the chicken they'd prepared and discussed other things. It was late afternoon when Avery left, but not before squeezing her grandmother into a tight hug.

"I love you," she said.

Gloria melted into Avery's arms. "And I you. If you find out any dark secrets in the family files, please don't tell me. I don't want to know."

Avery wasn't sure if she was kidding.

CHAPTER THIRTEEN

Imma had another sleepless night, thinking about the awful Sunday she'd had. She not only felt terrible about upsetting Avery, but mortified she'd called the emergency meeting in the first place. What business was it of hers? And what must her friends think? Mac had salvaged the day by giving some credence to Imma's theory, but her claims had clearly befuddled her friends.

It had been a long Sunday, with more rain, but she did use it wisely. Even though she never wanted to see another Fabergé egg, she spent the day working on her article for the newspaper. She'd promised Johnny, and she was determined to finish the piece. It was just a little bit different than she'd intended it to be. Instead of something about the tie to Garden with a quote from Avery, she was doing a simple story. Yes, she'd mention Jonathon Giles and his family's connection to Garden, but it would be a mere fact rather than a focus of the article.

She spent her morning on her housework, and at lunchtime she decided to check her e-mail. She didn't expect a response from the MMAA, but she planned to hold out until Wednesday afternoon. At that point, she'd have to send the final article for editing.

To her surprise, when she checked her in-box, she found a lovely correspondence from the director's assistant. She thanked Imma for her interest, attached a press packet for her to review, and instructed Imma to reach out at any point if she had additional questions.

Imma wiggled her fingers excitedly before clicking on the file, but then she groaned as she saw the information. The font was practically microscopic, and even after zooming and screen-shotting, she couldn't decipher it. It was time to seriously consider a home computer and printer.

Searching the house, she found Jo napping in the recliner. She touched her shoulder gently, and Jo awakened with a start. "We have to go back to the library. I need to print something."

Imma imagined one day Jo was going to refuse her odd and random requests, but it hadn't happened yet. She hopped up, freshened up in the bathroom, then joined Imma in the car.

"What are you printing?"

"Something for my article."

"Sounds important. Should we have lunch while we're out and about?"

Imma's appetite hadn't been good since the day before, but she supposed she had to eat. And the fact that Jo requested food amazed her. Maybe her new medication was working. She seemed quite alert, with no significant memory issues in the past weeks. Imma could only hope.

They cruised by a sandwich shop before heading to the library, and Imma decided to test Jo with the credit card. She did well, bringing their tray of food to the table, complete with condiments and utensils.

"They say we should stop eating all this processed food, Im. It's not healthy."

"What did you order?" Imma asked.

"The Godfather. Italian with hot peppers and oregano-infused EVOO."

Imma laughed. "Well, if that doesn't do you in, I think you'll be fine." She had completely other reasons for laughing, though. Jo really did seem to be doing much better. Everything from her appetite to her commentary on unhealthy foods indicated that her brain function was much better than it had been over the winter months, when she started to decline.

"Why are we heading to the library?"

"I have to print something."

"I know that, silly. What do you have to print?"

Imma paused, realizing how much she missed these little interactions with Jo. She'd developed the bad habit of not discussing things, because Jo wouldn't remember what she said anyway. It saved Imma a lot of frustration.

"An e-mail." She decided to share her thoughts with Jo. Two brains were better than one. "I reached out to the museum in New York to get more information about the Fabergé egg exhibit. The director has e-mailed me already. I want to know who was on the VIP list so I can include it in the article. I'm also curious to identify that man who abducted Henry. But I can't read the damn packet because the font is too small. I have to print it."

Jo nodded while she chewed, then wiped her mouth before replying. "Man, this sandwich is great. And I can see why you're so interested in the eggs. It's kind of amazing that the owner of such treasures used to run naked through the woods just a few miles from here."

"Don't repeat that," Imma said with a giggle. She'd heard that story many times, but she was impressed that Jo remembered it. "How did you even hear that?"

Jo shrugged. "Your sister brought it up, when we were talking about Jonathon Giles after his death." Jo paused and took another bite of her sandwich while Imma did the same.

"I think it's funny. And I think you should reach out to Avery and apologize, and when you see her again, you should tell her the story."

"I'm not sure," Imma said, laughing again. "About the story. But I will apologize. I don't know what I was thinking."

"Sometimes you just get excited."

"Thanks for the encouragement. And thanks for lunch."

"Anytime."

The library was just a few blocks away, and Imma parked in her usual spot near the rear. They were heading through the front door when they nearly ran into Blanche.

"Hey, friend," Imma said.

"Hey, yourself. Hi, Jo. You're not going to believe this, but I was about to call you."

"Oh?" Imma said. "What about?"

"Imma, I did some reading last night about the Giles eggs, and the insurance claims after 9/11. Something funny happened with those eggs."

"Really?"

Blanche nodded. "Some of those claims were settled within weeks of the attacks. The Giles claim took nearly three *years*."

"Why would it take so long?"

Blanche nodded. "I knew you were going to ask that, so I called an insurance adjuster I know and talked it over with her."

"And?"

"She said the most likely reason was suspected fraud."

"What does that mean?" Imma asked. "Speak English."

"The insurance company suspected it was a fraudulent claim. That the eggs weren't actually destroyed when the North Tower collapsed."

Imma felt her jaw drop. "Get outta Dodge!"

"Now, it was eventually paid, so there was some merit to the claim, but enough doubt to hold up the payment for a very long time."

"Blanche, thank you for telling me this. I feel like such an idiot after yesterday."

"Why? It's a good little bit of intrigue, Imma. Why does a billionaire have fake eggs on his desk? Maybe there's a reason, and maybe they aren't fake."

"But the insurance paid the claim. The eggs must have been lost."

"Listen. There was almost forty billion dollars' worth of loss on 9/11. You saw the pictures of the rubble. Two million tons. How could they ever find the remains of three little eggs? Plus, Jonathon Giles's office was above the impact zone. Everything burned, so what would be left to find? I'm sure the insurance company couldn't legally deny the claim, so they were forced to pay it. But that doesn't mean the eggs were actually lost."

"So you think the ambassador bought them?"

"Perhaps. Who knows? But it's certainly possible."

Imma hugged her. "I feel so awful after yesterday. I'm writing this article for the *Gazette*, and then I'm hanging up my detective's cap. But I am so happy you shared this info with me. That you think I'm not crazy."

A big smile brightened Blanche's face. "At our age, Imma, it's important to have daily reminders of our sanity. So I'm glad I could help."

Imma laughed. "I'll see you at book club."

As Blanche walked away, Jo laced her arm through Imma's. "Feel better?"

Imma squeezed her elbow, pulling Jo closer. "Maybe a little."

At the desk, Jenn greeted Imma and Jo with a smile. "One day, I'm going to get a printer. But until I do, can you print something else for me? Please?"

Jenn laughed, and they decided for her to forward the e-mail to the library account. A minute later, Jenn handed Imma a pile of papers a quarter-inch thick.

"That's quite a press packet," Jo commented as they walked away.

"Would you mind if I leaf through this while we're here? Just in case I have to print something else?"

"Not at all."

Imma suspected Jo liked to get out of the house, no matter how trivial the reason. And she had always loved the library. Imma had worked many evenings during her career, and Jo would often drop by with something she'd cooked, or sit in one of the cozy chairs where they could peek at each other as Imma took care of the citizens of Garden.

Taking a seat on one of the couches, Imma began leafing through the paperwork. It contained pages and pages of information, and Imma thought it would all be exciting to read. She'd do that at home, later. Twenty-six pages were dedicated to information about the eggs and how the exhibit was put together around them. Yet, even though she'd vowed to give up her obsession with the former ambassador and his eggs, it was the last page of the file, the list of attendees for the opening celebration, that interested Imma most.

CHAPTER FOURTEEN

A very sat in the hospital library, and instead of reviewing her clinical hematology textbook, she was engrossed in the stack of paperwork her grandmother had given her the day before. Much of it was easy to get through, short e-mails about the status of her grandmother's insurance claim, but the bulk of the papers was a report issued by an insurance investigator.

After listing her credentials, the investigator, a woman named Maxine Browning, who worked for an agency in London, relayed an interesting tale. An informant known to have details about stolen art shared with her agency that Mikhail Bichefsky, the Russian ambassador to the United Nations, had acquired the Giles eggs. The ambassador had the eggs at his office in New York and was looking for a way to smuggle them back to his homeland, because he didn't want to pay off corrupt officials to bring them in.

The report about the eggs was contrary to reports that the eggs had been missing since the collapse of the North Tower, their last known location. Upon receiving this information in early October 2001, Ms. Browning notified her superiors. They, in turn, notified the company that insured the eggs.

After receiving the approval from her superiors, Ms. Browning met with her contact. She let it be known that she could facilitate moving the eggs from New York to St. Petersburg. Making contact and setting up a meeting took approximately three months. At that time, in early 2002, she traveled to Philadelphia, where she met with Nikolai Orlov, the ambassador's assistant. When he asked the nature of her business, she told him she was in the transportation industry. He informed her he might need something transported.

They discussed options for moving a piece of art, including by air, private boat, and large shipping containers. Nikolai informed her he would be in touch if he needed her help.

Six months went by without further information, and then in the summer of 2002, Nikolai contacted her again, stating that he needed her to transport some artwork. They met for the second time, this time in Boston. Maxine asked for more specifics, such as the size and weight of it, and Nikolai stated only that it was small. It could fit in a carry-on suitcase and would weigh less than ten pounds.

They agreed to meet again in a week's time, in New York City.

Sure that the art he was speaking of was in fact three items, the missing Fabergé eggs, Maxine reported the information to her boss. Then she began formulating a plan to transport a suitcase from New York to St. Petersburg.

First, she created a fictional company with business cards and letterhead, established a phone number that would be answered by a service, and set up a post-office box for mail. Her business: art. As a legitimate art dealer, she could certainly transport art from one country to another.

Next, she purchased three replica Fabergé eggs, complete with padded boxes and information about them. She discarded the eggs and brought the suitcase with the empty boxes to her meeting with Nikolai a week later.

Maxine was taken aback when, instead of Fabergé eggs, he handed her a small painting by American artist Andy Warhol. In addition, he had all the paperwork he needed to legitimately transport the painting—a sales receipt with proof of taxes paid, the provenance of the work, and the address of the house to where the painting was to be delivered.

Maxine accepted the assignment, easily transported the painting to the destination, and was paid a sizable fee for doing so. Then she waited several weeks, hoping to hear from Nikolai again. When he failed to contact her, Maxine reached out to him. He told her his boss was very pleased and grateful for her help, and that he would be in contact if he had further need of transportation services.

A month later, in August of 2002, Mikhail Bichefsky announced his resignation as ambassador. Surveillance was placed on the ambassador's residence, hoping he might be caught with the missing eggs, but after days without any sight of him in New York, he was spotted in St. Petersburg.

No one knew if he had the missing Fabergé eggs, or if he had taken them with him back to Russia.

An effort was then made to establish a contact within Mr. Bichefsky's home and business staffs. After many months, a member of Mr. Bichefsky's household staff became a contact but, during a several-month period after that, reported no visual confirmation that the eggs were present in Mr. Bichefsky's residence.

In the meantime, efforts were being made to establish a contact within his office. One such person was persuaded to provide information and reported back that Mr. Bichefsky had four objects on his desk, which appeared to be Fabergé eggs. The informant could not get close enough to the eggs to give any specific details about them and didn't have the knowledge to speculate about their authenticity.

It was noted in the report that Mr. Bichefsky was known to legitimately possess two Fabergé eggs, and the report gave specific details about them. The investigator stated she could not have any way of knowing which eggs, if any, were present in Mr. Bichefsky's office.

This information was passed along to the insurance company in June of 2003. In turn, the insurance company reached out by mail to Mr. Bichefsky to determine if he did, in fact, possess the Fabergé eggs they had insured. When Mr. Bichefsky failed to respond to multiple letters, the insurance company asked Ms. Browning to further her investigation.

Ms. Browning then boldly appeared at Mr. Bichefsky's office and asked for an audience with him. To her surprise, her request was granted, and in January of 2004, she met with him.

Ms. Browning was ushered into Mr. Bichefsky's office and immediately noted the presence of five eggs in the Fabergé style displayed on his desk. He guided her to a sitting area and offered her tea, noting that she was British. She declined the tea and instead asked about these eggs. Mr. Bichefsky seemed amused and offered to allow her to examine the eggs, but declined to allow her to take the eggs from his office.

Mr. Bichefsky arose from his chair and very carelessly retrieved three of the five eggs. After placing them on the table before her, he poured himself a glass of vodka and returned to his seat.

Ms. Browning said it was immediately evident that the eggs were cheap replicas of the Fabergé masterpieces. She made a show of examining the eggs and thanked him for his time. Before she left, she looked around his office, which was adorned with multiple pieces of art, and asked why he had cheap replicas of Fabergé eggs in an office adorned with genuine masterpieces. He told her he kept them for sentimental reasons.

As she was leaving, she saw Mr. Bichefsky's assistant, Nikolai Orlov. He greeted her enthusiastically, as if they were old friends. Even though she had never shared her true identity with him, he greeted her by name. She was not certain how he'd learned who she was, but she surmised it was through the same informant who first told her about the eggs.

Ms. Browning stated that she could not offer any more evidence on this matter. She had spent nearly three years investigating the claim and was no closer to knowing the truth about Mr. Bichefsky's connection to the Giles eggs. She wasn't sure if Mr. Bichefsky had deceived her, but she had no evidence that any rumors were true. She could only state that three eggs on his office desk in St. Petersburg were cheap replicas and not the Giles eggs.

The report was signed and dated in March 2004. Avery looked through her paperwork and found a notice from the insurance company that her grandmother's claim had been settled and she would be issued a check for her loss. That was in July. A copy of the check was among the paperwork, dated a few days later.

Avery sat back in her chair and took a deep breath. She'd been so angry the day before when Imma Bruno had suggested the ambassador might have the Giles eggs. Yet, the insurance investigator had had the same question. Why fakes among all that authentic art? And, to be honest, so had Avery. Now, she felt rather relieved and sighed.

She supposed it was terribly selfish, but Avery was happy the ambassador's eggs were fakes. If they were real, it would have devastated her. The legend of the eggs was huge, the generosity of her grandfather for purchasing one for each of the women in his life. What would it mean if he had sold them and kept the sale a secret from the women to whom he'd gifted them? It would have changed so much for her, and she was happy she didn't have to deal with all that reckoning.

Avery supposed she owed Imma an apology. Of course, she'd been taken off guard the day before, but she knew the woman hadn't meant any harm. She hadn't accused her grandfather of anything illegal. If the eggs on the ambassador's desk were real, her grandfather might have had a legitimate reason to sell them. Others had had access as well, and one of them could have stolen the eggs and sold them to Bichefsky. The UN was just a few dozen blocks from the World Trade Center. They could easily have met up with the ambassador.

Avery picked up her phone, prepared to text Imma, and saw that she had several messages waiting. Laughing, she read the first one. It was from Imma.

"I'm really sorry about yesterday. If you'll forgive me, I'll tell you a funny story about your grandfather running naked across a cornfield while being chased by a dog. Unfortunately, there's no video, but it'll still make you laugh."

Avery laughed just thinking of it, the tension of the past twenty-four hours leaving her.

Her fingers flew across the keys as she typed a reply, and then she stopped. Beyond the tinted glass of the hospital library windows, it looked like a nice day. She grabbed her wallet and headed for the doors. Before she reached the sunshine, she'd dialed Imma's number.

"Hello," Imma said in greeting. "I'm so sorry, Avery. I was rude to say those things." Imma pushed aside her work and sat back in her chair, relieved that Avery had responded so quickly to her text.

"No. It was actually an amazing observation." Avery quickly relayed that she'd spoken with her grandmother and read the investigator's report from all those years ago. She shared the conclusion with Imma. "So Maxine Browning made the same observation as you. And you're not even a trained professional."

The warmth of the praise infused Imma, and her spirits lifted. "What else did the report say?" she asked.

"It was pretty interesting, actually. I've never read anything like this before. It gives all kinds of details, such as dates and times of meetings, but mostly it's a story. I'm really happy my grandmother shared the paperwork with me."

Imma would love to read it too, but she wasn't about to push her luck. She'd just gotten back into Avery's good graces, and she intended to stay there. Instead, she asked if Avery was interested in offering a quote for her article. Avery was silent for a moment, then replied.

"The MMAA's Fabergé egg exhibit is a wonderful tribute to the works of the House of Fabergé, including my family's eggs. Even though we are saddened by their loss, we are thrilled to see so many people have the opportunity to step into the world of Imperial Russia and glimpse the glamour and beauty of these works of art."

Imma jotted down the words as Avery spoke slowly, then re-read them to her. "It sounds perfect," Imma replied. "Thank you, Avery. A quote from you means a lot."

"I can't wait to read the article. To think, I'm friends with a famous local reporter."

Imma was warmed that Avery called her a friend, but she didn't dwell on it, as she laughed at the praise Avery heaped on her. She did love it when people commented on her book reviews. This would be her first venture of this sort, and she hoped it would be well received.

"It's due Wednesday, for publication on Thursday. Do you get *The Gazette* online? It's only fifty dollars a year, and we publish every week."

"I don't, but I should subscribe. I usually read it at Tori's when I go for coffee, or sometimes at the library. But that would make it easy to keep up with the local news."

"Something's always going on here, that's for sure. It may not be New York, with huge galas and such, but we stay busy."

"Oh! That reminds me of another coincidence. My grandmother actually met Mikhail Bichefsky. At the Met. She was there with my parents, for a fund-raiser, and she spoke with him. They discussed the ballet. My grandmother was a dancer back in the day."

Another crazy coincidence, Imma thought. "That's just unbelievable. Do you think that's why he has those eggs on his desk? Because he knew your grandparents?" It was a wild assumption, but who knew?

"I have no idea, Imma. He seems to be a man of mystery."

"I suppose only Mr. Bichefsky knows," Imma said with a chuckle. She changed the subject. "I so enjoy talking with you, Avery. When will you be back in Garden?" Imma asked.

"Funny that you ask that. My wife, who's a surgical resident, is off this weekend, and we're coming up to the Pocs Friday evening."

"Well, Jo and I are around. If you'd like to get together for dinner, we'd love that. There's a new Asian restaurant I've been thinking about. But it's also great grilling weather, so we could cook."

"Let me talk to Lauren, and I'll text you later in the week."

"It gives me something to look forward to. Talk to you soon."

Imma was smiling again and about to disconnect, when Avery spoke again.

"Imma, I know you've been very curious about my family's eggs. Would you like to read the investigator's report? I can fax it to you."

Excitement coursed through her. It was just what she'd been hoping for. "Oh, yes. That would be really interesting."

"I'll send it over now, and text you on Thursday."

Imma recited the number for the Garden Library's fax machine and disconnected the call.

How quickly the world turns, she thought. Twenty-four hours ago she'd felt like an idiot, and a mean one at that. Now she'd found out she hadn't been so crazy. Even if the ambassador's eggs were fakes, it was smart to question why he had them on display.

Stretching, Imma looked at the papers spread before her. The press pack had been so helpful, and she was close to finishing her article. Then, she planned to look up the names on the VIP list and learn more about them. It might add something to the piece.

"Time for a break," she said aloud. She couldn't wait to share Avery's information with Jo.

She'd been in the sunroom, working on her article, when Avery called. Now, she stood and searched the house for Jo, with no success. Opening the front door, she called for her but had no response. Dread filled her for a moment as she walked across the wide front porch and scanned the yard. Jo had never wandered away, but Imma had found her in the yard a few times, seeming confused about how to get back to the house, or wherever she'd planned to go. Her limbs grew weak when she saw the open barn doors.

Had Jo taken the car out? Imma had alarms on all the house doors, so how had Jo even gotten out without her hearing?

Walking briskly, she headed toward the barn.

The house was ancient, built a hundred and fifty years ago when the land was actually worked as a farm, and when one of her ancestors decided to parcel the property, Imma and Jo took the area with the house and barn. It was too charming to add a detached garage without changing the style and character, so every morning they hiked a hundred yards to the barn to get into their cars. Much of the time, Imma just pulled into the driveway in front of the house and parked there.

Since Jo's illness, her Jeep had sat idle in the barn. Imma found her there, detailing it. Her relief to find Jo well was instantly replaced by dread. Jo wanted to drive again.

"What are you up to?" she asked, trying to keep the terror from her voice.

"I told you I was coming out here, but you were too engrossed in your search to hear me. I thought I'd clean up my car. Take her in for service. She's due."

Imma's heart pounded. She'd thought of selling Jo's car, but it had been too heartbreaking a concept. She'd bought it brand-new when she retired, complete with a tow package, so they could pull the small camper they loved so much. And they'd had wonderful times in that camper, from Acadia National Park with one pair of friends, to the Gulf Coast of Florida with another one. The idea of taking the camper out now, with Jo's health so shaky, terrified Imma as much as the thought of Jo driving.

Imma decided it best to avoid discussing the situation. In an hour or so, the idea might be gone from Jo's mind again.

"I have exciting news," she said instead.

Jo stopped what she was doing and stood, giving Imma her full attention. "What's that?"

Imma told her she'd texted Avery, then relayed the details of their conversation. "Not only does she forgive me, but she's sending me a copy of the investigator's report! She's faxing it to the library."

Jo looked down at her hands and then at her car. "Let me clean up, and I'll drive you over."

Imma swallowed all her fears and nodded. "We'll go out for dinner. I don't feel like cooking."

CHAPTER FIFTEEN

Curt walked the perimeter of his house, checking all the locks and windows and security cameras. No one was here to tamper with them—no kids being kids, or a busy wife who forgot to lock a door behind her. It was just him, and he seldom spent time on the deck anymore, and never opened windows, so these safety measures were just part of his routine. Something to pass a little of the endless time he had on his hands, and to settle his nerves and steer him from near-constant thoughts of his recent encounter with Nick.

They'd agreed to meet the following Sunday, and Curt had contacted the diamond dealer who'd helped him before. Nick was to transfer the money to the man's business account, and then he would pay Curt once the egg was delivered. A simple plan, but so many things could go wrong. Not the least of which was a violent death. Hopefully Nick's guys with guns and the diamond guy's guys with guns would cancel each other out, and they'd all walk away happy. Nick would have the Imperial Palaces egg, Curt would have his money, and the diamond guy would have a million dollars for his troubles.

Satisfied that his home was secure, he walked down the grand staircase to the ground floor, made a turn, and opened his garage door. With his small SUV the only vehicle in a garage intended for three cars, it looked barren. His tools and toys—the riding lawn mower, the ATV, the snowmobile—were all in the barn. His garage was as empty as the rest of his life.

He longed for people again. The solitude of his mountain retreat had been exciting at first, as he and Yvonne built their own little sanctuary. The house had a wrap-around deck to enjoy the views and good weather, a luxurious pool with a hot tub and waterfall, and the inside was customized to all their various fantasies. A huge kitchen with everything they needed to make gourmet meals—because they wouldn't be eating out much. A living room with a huge television and surround sound, recliners and a couch, and a beanbag chair for Yvonne. A Jacuzzi tub and a game room and master bedroom with two walk-in closets, to fill with clothes they seldom wore.

Yet, he'd been happy at first. It was a new, exciting chapter in his life, and even though he'd been in shock over his narrow escape on 9/11, and truly grieved for the people who died, he'd still been happy. Now, he was just lonely.

Perhaps with this money from the Imperial Palaces egg, he'd make a move. He couldn't buy a new property—he was too afraid of a background check. But he could rent a house. Maybe he'd become a snowbird and spend winters in Florida. He had a little golf green in his backyard, he was pretty good at chipping and putting, and he could drive the ball fairly far into the woods behind his house. He'd join a golf club and meet friends and, perhaps, a woman to fill his time.

Why not? Why was he sitting around Garden? His kids were grown, Jonathon never visited the mountains, and Avery's visits were more and more infrequent. When she was here this past weekend, he hardly saw her. Although he'd crossed the state game lands to the Giles property and hiked to the house, she'd spent most of the day inside. Finally, when it was time for dinner, she made something on the grill and sat on the deck, seeming to relax for an hour. But as soon as the sun set over the lake, she went into the house, and that was the last he saw of her. When he checked on her the next morning, she was already on the road.

So why keep the house? Why keep struggling through this miserable existence? If he wanted to leave, he'd have to do some work around here, like getting rid of all the evidence of Curtis Hutchins. His files about 9/11 and Avery and Jonathon would surely raise some eyebrows in the event of a fire or a break-in. But with the egg gone, there was one less piece of evidence for a burglar or fireman to discover. Diamonds were so much easier to hide.

He laughed at the irony of that thought. Indeed, they were.

Satisfied that the house was in order, Curt got into his car and backed from the garage.

One thing that brought him joy in his chosen isolation was the printed word. Books were his salvation, an escape to places he could never travel, an interaction with people he could never dare. He pulled out of the driveway and headed toward the library, where he'd find solace in a good book.

It was still overcast, a fact that surely contributed to his mood. Like most days, he'd risen early and enjoyed coffee while reading all the awful news of the world. He decided to skip the lawn, since it was still wet from yesterday's rain, but he did weed his flowerbeds. He'd discovered that a combination of select flowers and deer deterrent kept the four-footed poachers from his garden, but it required constant upkeep. The rain had surely washed away the spray he used, so he'd generously reapplied it. Doing something, even something so small, improved his mood. He just knew it wouldn't last.

At the library, he parked and walked in, careful to silence his cell phone. Not that he had any calls, but he didn't like to draw attention to himself. Heading toward the check-out desk, he noticed both the head librarian, Jenn, and the part-time clerk, Arlene, were there. As Jenn slipped on her raincoat, she spoke to her co-worker. "I almost forgot. A fax came in for Imma Bruno." Jenn laughed. "It's from an insurance company. Something about an investigation into the Fabergé eggs that were lost in the World Trade Center."

Curt stood perfectly still as the world seemed to spin around him. Steadying himself at the counter, he smiled politely as Arlene answered. "Are we Imma's personal secretaries now?"

"She's writing an article about Fabergé eggs for *The Gazette*. I guess this is for her research."

"What an odd topic," Arlene responded.

"Ask Mr. Henry about it," Jenn suggested with a nod in Curt's direction. "He just borrowed a book about the eggs."

Both women turned to him, and he swallowed, his mind racing. After a moment, he decided the truth was the best option. "I read about the exhibit at the museum in New York. I thought I'd learn more information from a book."

"Did you go?" Arlene asked, her eyes dancing with excitement. He was sure whatever he said would be passed to everyone she saw for the foreseeable future, so he kept his response brief. "No. I just read about it. But maybe I will in the fall." He smiled to tell her he had nothing more to say, and she seemed to understand his intentions.

"I'll save these for Imma, Jenn. You have a great night." Then she turned to Curt. "How can I help you, Mr. Henry?" she asked.

Curt handed her his library book, then asked if it was possible to order a title he hoped to read. He was distracted, though, looking at the stack of papers Imma Bruno had received from an insurance company. Why was that woman always meddling? Why could she possibly care about the Giles eggs?

"What?" Curt asked. "I'm sorry. I was thinking about something. I missed what you said."

"I can have that book by Wednesday afternoon."

"Okay. That's great. Thank you," he said as he turned away from the counter.

In front of the library was a series of cubicles and tables, intended for people who needed to write something or work in private. Curt headed to the farthest one and sat down. He had to get that fax, but how? If he took it, surely someone would suspect it was him. He glanced up and saw the camera facing the check-out desk. If Arlene was curious, it was easy enough to review it. It might not get him into any legal trouble, but taking that report would certainly draw unwanted attention his way.

He had to copy it. But how? He certainly couldn't ask. He looked at the photocopy-fax machine and bit his lip. It was positioned on the wall behind the counter, adjacent to the door to the office where Arlene was focused on her computer. If he could snatch the report, which was sitting on a desk directly in her line of vision, he could send it through the copier without her seeing him. But how would he explain what he was doing if she stepped out and found him there?

A chime sounded, and he watched as Arlene picked up the phone in the office to the rear of the check-out desk. Since the library was small, with only one staff person, the chime was necessary to let them know when the phone rang. The staff of the quiet little Garden Library seemed to field phone calls every ten minutes or so.

That gave him ten minutes to formulate a plan, because he was sure of two things: one—having Arlene on the phone would be just the distraction he needed to snatch the report and copy it, and two—it wouldn't take Imma Bruno long to show up at the library looking for it.

Counting the seconds, Curt walked from the cubicle toward the men's restroom. Three restrooms were located at the front of the building, adjacent to the office where Arlene now sat. It took him six seconds to cover the distance. He opened the door, walked inside, and looked at his reflection in the mirror.

Old, he thought. You look old. After 9/11, he'd cut his hair very short and grown the beard that had slowly turned gray. He kept that short, too. No use calling attention to himself by looking like a crazed mountain man.

He imagined the sounds of a copy machine processing papers. He had one at home, because the Internet was so spotty in the mountains, where he often printed maps of hiking trails and directions to places he wanted to visit. Not good to end up lost with no map to lead him back home. In his mind, the machine copied a page every five seconds. The report on the desk was fairly thick, maybe about a quarter of an inch. He figured that was about twenty pages. So, two minute's worth of copying. It would take him a few seconds to punch the necessary buttons, but then he could walk away, minimizing his risk of discovery, while the machine did its thing.

Sighing with relief, or perhaps to pump himself up, he opened the door and walked out of the bathroom. Then it hit him. The copy machine was sitting right there in the open, with nothing to stop the public from using it. Nothing except perhaps a security code to unlock it.

Glancing around to be sure no one was watching, Curt approached the machine and looked down. Sure enough, he saw a message instructing him to enter the code.

"Fuck!" he murmured, then headed toward the new-release section. It was in the front, so he could pick something out and spy on Arlene at the same time. His mind raced as he debated stealing the papers. It was a bad option but perhaps his best. Then another thought occurred to him. Perhaps he could do what an old-fashioned spy would do, take them into the men's bathroom and snap pictures with his phone.

He mimicked that process in his mind. It wouldn't take longer than photocopying and would be less noisy. Hell, his cubicle was near the wall. He could just take the papers there and photograph them in relative privacy.

He grabbed a new release that looked interesting and headed toward his cubicle. As soon as the bell chimed, he had to be ready to move.

A few seconds later, it did. After checking to see Arlene's attention was on her computer, he grabbed the clipped packet of papers from the counter and tucked them inside his large, hard-cover book. Back at his cubicle, he pulled out his phone and spread them across the surface, quickly snapping pictures. When he finished those, he looked up and glanced around. No one seemed to be paying attention to him. He piled the papers and spread out the next batch and quickly photographed those, too. He looked around again, and seeing no one, he spread another pile and took more pictures. Finally, he finished them all. Without putting them in order, he piled them, put the clip on the corner, and tucked the document back in his book.

Just then, he looked up and saw Imma Bruno and her wife walking through the library's main door.

"Fuck!" he whispered.

Standing quickly, he rushed toward the counter and slipped the fax from his book. After he gave it a gentle push, it fell from the top counter to the bottom one and came to rest there.

Arlene hung up the phone and turned to him just as Imma Bruno greeted him. "Hello, Mr. Henry. How are you? How did you enjoy the Fabergé egg exhibit?"

Curt had been expecting Imma to question him, and he decided the best approach was denial. Even if she knew he was lying, it was nothing she could work with. There were no further rumors or information for her to investigate. She might argue and call him on it, but he doubted it. If anything, Imma was polite. "I'm not sure what you mean."

Arlene arrived at the counter. "Hello, everyone. Imma, I have your fax right here. Mr. Henry, this is a new release so it's due back in one week. That's seven days."

She didn't even ask his member number; she had apparently committed it to memory. She simply typed something in on the computer and handed him an appointment card with the return date on it. He took it and fled, leaving Imma and her wife standing there.

Practically running, he hopped into his car and put it in reverse, then backed out of the parking lot before she had a chance to question him. It took nearly ten minutes to drive home on the winding roads, but it wasn't until he was parked safely in his garage that he breathed freely.

That was close! But he'd made it, and he hurried into the house so he could read the pages he'd photographed. He opted for his iPad, since the font would be bigger, and pulled up the pictures. Not skipping a word, Curt read the report issued by Maxine Browning from Empire Inquiries, Incorporated. Page after page, he looked at the words without even pausing to think about their meaning. Only after he'd finished did he allow himself to relax, to sit back and digest the essence of the report.

It had never occurred to him that someone would connect the eggs to Bichefsky, but he supposed it was bound to happen. He just couldn't believe the insurance company had started investigating him so soon after 9/11! And that they'd waited so long to pay the claim.

He didn't often think of his former wife, but he wondered how Morgan had survived for three years. He'd been salaried by his father-in-law at a flat one million a year. And while that was an exorbitant amount of money, after taxes it was only about fifty thousand dollars a month. He did invest some, and paid a small mortgage, but they squandered the rest of it. Food, clothing, cars, spa days, private school for both kids, the ever-changing decor of their house in Short Hills.

He supposed he'd had somewhere near a million dollars in his retirement account when he left, enough for a normal person to get by, but not for Morgan. She'd spend that in a couple of years, maybe more quickly without him there to rein her in. He'd always assumed she'd be fine, with Jonathon to take care of her. But Gloria was a different animal, more conservative in every aspect, and less indulgent with her daughters. Where Jonathon and Curtis were unwilling or unable to control Morgan, he was sure Gloria kept her in line.

He laughed at a sudden thought. Maybe that's why she'd remarried so quickly. She was broke.

Not as broke as him, though. He needed to sell this egg and move on to the next phase of his life.

He looked once again at his phone, reading the conclusions of the report. Maxine Browning had determined the eggs in Mikhail Bichefsky's office were not the Giles eggs, but she hadn't been able to prove he didn't have the eggs hidden somewhere else. Was that a reason to worry? He supposed not. The report was written twenty years ago, and he'd never heard anything on the news to suggest there was a concern about the Giles eggs or the insurance claim.

This report was nothing to worry about. He had two other worries, though.

Nikolai Orlov and Imma Bruno.

Both were potentially dangerous in their own ways.

The first time he'd done business with Nick, Curt had the security of the third egg. He'd been worried during their first meeting, but in the back of his mind, he felt sure that Mikhail Bichefsky wanted the third egg enough to keep him alive. After the terrorist attack on the World Trade Center, Curt hadn't had to deal with the potential dangers of another meeting with Nick.

Now, that moment had come. Curt had contacted his man in the diamond district and explained the situation to him. He hadn't hesitated about coordinating the deal. In reality, this was probably a routine transaction for him. And Curt had seen the armed guards at his store. He had no doubt he could handle Nick. Curt was sure he'd handled worse.

Then there was Imma Bruno. Why was she so fascinated with the eggs? He knew she hadn't believed him when he'd denied being in New York. But what would she do with all that curious energy, and how much did he have to worry about her?

Filled with a sudden rage, Curt slammed his fist into his counter. "Don't make me hurt you, Imma," he whispered.

CHAPTER SIXTEEN

Imma turned to watch Henry leave the library and shook her head.

"What a peculiar man he is," Arlene stated.

Imma agreed. "Isn't he?"

"You two are mean," Jo said. "He's just different. Maybe he has autism or something like that."

The comment caused both Imma and Arlene to pause, and they looked at each other, contemplating Jo's remark. Since the diagnosis had become so prevalent, Imma had thought about many peculiar people she'd known in her life and wondered if they might have warranted the diagnosis. There had been no explanation for their odd behavior seventy years ago, so they were just labeled misfits or strange.

But Henry wasn't that sort of strange. He seemed to have had a good relationship with his wife. They'd talked and laughed together, hiked together, explored the woods on foot and ATV. They'd skied, both downhill and cross-country. Henry went to her fitness classes, going through all the moves like the rest of the group, but without interacting. He just ignored people. That wasn't autism. That was rude.

"I don't know about that, Jo," Arlene finally said. "I think something's up with him. How he and his wife just showed up here out of nowhere, building a house in a place they'd never been before. It's odd. I always felt like he was a criminal, hiding from the law. Like a mafia guy. Isn't that what they do? Find a small town and disappear?"

Imma gasped. Of all the thoughts she'd had about Henry, that one had never occurred to her. But she supposed Arlene's train of thought was as valid as any.

"Maybe he's in witness protection," Jo said.

Imma was startled once again.

"Whatever his story is, it involves money. He spent a fortune on that property, and I heard from the contractor's wife that the house is spectacular. Top-of-the-line marble and stone and custom cabinets and all that expensive stuff."

"I can't argue with you on that point. He was a young man when they moved here, and he's never worked. I'm sure Yvonne's business made a profit, but not enough to pay for that property."

Imma felt a little guilty for gossiping, but, just like with the eggs, it felt good to have her feelings affirmed.

"It could be lottery money, too," Jo said.

Arlene pursed her lips, and Imma considered the point as well. "Why so secretive, though? Does he think the next question after 'How are you?' is going to be 'Can you lend me some money'?"

Both Arlene and Jo laughed.

"Imma, I hope you don't have anything top secret in this report. Because whatever it is, Mr. Henry had a look at it."

"What?" Imma asked, startled.

"I guess he's unaware that the security cameras are motion-activated. I was in the office, and he started prowling around. Then when I was on the phone, he grabbed the report. Truthfully, I should have stopped him, but I was curious to see what he would do with it."

Shocked, Imma was silent for a moment. It was difficult to believe. "Tell me again. From the beginning."

Arlene relayed the events at the start of her shift, with both Henry and Jenn at the counter when Jenn told Arlene about the fax. After that, Henry seemed to be canvasing the desk, and sure enough, when her attention was diverted, he took the fax. Arlene watched him on the surveillance video as he photographed the papers and returned them just as Imma came through the door.

"Do you want to see the security video?" Arlene asked.

"Of course," Imma said.

She and Jo walked behind the counter and looked at the twenty-four-inch computer screen. There were eight blocks on the screen, one from each of the cameras watching the library. The first four focused on the outside of the building, and the last four on the inside. One showed the front desk, and the other three scanned the stacks and the lobby.

Arlene clicked on the image of the lobby, and then Imma and Jo watched a rapid rewind as Arlene studied the image. She stopped on a frame where Henry walked out of the men's restroom, and then she played the video.

Huddled together, the three of them watched Henry look around the lobby, then walk to the photocopy-fax machine, then back to his cubicle. "I think he was checking to see if the machine needs a code," Arlene said before Jo or Imma could ask what he was doing.

Arlene began forwarding through the images again. "I think he was going to copy the report. I guess he thinks I'm deaf as well as old and wouldn't hear the copy machine next to my door."

They chuckled, and Arlene stopped the video again. When she pressed *Play*, the small images on the screen disappeared, and the image in question filled the entire space. They watched Henry reach over the counter, tuck the fax into his book, and walk quickly back to his cubicle. He remained standing.

The camera's view was blocked by the cubicle, but it appeared that Henry reached into his left back pocket and removed his phone. He looked down, and it was unclear what he was doing, but he was using both hands. After about fifteen seconds, he looked up, then went back to work.

They continued to watch as he emerged from the cubicle and sprinted to the desk, then clumsily returned the faxed pages.

"I have to say, Arlene, this is bizarre." Imma said.

"I suppose I should have stopped him at this point, but like I said before, I was curious to see what he was up to."

"Yes. I'm glad you didn't. I wonder myself—what's going on? I don't know why, but Henry has a thing for Fabergé eggs. He borrowed a book about them, and we saw him at the exhibit in New York. Now he steals my report."

"But he said he didn't go to the exhibit," Arlene replied.

"Well, he lied. The entire Tuesday Night Book Club saw him. He was there."

"Then why deny it?"

"It's just another Chris Henry mystery," Imma said.

"What's in this report, anyway?"

"I'm not sure of all the details—I haven't read it yet. But it's from an investigator who was looking into the Giles eggs. Apparently, there was some question that Jonathon Giles might have sold the eggs to the Russian ambassador without his family knowing. Then, when the Twin Towers collapsed, Mrs. Giles filed an insurance claim for the eggs. Obviously, it was a big claim, so the insurance company spent three years investigating before they paid."

"Well, if they paid in the end, the eggs must have been destroyed. It's not easy to get money out of insurance companies."

"Yes, agreed. And Blanche tells me the insurance industry really stepped up after 9/11. They settled most of the claims quite quickly to spare the families more grief."

"That's nice to know. I think post-9/11 was a pleasant time to be an American. I know we were all grieving for something—the loss of someone we knew, or something we knew. The heartbreak for all those people who died. The shock and fear of a terrorist attack on American soil. It was all awful. Yet, for the first time in a long time, we were all Americans again. We set aside our differences for a little while."

Imma smiled at Arlene. "That's a nice thought. And here's one. If you get tired of shelving library books, you can open a detective agency. You're on the ball."

Arlene playfully swatted away the praise. "I'm already collecting my Social Security. I just work here to keep up on my gossip."

"It's a good source, that's for sure." It was one of the things Imma missed most. When she'd worked at the library, she knew everything going on in town.

"Well, I can't wait to read your article," Arlene said as a patron presented a book to borrow.

"Thursday morning. Thanks for everything," Imma said as she turned to leave.

"See you next time, Detective," Jo said.

Imma linked arms with her and led her through the library doors and into the cool, summer night. The elevation in the Poconos was over 2,000 feet, and it tended to cool off in Garden once the sun cleared the mountains.

"I feel like we just ate lunch, Jo, but I am a little hungry."

"You only picked at your sandwich."

"I was glum."

"Yes, you were. I'm happy Avery reached out to you. You have a kind heart, Imma, and I know that was weighing on you."

Imma squeezed her elbow and pulled Jo a little closer. "Thanks for saying so."

"I wouldn't mind eating again. Do you want to go to the diner? It's a night for comfort food."

"Agreed," Imma said. Though the rain had stopped, it was foggy and cooler than usual in the mountains.

They made the short drive to the middle of Main Street and parked, then strolled a short distance to the diner. It was an old-fashioned, tin-can style, small but cozy, and an anchor of the downtown business community. When they walked in, the server greeted them by name and told them to choose a booth.

Imma spotted an empty one in the corner and steered Jo that way. She'd have a street view and be able to see everyone in the restaurant. They'd taken only a few steps in that direction when they stopped short. Rio and her wife Karen were seated across from each other.

After exchanging greetings, Karen invited the newcomers to join them. Imma looked at Jo, who nodded, and they sat beside their old friends.

"We haven't ordered yet, so your timing is perfect."

"I don't need a menu," Jo said. "I'm having a burger."

"Me, too," Imma said.

"So what's new?" Karen asked. "I hear the field trip was fun."

Imma rubbed her hands together excitedly. "It was a blast. And now I'm writing an article about the exhibit for *The Gazette*."

They both murmured their approval. "Is this going to be a regular thing now?"

"Maybe," Imma said. "I can write something monthly about the adventures of the book club."

"It's a great idea," Karen said. "You're always doing something fun. People would enjoy knowing about these places you go to."

"We'll see. It's a lot of work just doing the weekly column, because it means I have to read a book every week so I can review it. But maybe I'd substitute this and see how the readers enjoy it."

"I'm surprised to see you guys out tonight. It's a perfect night to stay in and watch television."

"I had to stop at the library, so this was easy."

"New book?" Karen asked.

"Actually, no. I had to pick up a fax." Imma told Karen about the debacle at her house when she'd called the emergency meeting of the book club. If Rio had shared the details with her, Karen didn't let on. "So, Avery not only forgives me, but she shared the report with me."

"What did it say?"

"I haven't had a chance to read it, but it basically says the eggs in the ambassador's photo are fakes."

"Well, I'm surprised," Karen said, and Imma knew then that Rio had indeed shared the whole story of the day before with her wife.

A licensed investigator had the same suspicion. I don't have anything to be ashamed of. And Mrs. Giles knew the ambassador. There certainly could have been a secret sale and a fraudulent insurance claim.

Rio jumped at her wife's remarks. "I was talking about this with Karen, Imma, because I really do think it's all intriguing. Yes, those eggs in the picture are out of place. But there's more. What about Henry? What was he doing there, and why did that man abduct him?"

Imma nodded. "It is peculiar. There are so many questions. That's why I'm so fascinated. Since I'm writing an article about the exhibit for *The Gazette*, I had the museum e-mail me a press packet. It has a list of all the VIP attendees. Hopefully, that will clear up the mystery about who took Henry home that day."

Rio leaned back and looked at Jo. "So there is more to this than an article about the eggs, Imma. You're investigating Henry?"

"I just want to know all the facts. What was Henry doing there? It's so mysterious."

"Maybe you should interview him and ask him about his trip to New York," Rio said with a laugh.

"You won't believe this, ladies, but he denies being there. First to Jenn and Arlene at the library, and then to me."

"That man is very strange," Karen said.

"Did you get to know him at all when he was house-hunting?" Imma asked Rio.

Rio shook her head. "I didn't. Yvonne made several trips to Garden, and we visited a ton of houses before they finally decided on that property next to the game lands. But she vetted everything, and he simply came up a few times to give his approval with the place, and then to sign the paperwork."

"He must have been working then. Maybe that's why."

"Who knows? I always thought Yvonne was the one with the money, because she really did make all the decisions. And they did have money, because they paid cash for the house. And they spent a fortune remodeling, too. But when I saw Henry the other day, I started thinking about it. Maybe he had the money. Maybe before he came to Garden, he hung out with the one-per-centers, like people at the museum."

"Interesting thought. I have to confess, I've googled Henry, and nothing comes up. Actually, a lot comes up, but nothing about *our* Henry. The name is quite common. But I wondered if he'd founded some tech company and sold it, or something like that. I suppose we'll never know."

"Why do you think he hangs on to the firehouse?" Jo asked.

Yvonne's studio was never called The Lotus Garden, its official name. It was always called the firehouse. People went to classes at the firehouse. The firehouse donated a basket to a raffle. The firehouse was closed due to a power outage in town. It was always the firehouse, and probably always would be.

"That's a really good question, Jo. I approached him about selling twice. People made solid offers on the building, but he wouldn't even talk about it."

The server arrived, and they dug in, but the conversation continued unabated.

"Maybe he keeps it because he hopes she'll come back," Karen said.

"It's been a while," Imma said.

"Does anyone know where she went?" Jo asked.

"I don't think so. Gigi says she still gets mail. Mostly junk stuff, but she didn't leave a forwarding address, so she just puts it in the box with Henry's mail."

"If I hadn't talked to her myself before she left, I'd worry he harmed her," Rio said.

Imma turned to look at her. "Really?"

"Oh, come on, Imma. Don't you watch television? That sort of stuff happens all the time."

"Oh, I don't know, ladies," Karen said. "If he murdered her, he would have found a replacement by now. I think he's waiting for her to come back."

Imma had never thought about it before. Yvonne had let everyone know she was leaving, and she didn't seem unhappy or scared as she made her plans. She seemed at peace, like the decision had been hard, and a long time coming, but it was the right thing to do.

Imma might not watch that much television, but she did read her share of mystery novels. Yvonne's leaving didn't seem so mysterious. Who would be happy with a hermit like Henry? It was only surprising that a beautiful and vivacious woman could last as long as she did, living such a strange life in a small mountain town.

Still, you never knew.

CHAPTER SEVENTEEN

The eerie mist floating above the river seemed to keep the joggers away, and Curt found himself alone on the path that led to town. Some people parked at a designated lot at the trailhead in town and rode bikes and jogged in this direction, toward the state game lands. For Curt, picking up the trail near his house required only a short trek down his driveway and then a little hike through the woods. The jog to town was about six miles along the trail, a beautiful journey beside the small river.

The Delaware River near Trenton was probably a quarter mile wide, a clear barrier between New Jersey and Pennsylvania. This river, The Arrowhead, was more like a large stream, one he could cross on foot by hopping along a few well-chosen rocks. He often laughed when he saw the sign.

Running had never been his thing before he moved to Garden, but he'd started the September he'd moved. First of all, he'd been frazzled by his near escape and the loss of so many people he knew. Running required an effort then, and that effort required concentration, and that took his mind off everything else. It was also a great way to stay in shape, something he could do with Yvonne or on his own. And it was a great way to spend time. He had lots of time.

Slowing at a bridge, Henry took the fork in the path that continued to the parking area, but instead of going into the lot, he skirted around the boulders that marked the space and headed to the rear entrance to the firehouse.

After he pulled the key from his pack, he let himself inside and quieted the alarm, then reset it to "stay" mode.

He looked around Yvonne's office. It was a large room, twenty by thirty feet, once used as the bunk area and kitchen when the firemen took overnight shifts in the building. Yvonne had painted the wall with the sink and the disgusting old refrigerator a cheerful yellow, then put in a granite counter and a single, pantry-style cupboard. A small fridge sat at the edge of the counter, and inspirational artwork decorated the walls. The middle of the room housed her desk, and she'd added a private bathroom and storage closet on the other side. Small windows at the top of the twenty-foot-high wall let in some light, but not much, especially on a gloomy day like today. He turned on the overhead lights, dangling spheres that bathed the floor in light but left the ceiling in shadow.

Sitting in the comfy office chair, Curt leaned back and surveyed the room. He knew it so well he was sure he could draw the floor plan to scale if he had to. He'd been studying the place for years.

Looking up at the shadows, he studied tiny windows so high up near the ceiling. They marched neatly across the wall, a perfect line from one side of the room to the other. He often wondered why they were placed so high up. Someone in town probably knew—probably nosy Imma Bruno did. But he'd never ask her, and so he'd never know.

Curt looked at the kite next. It was a satiny number, bright purple with exotic colored flowers, and a tail that matched. Yvonne had filled the space above her with whimsical decor—the kite, a hot-air balloon, a mobile, a birdhouse. The objects made the large open space seem cozy and friendly.

Closing his eyes, Curt thought about the early days of their relationship, just after they'd moved to Garden. They'd bought the building against his wishes, but Yvonne had been so excited about it, and he'd had a hard time saying no to her. And as she'd predicted, the property value had soared. He laughed aloud. If only he could sell it.

If only he could go back in time, to the days when they'd worked together side by side, making this space a welcome place for Yvonne to work and escape. To the days he'd sneak in through the back door and surprise her, or when they'd make love right here in the office between classes.

His problem, he'd come to realize over time, was that she was his life, and he wasn't hers. Curt quite simply had nothing else, and Yvonne had so much. When they'd moved, she still had a family, and once a month she'd go visit her parents and come back with interesting stories and slices of her mom's homemade chocolate cake—one of Yvonne's rare indulgences. Curt had gone with her, of course—he was the new boyfriend for whom she'd abandoned life in Jersey City to settle with in Garden. But those visits were strained, with Curt so afraid of saying something telling that he rarely spoke. It was no different than talking to people here—he had to be on guard constantly.

He supposed now, so many years later, if they were still alive, he'd have a lot to discuss with them. But back when he'd first become Chris Henry, his nerves were too on edge to engage in any meaningful conversations. Yvonne understood and asked him to make the trip to her parents' only on the rarest of occasions. Christmas, of course, and then for a birthday or wedding. She'd still gone, though, while he'd stayed at home like a dog, waiting for his master to return.

A pen holder sat on the edge of Yvonne's desk, collecting dust. A large desk calendar took up much of the writing surface. The calendar no longer marked the passage of time—in here, nothing changed. It was still August 2018. She'd been recovering from her breast-cancer scare then, and the calendar that month and the months before were pristine, with no entries. One of the last was in January of that year, when she'd scheduled her first mammogram.

With a prolonged sigh, he stood and walked to the studio. "Yvonne," he whispered. "What the fuck did you do with those diamonds?"

Flipping on the light, Curt looked around as he bit his lip. Three of the four walls were brick, and he'd checked each one for new mortar, climbing on an extension ladder to reach the top row, tapping with a hammer to find the loose one. He got nothing for his efforts but some crumbs of brick on the floor. That floor was hardwood, and he'd supervised the installation before Yvonne opened the studio. It sat on a double layer of foam padding over the concrete beneath it. If she'd pulled up the floor somewhere, he couldn't locate the spot. He'd been tempted to jerk it all up and jackhammer the concrete beneath, but Yvonne wouldn't have been able to pull up the floor and repair it by herself.

And he was certain she was working alone. She didn't have anyone to share this story with. She wasn't leaving for another man, or a woman. She'd simply had enough, she told him, and he believed her. Her breast-cancer scare had helped her clarify her vision, and she was able to see that she needed to move on from him. Start over someplace new, where she could just be herself and not have to carry the burden of all Curt's secrets.

She'd been calm as she explained it all to him, and they didn't fight that day, or in the weeks to come as she'd closed the studio and notified her students that she was leaving Garden to pursue new opportunities.

During that time, Curt had been in denial. He kept hoping she'd change her mind, see that they could make things work. He'd move with her, and they'd start over. It had been years since 9/11, so he could go anywhere, and no one would ever suspect a thing. But she'd insisted that this was about following her dreams, and that he should start thinking about his own future.

One day, a few days before she was scheduled to leave Garden, taking her clothes and a few personal items and her Jeep, something started nagging at Curt. "We'll split it all, fifty-fifty," she'd said. She'd made up her mind, and he just had to accept her decision. And he had, like everything else.

Then, he'd started questioning her. Where she was going no longer mattered. She was leaving, and that was her final answer. But when he asked her about their cash, the money they'd been laundering through her studio, some million dollars over the years, she'd become defiant. That was *her* money, she'd said. It was from the studio. He reminded her they'd sold diamonds, millions of dollars' worth of diamonds, to fund their life and pay her expenses at the studio. And to legitimize some of their cash, they'd laundered it, mixing the diamond money with the ten-dollar bills Yvonne got paid for teaching yoga and Pilates and fitness classes. They'd had hundreds of thousands of dollars in that account, and they were as much Curt's as Yvonne's. More than that, though, he needed some cash. He could take diamonds to Manhattan and sell them just as easily as she could, but it would require a little time. He'd have to call and arrange a meeting, just as she'd done over the years.

For the first time since she'd told him her plan to leave, they argued. It was also the last. He didn't mean to hurt her, but when he pulled her, she'd fought back, and when he'd let go, she'd hit her head. Then she'd gotten angry at him and pulled a knife from the block. "You can have the egg," she said. "I'm taking the cash and the diamonds."

"That's ten million dollars in diamonds, Yvonne. And what am I going to do with the egg? I can't eat it. I need to live."

"You can sell it, just like last time. It's worth fifteen, twenty million. I don't care how much you get—it's all yours. I just want out. I'll leave you some money in the account, to hold you over. But I'm leaving, and I'm taking the diamonds."

If he'd known beforehand that she'd already taken them, he wouldn't have strangled her. It was only after he buried her body in the woods of the Giles estate that he discovered the diamonds were missing. He'd been searching for them since.

Shutting off the light, Curt walked back into Yvonne's office and sat at the desk. Soon, he'd have more diamonds. He was in his mid-fifties now, so the money from Nick would last him until his death. Even if he never found the others, he could live comfortably for thirty years. And someday, maybe someone's dog would start digging and unearth a hidden treasure in diamonds that was virtually untraceable.

Curt drew his hand back and, in a sudden act of violence, swatted the cup from Yvonne's desk, sending it flying. It broke noisily on the hard floor, and pieces of ceramic and pens scattered in all directions, but he hardly noticed as he brought his hand to his mouth in pain. He'd caught the cup directly on the knuckle, and the sturdy ceramic had fought back.

"Fuck!" he screamed as loud as he could. Shaking out the pain, he looked down and saw a bruise already forming, a lump growing across the back of his hand.

He rose and ignored the mess on the floor. Instead, he opened the freezer. It was empty. He closed the door and pressed the lever for the ice machine on the door, and a few cubes fell into his hand. Shifting to his left, he pulled two plastic bags from the cupboard, added more ice, and made himself a double-thick ice pack.

Satisfied that it wouldn't leak all over him, he shut off the lights and locked up without even sweeping up his mess.

It was a long run home, with the fingers of his left hand freezing as they held the ice on the right one. Halfway there, just past the picnic area and car park, he stopped and dumped the ice. It didn't seem to be helping, and it was impossible to run with it anyway.

Flexing his fingers, he looked at his swollen right hand. He hoped he didn't need an X-ray. He didn't have insurance, and a visit to the ER would cost a small fortune. He tried to hold onto his cash. Until he sold that egg, he didn't have any more coming in.

CHAPTER EIGHTEEN

After a breakfast of oatmeal with fresh fruit and nuts, and two cups of coffee nursed over the course of the entire newspaper, Imma started working on her article.

Since it wasn't due until Wednesday afternoon, she technically had a day and a half, but she hoped to finish it by this afternoon. It was Tuesday, and Gigi was hosting the book club, but it was potluck, so Imma had to make a small dish. Cooking it would be easy, but deciding what to cook would take time.

For now, though, she'd focus on her article. She planned to look through the names on the VIP list, google some of them to learn more of their stories, and then pepper her article with some juicy factoids.

Glancing at the list of over two hundred VIPs, she typed in the first name. Lev Aaronson. Imma had never heard of him, but she learned he was a wealthy philanthropist who donated generously to many causes, including the MMAA. A holocaust survivor who learned to speak four languages while in the Nazi camps, Aaronson had made a fortune in international banking. Imma found a photo of him and his wife and knew she hadn't seen him at the museum on Friday. He was unmistakable with a shock of white hair reminiscent of Albert Einstein, and he seemed to use a cane to walk.

Imma soon found herself engrossed in Mr. Aaronson's life story, and twenty minutes later, she shook her head. "You'll never get through this list if you read about everyone." Yet she wanted some details for her article, so she made a few notes about the man before moving on.

Next on the list was Douglas Abel. Imma had never heard of him either, but she soon learned he was a renowned artist. He'd contributed to the MMAA in the form of the hammered-copper facade that adorned the building's entrance. Imma found his picture on his web page and knew she hadn't seen him at the show, either. He was mid-fifties, slim, with salt-and-pepper hair and a neatly trimmed beard, and shockingly handsome. Imma would have remembered him.

On Imma went, through Adcrofts and Amblers, Andersons and Angersons, through all the *A*s and *B*s and *C*s, learning interesting things about many of those people, but not finding the man who pulled Henry into the limousine.

When she finished the final name in the *C* column, Imma stood to stretch. She'd been at her research for nearly three hours, and obviously she wouldn't get through the list of VIPs by the evening. Oh, well. She'd done the first three letters of the alphabet, and if she randomly picked a few other names from the *G*s and *O*s and *W*s, she'd have what she needed. Then she could finish her article and focus on finding the man in the limo.

It had been a foggy morning, but now the sun was shining brightly, and it would be nice to feel the warmth of the sun after days of clouds.

"Jo," she called, without a reply. Walking through the living room to the base of the stairs, she called out again.

"Hmm," she said. She hadn't heard her leave the house, and since all the doors had alarms, she should have been alerted if one of them was breached. Still, she opened the front door and peeked into the yard. Once again, the barn door was open. "Damn," she muttered. "We need a new alarm system."

The warmth of the day hit Imma as soon as she stepped onto the porch. After days of clouds and rain, it felt good. She descended three stairs to the sidewalk, then followed it to the garage. Once again, she found Jo working on her car.

"What are you up to?" she asked.

"I want to take her in for an oil change. I'm ready to start driving again."

Imma's throat went dry, and she swallowed before replying. Still, her voice cracked. "Do you think that's a good idea? Maybe we should check with the doctor."

"I feel really good, Im. I've got energy, and my appetite is back. And I'm less forgetful."

Imma couldn't argue with any of that, but the changes Jo mentioned had been recent ones. How long would they last? Would she relapse? How could they know?

Jo swatted away Imma's concerns.

"At least let me talk to Jessica. Why don't I call her? Perhaps she and Mac would like to join us for dinner tomorrow. The forecast looks good for the next few days, so we can cook out and catch up with them."

"She's probably working."

"I can check. If not tomorrow, then the next night. One night this week. What's the hurry? But in the meantime, we can take the car in for an oil change. I'm sure it's overdue."

Jo seemed to accept her answer, because she stood and began putting away the supplies she'd been using to restore the car's interior. "How's your research coming?"

Imma realized she'd been ignoring Jo for days and suddenly felt guilty. Truthfully, the article was nearly perfect. She was just adding fluff now. "Almost done. But instead of spending my time over the computer, we should be enjoying this beautiful day. How'd you like to go for a hike? We can take a picnic."

"That sounds good to me."

Back at the house, Imma dialed Jess's phone number, and she answered immediately. "What's going on?" she answered in the direct manner Imma loved about her.

Imma told her about her idea for dinner.

"I'd love to see you guys," she said. "I'm on day shift, but I can check with the night guy and see if he can come in an hour early. And I'll call Mac and run it by her. I'm not sure if she's made any plans."

"I can call her. I'm sure you're busy saving lives."

Jess laughed. "It's actually not busy right now. I'm eating my lunch."

"I hope you'll be able to make it to book club tonight."

"You know me, Im. I might be late, but I'll show up eventually."

"I know it's hard to ask your colleagues for so many favors so you can have time off for your friends. We'll take what we can get."

"I appreciate you guys being so flexible. I'm sure it's disruptive when I walk in during the middle of the discussion."

"Nonsense. We all understand."

"Thank you."

"You're welcome. But Jess, if you have a minute, can I discuss something with you? It's a medical issue."

"Of course," she said.

"It's Jo." Imma shared the news about her progress and that Jo wanted to start driving again. "What do you think?"

"It's a concern. The doctor said she shouldn't drive, but her symptoms were worse then. I'm not sure what the specialists say about when or if people in treatment can resume activities like driving if they're doing better. It's probably a good time for a checkup."

"She's scheduled in two weeks. I think I can delay her until then." Imma paused. "Can I leave her alone at all? I don't mean for hours, but if I want to go for a pedicure or run to the store. I'd be gone an hour."

"That should be okay. Her disease is very early, Imma. And from what you're telling me, she's doing better. Some people in the early stages of Alzheimer's actually live on their own."

That was a relief. Imma hadn't left Jo on her own in more than six months, since a scary episode when she wandered to the barn in a snowstorm and didn't seem to know how to come back to the house. Imma had found her sitting there, looking lost, and it had scared the crap out of her.

"Thank you, Jessica. I can't tell you what a help you are."

"Anytime. And hopefully, I'll see you tomorrow."

"Love you," Imma said before disconnecting the call. She immediately called Mac.

"Mac here," she said.

"Hi to you." Imma replied before asking Mac how she felt about coming over for dinner the next night. Mac loved the idea, and they settled the plans, including the time and the menu, contingent on Jess getting coverage at the hospital. Wednesday was her last day until the weekend, so Mac suggested Thursday if the coverage didn't work out. Then she offered to bring all the fixings for cheeseburgers, as well as dessert. Imma had the burgers and rolls, and would put together a pasta salad.

After hanging up, she threw water on to boil. She'd take the salad on her picnic, too, and use it for her book-club dish. She was inspired.

While the water heated, she found her backpack cooler in the closet, wiped it down, and threw the pasta into the pot. Next, she made two sandwiches. She didn't even bother to ask Jo what she wanted; it was always the same. Italian.

Scooping out a spiral noodle, she tested it by taking a small bite. "Perfect," she said. She dumped the noodles into a colander in the sink, then ran cold water over them. After chopping a few garden vegetables, she cut cheese from a block and pepperoni from a stick, and tossed it with oil and balsamic vinegar. After tasting it, she divided it into three portions and finished packing her cooler.

When she emerged from the house in her hiking shoes and bucket hat, she found Jo waiting on the porch, dressed in a similar fashion. It was a short walk to the trail, just down their driveway and across the road. Years earlier they'd cleared a path and laid down stone pavers, so they wouldn't slip when the path was wet, and they easily descended the stairs they'd made and met the main path.

The Arrowhead River, swollen with recent rain, roared beside them as they walked under the canopy of trees. Dappled sunlight lit their way and danced off the wet rocks in the river. Birds called, and squirrels scampered into the underbrush as they approached. They walked in silence, and Imma breathed deeply and took in all the beauty around her.

This town was one of her greatest blessings. Jo had been born in the city and had adapted to the country like a pro, but Imma felt a connection to the land that she knew Jo didn't have. Exploring the place as a child had made it truly hers, and Imma couldn't count the times she and her friends had thrown down their balls and bats and jumped into this river to swim. It wasn't very deep, and even now, when it rushed like this, it was still crystal clear. If she was thirsty, she wouldn't hesitate to take a drink. She'd done it before, and so far, it hadn't killed her.

There was a picnic area along the trail, but Imma and Jo preferred to make their own place. They had a special rock, one that sat at the perfect height from the ground. It was flat, and if they knelt next to it, they could eat beside the river in relative solitude, with only an occasional curious squirrel coming by to see if they had anything to share. Today, with the wet grass, they'd use it as a bench and eat off their laps, but they'd make it work.

They'd almost reached their spot when they noticed a commotion ahead. The Garden Police ATV was parked with its lights flashing, and a dozen people were gathered. Oddly, some were on their hands and knees, searching the ground.

"What do you suppose is going on?" Imma asked.

"It looks like they're hunting something."

After another minute of walking, Imma spotted Johnny, talking to a woman who stood bouncing a baby on her hip. A large dog sat calmly beside her, watching all the activity.

Imma nodded to him as they reached the group, and she spotted Mac on the other side of the ATV, speaking with the police officer.

"Hey. What's going on?" Imma asked.

"I'll let Mac fill you in," the man said.

Mac stepped in her direction and gave them both a gentle hug before answering. "That lady with the baby found a bunch of diamonds on the trail."

"Diamonds?" Imma asked. "What kind of diamonds?"

Mac pulled on Imma's left hand and rubbed her ring. It had been her grandmother's, but Jo had placed it on her fourth finger the day they made their commitment to each other. "This kind of diamond, but loose."

"Just lying on the trail?" Jo asked.

"That's what she said. She brought the baby and the dog out, and when the dog stopped to do his business, she noticed something shiny. There were twenty-eight of them, all within about two feet of each other. She called the police, and I heard the conversation on the scanner. I thought I'd come out and see what was going on."

"Are you sure they're real?" Imma asked.

"Who knows? People are searching for more, and the police are looking around to make sure no one's dead in the woods, or anything else suspicious. Then they're going to take them down to the jeweler to see what he says."

"This is so strange."

Mac shook her head. "It is. And I've seen a lot of strange things in my day."

Imma leaned closer and whispered. "Do you think it's drug-related?"

"It wouldn't surprise me," Mac said with a frown.

"That woman is possibly the most honest person in Garden." Jo chuckled.

"Well, if there's no evidence of a crime, and no one claims them, I think she'll get to keep them."

"Get out!" Imma said. "How much are they worth?"

Mac laughed and showed Imma her phone. "You'd be a great detective, Imma. I was wondering the same thing. According to the experts at Google, a one-carat diamond is worth anywhere from a couple of thousand dollars to sixteen thousand. And these diamonds are pretty big. I'm guessing it's a couple of hundred grand, if they're real."

"Wow!" Imma said.

"Wow is right," Jo added.

An elderly couple moved past them, and Imma watched as they held onto a rock and dropped to their knees, searching the vegetation beside the trail.

"Do you think there are more?" Jo asked. "Should I be looking?" Imma saw the twinkle in Jo's eyes, and it made her smile.

"I heard the call on the scanner right after I got off the phone with you, Imma, so it's been about an hour. I think we're a little late to the party. In fact, no one has found any except the lady with the baby."

"Mac, this is why I love life so much," Imma said. "You just never know what the day's going to bring."

Mac laughed. "You're right, Imma." Then she nodded at the backpack. "Picnic?" she asked.

"Yes, and we'd better get to it, because before you know it, it'll be time for book club."

"See you tomorrow," Jo said.

"See you."

"Good luck," Jo said to the treasure hunters as they picked their way through the crowd.

"Can you believe this?" Imma asked. "In Garden."

"It must be drug-related," Jo said. "Because who else has that kind of money tied up in diamonds?"

"I just hope they don't find a dead body," Imma said.

CHAPTER NINETEEN

Curt liked to watch television in the evenings. He'd start with the local news, followed by the world news. If he couldn't be out there living, at least he knew what was going on.

So he'd broiled a chicken breast and steamed some vegetables, and he'd eat in front of the television, like he did most evenings. Using heat-resistant gloves, he emptied the contents of the broiling pan to his plate, then closed the oven and turned it off.

In his kitchen, he poured himself an inch-and-a-half of wine, one of his rare luxuries. He often drove to liquor stores in distant cities to buy bottles not available in Garden. He particularly enjoyed the store in Clarks Summit. It was almost an hour away, but they had a fabulous selection, and he enjoyed talking to the wine specialist there. He usually picked a bottle from the temperature-controlled "cellar" in the store, and he'd uncork it as soon as he arrived home, then spend the rest of the week enjoying it.

He took a seat at the end of the island closest to the living room. Using the remote, he turned on the television and sipped his wine. This bottle was a South African red blend, and even though he was eating chicken, he knew he'd enjoy the wine anyway. A wine expert had once told him that the food pairing wasn't as important as drinking what you preferred, and Curt definitely enjoyed this wine.

As he took his first bite of the chicken, the newscaster came on the screen. "Treasure discovered in the Pocono Mountains. We'll have the full story, coming up next."

The news broke to commercial, and it hadn't even started yet. *Typical.*

He enjoyed his dinner and his wine while he waited, and in just a few minutes, the same news woman came back on. He stopped chewing and listened.

"It was a lucky day for one woman from Garden, Pennsylvania, who discovered a fortune in diamonds while walking her dog. Reporter Jimmy Cross is on the scene. Jimmy, what can you tell us?"

Hopping off his stool, Curt walked toward the television while pointing the remote to turn the volume up. The reporter nodded and began. "Just after noon today a woman walking her dog along the Arrowhead River made a surprising discovery—a pile of diamonds scattered on the trail near a popular picnic spot."

Curt watched as the camera panned to the familiar scene along the trail where he'd been running this morning.

"Police in Garden say they're not sure how the diamonds got here on this walking trail, or who they belong to. I was able to talk to one woman, who was here just after the discovery. She informed me that a wide area was searched, but the diamonds were all found along the trail, where it meets the forest, in a space about two feet by two feet. The search turned up nothing else unusual. Mark Hayes, who owns Hayes Fine Jewelry in town, says Garden police brought him the diamonds to verify their authenticity."

Curt leaned closer as Mark began to speak. "It has to be the strangest day I've ever had in the twenty years I've been in business. Two police officers came in and asked if I could look at some stones they'd found. They dumped a paper bag of diamonds on my counter, and I thought there's just no way. Then I looked at the first one and was in shock. It was one of the most perfect stones I've ever seen. So were all the others."

"How many in total?" Jimmy asked.

"Twenty-eight."

"And what would you say is the value of these diamonds?"

"I'd say it's three-fifty or four hundred thousand dollars."

The camera cut to the *Welcome to Garden* sign on the edge of town. "Police are still investigating this strange discovery, but they say that if no one claims the diamonds, that lucky dog walker is entitled to them."

"Thanks, Jimmy," the newscaster said, and Curt flicked off the television.

Running his hands through his hair, he paced. He'd emptied the bag of ice beside the trail. At a spot just after the parking area. He was certain, because he'd entertained the idea of walking back to throw the plastic bag into the trash bin. It was the same spot. It had to be!

Had Yvonne hidden the diamonds in the ice dispenser? He laughed. He'd contemplated jack-hammering the concrete floor, but he'd never checked the ice maker.

He would now, though. The only way he'd know for sure was to inspect the rest of the ice, to see if the diamonds were there.

Without even bothering to clean up dinner, he bolted down the stairs to his garage and waited patiently for the door to open.

He shook his head as he thought about it. He'd searched that office from top to bottom with no luck. He'd searched the refrigerator, too. He'd had to clean it out. But it had never occurred to him to look in the ice maker. It was tucked into the door, out of sight. Her choice was brilliant.

He was laughing out loud as he backed out of the garage. He sped down the driveway and turned right toward town, slowing at the parking area for the trail. He wanted to stop, but why? The diamonds were gone, and he'd probably just run into people he didn't want to talk to.

A few minutes later, he pulled to a stop in front of the firehouse. There, he ran from the car to the back door, turned the key in the lock, and darted into Yvonne's office.

The broken glass was still scattered across the floor, as were the pens. Curt walked over them on his way to the refrigerator. Opening the freezer door, he flipped the lever that held the ice chest in place and carried it to the sink. Grabbing a bowl from the cupboard, he put a handful of ice inside it and ran warm water over it. Then he grabbed the sink stopper and inserted it. If he was right, he'd soon have a handful of diamonds, and he didn't want to lose his treasure down the drain.

Mesmerized, he stared as the ice cubes began to melt, revealing the shapes frozen inside. One, then the next, and another. It seemed that each cube concealed four diamonds.

Curt tilted his head back and cackled. He'd found them at last.

"Mr. Henry, is everything okay?"

Curt knew that voice and turned to find Imma Bruno standing in the doorway of the office. In his haste, not only had he failed to arm the alarm, but he hadn't even closed the door behind him.

Curt lost his voice and simply stared. It had taken him years to find these diamonds, and now he might lose them again because of being so impulsive.

"I saw you running and thought there might be an emergency."

Fighting the impulse to look back, to check the diamonds, he cleared his throat. The thawed ice was in the bowl, out of view in the sink. The only thing he could see was the ice chest. The ice and the diamonds were carefully hidden inside.

"Oh, yes. Sorry. I didn't mean to worry you. I'm just...making some frozen margaritas, and I'm out of ice at my house. So..." He made a motion with his hand toward the ice chest. "I'm just going to take this. Save myself two bucks on a bag from the gas station."

Imma nodded. "Okay. I'm glad everything's all right." She looked around. "It's very nice in here. Cheerful. It reminds me of Yvonne. How is she?"

Henry shrugged. "She doesn't keep in touch."

Waving, Imma offered another smile. "Well, I'm glad everything's okay." She turned and walked back out into the warm evening, and Curt collapsed against the counter.

With a loud exhale, he practically jumped across the room to lock the door, and this time he armed the alarm as well. Fuck! Had she seen anything? And why ask about Yvonne now, after all these years? No one had ever mentioned her after she left. By announcing her plans, she'd given him the perfect opportunity to get rid of her, because no one suspected a thing. They all assumed she'd simply left town.

"I gotta get out of this place," he said. "Soon."

Back at the sink, Curt smiled, and for good reason. At the bottom of the bowl, beneath the skeletons of the ice cubes he'd melted, a small mound of diamonds had formed.

He dipped his fingers in the bowl and pulled one out. Laughing again, he kissed it, then opened the cabinet beneath the sink and retrieved the dish strainer. It had a utensil cup, with small drainage holes, too small for a diamond to escape but large enough to let the water out. He poured the bowl of frozen diamonds, then turned on the hot water and filled the container, watching the water drain from dozens of small holes.

When the cascade stopped, he could clearly see the outlines of diamonds in the remaining ice, but he realized the bowl was probably a better way to melt the ice. He poured the contents of the cup back into the bowl and filled it with water again.

Impatient, he sighed. He had probably two pounds of ice to melt. At this rate, he'd be working for hours. Stuffing a paper towel over the drain stopper, he dumped the entire ice chest into the sink and filled it with hot water. Some of the ice floated, though most of it sank, but all of it began to melt. The sharp edges of the cubes rounded out and grew smaller over time. He didn't wait for the sink to empty before refilling it with hot water, and he helped the process along by grabbing a handful of ice and holding it directly under the stream flowing from the top.

Smiling, he watched the diamonds take shape in his hand.

He pulled a dish towel from the drawer and placed it neatly on the counter, then gently placed the diamonds on it. After that, he grabbed another handful of ice cubes and put them under the stream of water until they melted.

His pile grew slowly, until all that was left were a few fragments of ice in the sink. After those, too, had melted, he pulled out a plastic storage container from the cabinet and took great care while transferring the diamonds from the towel to the container. His hand was shaky, and more than once the diamonds spilled from his hand to the countertop and bounced away.

When he was done, he had a mound of diamonds as large as a softball. He pushed it flat and covered the container with the lid.

In the closet he found a broom and dustpan, then got down on his knees as he swept up the remains of the pen holder and its contents, searching every corner of the floor for a diamond. He didn't want to lose a single one. When he was satisfied that none had escaped, he carried the waste to the can and returned the broom and dustpan to the closet. After replacing the ice chest in the freezer, Curt turned around. Other than the missing pen cup, and the container of diamonds on the counter, the room appeared just as it had this morning.

"Okay. What now?" he asked as he looked at the diamonds.

The plastic was tinted blue, and he couldn't discern the contents with the lid in place. But it looked like the right amount. When they'd lived in his safe, the diamonds had been in smaller receptacles, velvet bags designed for jewelry. It didn't seem fitting to see them in the same sort of storage container he'd use for his leftover chicken. But then, who did he have to impress?

Another thought occurred to him. Should he move forward with the sale of the Fabergé egg? It was Tuesday, so he was scheduled to meet Nick in five days to make the exchange. But he didn't need to sell the egg now. When he converted these diamonds to cash, he'd have more money than he could ever spend.

Yet, why keep the egg? He'd have to think this situation over and weigh his decision. For the first time in a long time, he had options. It was a good feeling.

Then a dark thought brought his mood back to baseline.

Imma fucking Bruno.

He remembered thinking about his first life, the one with Morgan and the kids, contemplating what he'd miss when he left. He'd known he'd regret losing the view from his office. It was incomparable. And Avery. She'd made the decision a hard one, but in the end, he'd thought leaving was the right move for him.

Now, he had no reason to stay. And Imma fucking Bruno was a great reason to leave. That woman was infuriating! How, how, how did she keep turning up at the least opportune moments? It was like she had some sort of magnet, attracting her to him. It was a ridiculous thought, he knew, but he was starting to get a little paranoid.

The upcoming meeting with Nick wasn't helping either. Of course he'd thought it through, and he was sure the diamond district was a safe place to conduct business. But there was another issue now, as well—Nick knew he was still alive. He hadn't searched for him after 9/11 because he'd assumed Curt was dead. Now…

Curt walked across the room to the closet and found an old duffel bag hanging from a hook. He carried it to the diamonds and slipped the container inside before zipping it closed.

Walking to the studio, he set down his bag and leaned against the wall. "Fuck you, Yvonne," he said softly. "I found them. And if you'd only been fair…half of them would be yours."

Anger was rising in his chest, and he didn't need that feeling. This was a happy moment.

Closing his eyes, he breathed in and out, the way she'd taught him. Imagining crystal-clear blue waters beneath a matching sky, he thought of the next phase of his life. Florida. Golf. A girlfriend. Tension began to ooze from him, and after a minute he opened his eyes. It was the same old studio, but he was seeing it in a whole new light.

He'd once given up everything for Morgan. Then he'd done the same with Yvonne. This time, he intended to live his life for him.

After locking the office and setting the alarm, he walked out and got into his car, feeling much calmer than when he walked in.

Richer, too.

❖

Imma sat in the corner chair at the nail salon, watching the firehouse. She'd had to wait an extra fifteen minutes for that seat to open, but it was the one with the best view of Henry's car.

She'd just been walking into the salon an hour earlier when she'd spotted Henry speeding into the parking spot beside the firehouse. She was shocked when she saw him jump from his car and run around the building to the private entrance in the back.

Of course she was curious, but she was also worried. He had no one to look after him. Was he okay?

After a moment's consideration, she walked to the corner and crossed the street, then made her way to the back of the building. It surprised her to see the door open but reinforced her decision. Henry had been in a great hurry. She hoped he was okay.

Imma was sure she startled him when she called out to him, and he seemed nervous when he replied. She wasn't sure what he was doing with that ice, but she was pretty certain he wasn't making margaritas. Not unless he had the tequila at the firehouse, because he was still in the building forty-five minutes later.

Now she saw him strolling to his car, carrying a small black duffel bag. If it had that ice in it, surely it was slush by now.

The mysterious Christopher Henry never stopped intriguing her.

CHAPTER TWENTY

Imma sat with her iPad as she read about the next person on the VIP list, her new friend Avery Hutchins. Avery, her brother, and her grandmother were all listed, even though Imma knew the grandmother hadn't attended. She found enough information about Jonathon Hutchins to give a personal touch to the article, but little about Gloria Giles. Imma considered calling Avery to ask about her grandmother, but she supposed the woman preferred to avoid the spotlight. That's probably why she hadn't attended the exhibit's opening, and why there wasn't much to learn about her online.

Instead, Imma did a little research about Gloria's late husband and the Giles family. Then she paused to write. Johnny had given her a word count for the article, and if she exceeded it, entire paragraphs could be cut from her piece. It was much better if she did her own editing. Once she saw where she stood, she'd figure out how many more VIPs to profile, or if she should add a few more details about the exhibit itself.

An hour later, she paused and re-read, then nodded. She liked the piece. With ninety-one more words at her disposal, she started scanning the VIP list. It might be nice to include Max Montgomery, since he was world famous, and people might find it interesting to know he was more than just a handsome face. Max owned an impressive art collection and helped artists in third-world countries exhibit their works.

But as Imma had learned in her research, most of the people on the list led interesting lives. They were wealthy art collectors, philanthropists who supported the arts, and people who worked in the field. It would be hard to choose a single person to profile last, but with her word limit looming, she had to.

Scanning the list, she focused on the people in the second half of the alphabet. She didn't see any names she recognized until she came to the Os. Nikolai Orlov.

"Where have I heard that name before?"

Imma pursed her lips in concentration and thought for a minute. "It sounds like a Russian name," she said aloud as she worked out the puzzle.

Giving up, she typed his name into the search engine and found it. "That's it," she said. "The ambassador's personal assistant."

Though the article she read didn't say much about him, it did mention that he'd been with the ambassador since the early days of his business career and was "indispensable" to Mr. Bichefsky.

Interesting. Imma switched her search from news to images and scrolled down. Halfway through the first page, she stopped, opening her eyes as she pinched the screen to enlarge the image and the description beneath it.

Ambassador Bichefsky was pictured at a fund-raiser for the Metropolitan Opera with his assistant, Nikolai Orlov. The man Imma was looking at was the man from the exhibit who'd abducted Henry.

Imma stared out the window and recalled that day. They'd been people-watching at the entrance to the MMAA, excited after seeing Max Montgomery, wondering who they might spot next. Seeing Henry there among the museum crowd was surprising, to say the least, but when they'd called his name, and the man with him pushed him into the limousine, Imma had been truly shocked.

The mystery around Henry continued to grow, and Imma pursed her lips as she thought about what it all meant. Henry clearly came from money, the kind that allowed him to buy property for cash and bump elbows with a former ambassador. Or, at least, the elbows of the ambassador's indispensable assistant. So why move to Garden and give up that life?

The easy answer was 9/11, but Imma knew Henry and Yvonne had bought their property before the terrorist attacks, so that didn't make sense. They'd refurbished the house to live in it, not as a weekend home. There was another reason for their exile in Garden, and more than ever, Imma suspected Henry would rather keep that reason to himself. That was why he was so reclusive and unfriendly.

She shook her head. Maybe she'd solve the mystery of Henry one day, but she guessed she never would.

It took her another half hour to craft the sentences that completed her piece, and then she proofed it yet again. Satisfied at last, she saved the final edition and then e-mailed it to Johnny.

With a small smile, she sat back and looked out the windows at the trees beyond the backyard. Then she did a little dance in her chair. She was a reporter!

Even if Jo's illness progressed, if this turnabout was only temporary, Imma could write. A weekly column for *The Gazette* would involve some research, fieldwork, of course, but for the most part, she could do it from home. If she needed to be with Jo, to take care of her, she could still write. It was a bright spot in what sometimes threatened to be a bleak future.

For the last months, as she'd watched Jo struggle with her memory and saw the woman she'd loved for so long fading away, Imma had struggled as well. Not just because of her concerns about Jo, but because she was losing her own freedoms. Jo was easy, too. She needed a little direction at times, and reminders to eat and someone to cook for her—but the latter was nothing new. It was just the idea that another human being was totally dependent on her that she found so overwhelming. Having something like this little article to write gave her something back, made her feel like the old Imma.

She stood from her chair and searched for Jo, finding her in the kitchen.

"Whatcha up to?" she asked as she looked at the pile of lunch meat and condiments on the table. Her heart caught in her throat as she saw the confusion on Jo's face.

"Nothing."

"Are you trying to get me to make you a sandwich?" Imma asked playfully, but Jo didn't smile.

Swallowing the lump in her throat, Imma started assembling the sandwich, making excuses as she worked. Jo had never been much of a cook, she told herself. Even sandwiches were a chore for her, always had been.

After she finished, she looked up and saw Jo smiling. "It looks good," she said.

Imma pushed the plate toward Jo and began to make her own sandwich. Then she sat beside her, and they ate in silence. Then Imma looked into Jo's eyes and saw the spell had passed.

"Shall we get everything ready for tonight?" Imma asked as she began to clean up. "Then when Jess and Mac arrive, we can enjoy their company."

"When's book club at our house?" Jo asked as she wiped down their plates. "I don't like staying with Bev."

Imma knew Bev, Jo's sitter, was a little bossy, but she worried there was more. "What's wrong?"

"She treats me like I'm stupid."

"I think that's just Bev." Imma sighed. Finding people to stay with Jo in the evenings hadn't been easy. Some older people didn't like driving at night, some had trouble hearing, and some were just too limited for one reason or another. Bev, pushy as she was, was a gem compared to some others. But maybe it was time to give Jo a little more freedom. Imma told her about her conversation with Jess. "Do you think you'd feel comfortable staying by yourself? I might be gone a few hours."

"You'll leave the house at 6:15, and you'll be home at 8:45. You're like a clock, Im."

Imma pointed a stern finger in Jo's direction. "Okay. Next week we can try it. But I'm going to call you every seven minutes to check on you."

"Why not make it every five? It's a nice, divisible number."

Imma chuckled, stepped forward into Jo's space, and kissed her. "I love you," she said through laughter.

After they'd cleaned up the house and prepared a tray with condiments for their cookout, Imma hopped into the shower and put on a clean pair of shorts and a cozy T-shirt for dinner. She'd just reached the landing when the doorbell rang, and she opened the front door to find Jess and Mac on the porch.

"How are you feeling?" Imma asked by way of greeting. Jess had begged off book club the night before, claiming a headache.

"Better," she said with a nod toward Mac. "I have one heck of a nurse."

Imma hugged them and ushered them in, and they found Jo on the back patio, sipping a tall iced tea and watching the sun fall over their mountain. She stood to greet the guests, and Imma was pleased to see Jo was back to her old self.

After they exchanged greetings, Jo hurried to grab them all drinks. "How are you two doing?" Imma asked. "Really doing?"

Jess laughed, and Imma was happy. After Jess's struggle with opioid addiction, Imma had worried about her. Now that both parents were gone, Imma felt it was her job to look out for her. She knew Jess and Mac had a strong relationship, but Imma knew you sometimes need someone other than your spouse. For her, it was a lot of someones—all the ladies in the Tuesday Night Book Club. Imma had known them all since college, and they were more family than friends.

"I'm doing great. Really," Jess said and winked. "And Mac is... well, I'll let her tell you."

"Maybe we should wait until Jo gets back."

"Did I hear my name?" Jo asked as she rounded the corner carrying a small tub filled with drinks.

"All good things," Mac said as she pulled a beer from the ice Jo had prepared earlier that day.

Imma and Jess helped themselves as well, and Jo, mindful of the side effects of her medication, stuck with her tea.

After a moment spent enjoying their refreshments, Mac cleared her throat. "So, I have some news."

Imma sat up a little taller. "Do tell."

Mac nodded. "As you probably can guess, I've had a lot of time on my hands since Zeke died. I enjoy the self-defense classes I've been teaching at the community center. And I'm into fitness. Jess does a lot of meditation. There's been a void in town since Yvonne left. So we've decided to open our own place. We'll offer classes in all kinds of fitness and self-improvement."

Imma clapped. "How wonderful!" She was so happy to see Jess and Mac thriving, their relationship growing in another direction. "Garden can use something like that. And when Yvonne did the classes, they were so successful."

Mac nodded. "Speaking of Yvonne," she said with a chuckle. "We talked to Rio about a month ago, and she told us Henry wasn't interested in renting the firehouse. She said he'd refused a couple of offers to buy it."

Jo nodded. "Rio told us that as well."

"So, Rio knows, right? We looked at a few places and found something out by the vet clinic. We were supposed to sign the lease

Friday. Then…Rio called this afternoon and said Henry wants to sell. Not only the firehouse, but his house as well. Apparently, he's relocating."

"Wow!" Imma said. "Henry never stops surprising me."

"I don't think he has any reason to stay here, right? No family, and he certainly hasn't made any friends since he's been here," Jo commented.

Jess nodded. "You're right. Still…Henry's a weirdo, but he's our weirdo."

Imma laughed. "I agree. Yesterday when I went to have my nails done, I saw him rushing into the firehouse. I was kind of worried. I mean, what if he was sick or something? Who does he have to watch out for him?"

"So what did you do?" Jess asked.

"I went over to check on him, of course."

They all laughed.

"How'd that go?" Mac asked.

"As expected. It was a frosty reception. Literally. I thought he was going to throw a chest of ice at me."

Again, they laughed, but Mac puckered her lips. "What do you mean, Imma?"

Imma didn't want to be any more of a gossip by talking about Henry and his ice chest. She waved Mac off. "It was nothing. But anyway, he's leaving us. Good for him, I guess. And good for you. What are the details?" Imma asked.

"Rio says he wants to sell quickly. He's only asking what he paid for it, and Rio says it's worth double that."

"You better move fast, then."

"Tomorrow after work," Jess said. "We're meeting Rio at the firehouse, and then hopefully we'll make an offer."

"It's a perfect location," Jo said. "The first building you see when you come into town."

Imma chimed in. "Plus, it's already set up just the way you need it."

Jess and Mac were all smiles. "Yeah. It is," Jess said.

"I wonder where Henry will go?" Imma asked. "Back to New York?"

"Is that where he's from?" Mac asked.

"Somewhere in Jersey. Close to New York," Imma replied. "I think. He's never actually confirmed that point. It's just rumor."

"Well, maybe he'll be happier there." Jess shrugged.

"Maybe. He apparently has at least one friend in New York," Imma said. "Today, I found out our anti-social Henry was consorting after the Fabergé exhibit with a real VIP. The man who pulled him into the limousine was the personal assistant to the former Russian ambassador to the UN."

"Holy crap!" Jess said. "You've got to be kidding."

Imma shook her head.

"How'd you figure that out?"

Imma told her about the research for her article, and how she'd put a face to the name.

Mac sat back in her chair and shook her head. Imma knew Henry's arrival in Garden predated Mac's, and Jess had already left for school. "So he came from some big-time money, huh?" Mac asked.

"Rio says they paid cash for their property. Their house and the firehouse."

"A lot of money came into the Poconos after 9/11," Jo said. "People escaping the chaos. But we have our own chaos here. How about those diamonds on the trail?"

"Truly unbelievable," Imma said. "Mac, have you heard from the GPD? Any ideas about where the diamonds came from?"

Mac shook her head. "No one's claimed them. And so far, no dead bodies have turned up. Hopefully, none do."

"Do you suppose they just fell out of someone's pocket?" Jess asked.

Mac rolled her eyes. "Jess, who walks a trail in the woods with hundreds of thousands of dollars' worth of diamonds in their pocket?"

Jess shrugged. "It's as good an idea as any."

"Actually, the GPD thinks the diamonds were hidden in ice," Mac said.

Imma sat back in stunned silence, as the scene from Yvonne's studio replayed in her mind. Henry, with a chest full of ice. A bowl of ice melting in the sink.

She met Mac's gaze. "What makes them say that?" Imma took a sip of her beer to cure her suddenly dry mouth.

"Interestingly, when the woman found the diamonds, she was smart enough to realize it could be a crime scene. She put the diamond she found back where it was and called 911. When the first officer arrived at the scene, he took crime-scene photos. The state-police detective analyzed them. The diamonds were found in clusters of four, and there were wet spots on the ground beneath them, plus a few tiny shards of ice very close to them. So, that's the working theory. The diamonds were hidden in ice."

"And like I said," Jess said. "The ice fell out of someone's pocket."

Jo and Mac laughed, but Imma simply smiled politely. Should she tell them what she'd seen at the firehouse? Or would they think her a fool? After the emergency meeting of the book club, she wasn't eager to be the butt of anyone's jokes again anytime soon.

No. She wouldn't say anything. Except maybe to Henry. Imma had quite a few questions for Henry.

CHAPTER TWENTY-ONE

"Good morning," Jo whispered, and Imma tasted coffee on her kiss. "I have a surprise for you."

Imma blinked the sleep from her eyes and sat up. "I love surprises."

Jo handed her the iPad. "*The Garden Gazette.*"

Imma had been so preoccupied with thoughts of diamonds and ice cubes, she'd forgotten about her article. Yet there she was, on page five of *The Gazette*, her smiling face looking back at her from the iPad. "What's it say?" Imma asked.

"I didn't read it," Jo said.

"What? Why not?"

"I want you to read it to me."

Imma grabbed her eyeglasses, and Jo crawled back into the bed beside her.

"Okay. I'm ready," Jo said.

Imma started with the title. "'A Celebration of Russian Master Fabergé in New York City,' by Immaculata Bruno."

"I like that you used your name."

"Thank you. Shall I proceed?"

"Please do."

Even though Imma had already read the article about a hundred times, this time was the sweetest, as Jo added commentary.

When she finished, Jo squeezed her hand. "You're amazing, Imma."

"I'm glad you think so."

"I do, and now I'm off."

"Kiss me again, and promise me you won't fall in the lake."

Jo kissed her and crawled from the bed. Imma sat back, and closed her eyes, and listened as Jo descended the stairs and left through the front door.

She was excited to have the morning to herself. Last night before she'd left, Mac had made a fishing date with Jo. Mac seemed bored, and Imma hoped their business idea worked out. They were wonderful people and had so much to give to the community. The business would soar if they could get it to the launch point.

In the meantime, Jo was happy to keep Mac entertained, and Imma was happy to have a little freedom. She jumped from the bed and grabbed some clothes from the clean-laundry pile, then quickly dressed. Jo and Mac would be back by lunchtime, so Imma wanted to run her errand before then.

It was time to talk to Henry. But first, she wanted to see the firehouse. Since Rio planned to show the property to Mac and Jess, Imma hoped she'd get a preview.

She picked up her phone and dialed Rio. "Hello. I just read your article in *The Gazette*. It was fabulous."

Imma felt a little giddy. "Thanks, my friend. That's kind of you."

"Well, it's true. I'm going to pick up a printed copy so you can autograph it."

"Ha. Well, I'll give you an opportunity, if you're game. What do you think about showing me the firehouse? I heard it's on the market."

"Can you believe it? We were just talking about it the other day."

"We had dinner with Jess and Mac last night, and they told us the good news. They said you're showing it to them this afternoon. I thought maybe I could see it first."

"Imma, I can't let you steal it from Mac and Jess."

"I know…it's not that. I just want to see the kitchen area. I'll explain when I get there. Are you at work?" Rio's office was just a few doors down from the firehouse.

"I am. When do you want to meet?"

"How's fifteen minutes?" Imma was starving, but she'd head over to Tori's and get something after the tour. Maybe Rio would join her.

"I'll see you there."

Imma hurried down the stairs and out the door, and she was driving toward town a few minutes later.

She couldn't stop thinking about this newest development in *The Adventures of Henry.* Did the diamonds on the trail belong to him? If so, did he have more in the ice chest in his freezer? Did the diamonds have anything to do with his trip to New York and his meeting with Nikolai Orlov? Why was he suddenly selling property he'd refused to get rid of just a month ago?

She was so lost in thought she nearly missed the turn for the parking lot at the walking trail. She pulled in and found a spot just across the street from the firehouse. No sense drawing attention to herself by parking in front. Garden was a small town, and someone was bound to notice a car there. If word got around that the firehouse was on the market, Mac and Jess might find themselves in a bidding war. Or, worse yet, they might lose the building altogether.

Imma spotted Rio heading her way, and she crossed the street and met her on the sidewalk with a hug. "Hello, my friend," she said.

"Hello," Rio said as they walked. "Imma, you always intrigue me. Writing for the newspaper, calling emergency meetings, and now, shopping for an old firehouse."

"Can't you see me teaching yoga?"

"Honestly, Imma, I could see you doing just about anything. Now what's this all about?"

"Rio, did you hear the police theory about the diamonds they found on the trail? About them being hidden in ice?"

"No. What are you talking about?"

Imma relayed the information she'd learned from Mac.

"That's pretty crazy. But it still doesn't explain how they got there."

"I'm trying to figure that out."

"Detective Bruno?"

Imma shrugged and paused as Rio inserted the key into the lock and opened the back door of the firehouse.

When they were safely inside, Imma closed the door behind them and told Rio how she'd been in town for her pedicure and saw Henry running toward the firehouse, and how he'd been suspiciously melting ice in the sink.

"So you think Henry has diamonds hidden in his ice?"

Imma shrugged. "You have to admit, Rio, there's a ton of mystery surrounding him. I'm just curious."

Rio nodded toward the refrigerator. "Let's check it out, Detective."

Imma suppressed a smile as she walked across the kitchen toward the fridge. Opening the freezer door, she fiddled with the lever that held the ice chest in place, and after a few moments, she gave way to Rio.

"I can't figure this out."

"Everything is so complicated these days, isn't it?"

Rio jiggled the handle, and after a forceful push, it gave. The back wall of the freezer door seemed to separate from the rest of the unit, and Imma heard the clatter of ice as it came free into Rio's hands.

"What now?" Rio asked.

Imma looked in the sink and saw a stopper there. "Just dump it."

Rio did, and while she replaced the bucket where she'd found it, Imma turned on the water and watched as the cubes of ice in the sink began to melt. Fishing one out of the water bath, she held it up and examined it.

"Well?" Rio asked.

"I don't see anything," Imma said, dejected.

Rio pulled her own cube and pulled her glasses down her nose to examine it with her naked eyes. "Looks like ice to me."

Biting her lip, Imma watched the pile of cubes shrink and ran her hand through the chilled water, feeling for anything that sank to the bottom. "Nothing," she said, as she pulled out another cube to examine.

Like the first, this one looked like regular old ice. Dropping it back in, she loosened the stopper and let the water drain, her spirits going down with it. She'd been so sure there was a link between Henry and the diamonds on the trail, and she'd thought this was the place she'd prove it. "Damn," she said aloud.

Rio patted her on the back as Imma then turned on the faucet to refill the sink. "I think we should let them melt all the way, to be sure."

"Of course."

"So, you think Henry will take the offer from Jess and Mac? They said he was asking way below value."

"I told him where to price it, and he refused. Said he'd be happy to get what he paid for it."

"I'm thrilled for them. Especially Mac. She'll do great here, you know? Everyone loves the self-defense classes. And everyone loved the classes Yvonne taught. It's bound to be a hit."

"And a great investment, especially since they can get it at such a good price."

"Do you think Henry's house will sell as quickly?"

"It's pricey, but the house is absolutely magnificent. Everything's top-of-the-line and in pristine condition. Couple that with all the forested land he has, and I think it will."

"Is the house underpriced, too?" Imma asked as she swirled her fingers through the last remnants of ice in the sink.

"By about a million dollars," Rio said with a chuckle. "I wish I could afford it. I'd buy it myself."

"Rio, there are no diamonds here. This was just another crazy idea. Please don't share it with anyone."

Rio smiled kindly. "Not a word," she said.

Imma pulled the stopper from the sink and watched the water swirl, then reached for a roll of paper towels from the corner near the fridge. As she pulled the paper holder, it shifted slightly on the countertop, and something sparkling caught her eye. She gasped.

"Imma, what is it?" Rio asked.

Imma pointed, and Rio followed her gaze to the spot on the counter behind where the paper towels had been. Then she leaned forward and teased the diamond from the corner and held it in her hand.

"Rio, it's a diamond," she said with a trembling voice that matched the hand holding the jewel. She couldn't remember being so nervous as her pulse throbbed in her throat. "I can't believe it. I was right! Those diamonds on the trail are Henry's."

A voice behind them caused them both to jump. "I worried I might have lost one. Nervous fingers, you know."

Imma looked at Rio, who didn't seem alarmed to see Henry standing there in the doorway to the studio. Imma, on the other hand, was scared senseless. Henry was up to no good. She knew it.

Imma repeated her accusation. "They were your diamonds on the trail, Henry. Hidden in ice."

He shrugged, then held out his hand as he walked closer. "Hand it over," he said in a stern voice.

Imma did as instructed. "Now, your phones. Both of them."

"What?" Rio asked, and Imma looked at her, hearing the alarm in her voice. "Why?"

"Because you won't be needing them."

Neither of them moved, but Henry did, grabbing Imma's purse from Yvonne's desk before she had a chance to react. He held out his hand and wiggled his fingers toward Rio. "C'mon. Hand it over."

"Mr. Henry, what are you talking about? Why do you want my phone?"

Ignoring her, Henry pushed Imma out of the way and grabbed Rio's bag from the counter beside the sink.

Then he calmly opened a drawer and pulled out a large knife. "Now, both of you—walk."

Imma's mind was racing as she took slow, deliberate steps from Yvonne's office into the studio. How were they going to get out of this one? There were two of them, but he had a knife. She already knew they wouldn't be able to reason with Henry. Something wasn't right with him, and Imma knew he was out of control. She'd just have to be smarter.

"Mr. Henry, it's nine in the morning, and you're on Main Street. Dozens of people are driving by this firehouse every minute. Why, I spoke to three or four people before on my way across the street from the parking lot. And the people at Rio's office will miss her in a few minutes. Why don't you rethink whatever it is you're planning."

"You're so smart, Imma. I'm glad you're here, to help me figure it out."

Henry walked to the door at the front of the firehouse, urging them along with a circular motion of the knife in his hand. It was on the right side of the building, where the patrons of Yvonne's studio could tuck their bags into cubbies and change their shoes on a long bench.

"Not a sound, understand?" he said as he unlocked the door and peeked outside.

He quickly shut it and looked at them. "Now, here's what's going to happen. Imma, you're going to walk across the street and get into your car. And then you're going to bring your car over here and back it up close to this door. If you talk to anyone, anyone at all, I'm going to kill your friend. And then I'm going to hunt down your wife and kill her."

"What if someone talks to me? There are cars over there, someone could—"

"I guess you better make sure they don't."

Henry handed Imma her purse. "Now, very carefully, I want you to reach into your purse and take out your phone."

Imma did as instructed.

"Now, turn it off."

Again, she obeyed his command.

"Now, your car keys. Slowly."

Imma felt almost faint. Her chest didn't seem to be able to expand to take in air, and the blood seemed to pool in her chest, not making it to her brain. But she searched with her fingers, pulling the key out and reaching out to hand it to Henry.

He laughed. "I don't need that. You do."

"Oh, yes. Of course. Okay," she said, then turned to Rio. "Rio, don't worry. I'll be right back."

Once again Henry eased open the front door, this time a little wider. "Remember, not a peep to anyone."

Imma looked at Rio. "I love you, my friend."

"Blah, blah, blah. Go," he said.

Imma walked, deliberately putting one foot in front of the other, careful not to fall. By turns, she hoped she'd spot someone she knew yet feared she would. But she made it all the way to her car without seeing a single soul, other than a few cars that drove by too quickly to take note. If she survived this ordeal, she intended to have a word with the Garden PD about the speed limit in town.

Imma opened the car door and very slowly sat in the seat, removing her glasses from the cup holder as she did so. They were old anyway, and she needed new ones, so it didn't hurt her so much when she dropped them to the ground before closing the car door. She turned on the ignition and pulled across the street to the firehouse parking area, as Henry had instructed her. Then she made a K turn so she was facing out.

He hadn't told her what to do after she parked the car, so she sat there in silence, fiercely gripping the steering wheel with both hands. A few seconds later, the passenger doors opened, and Rio slid into the front seat, while Henry slipped into the back.

He said only two words. "Drive home."

CHAPTER TWENTY-TWO

I can't believe you got four days off," Avery said as she reached over and squeezed Lauren's hand.

"Dumb luck," Lauren said. "We can continue our honeymoon."

Avery liked the sound of that. They'd been finishing their honeymoon since they returned from their week in the Caribbean. It hadn't been enough, but with their work schedules, they couldn't spare any more time. Once they'd both started their training, finding time together had been a task. Whenever they had more than a few days, they honeymooned. It wasn't just about sex, though. It was about reconnecting. Avery missed her wife. Lauren had first been her friend, then her roommate, and they'd done everything from laundry to grocery shopping to studying together. The sudden conflict in their lives was a hard adjustment.

"I love honeymooning," Avery said.

"Yeah. I do, too." Lauren sighed. "We so lucked out."

The night before, Lauren had come home from her first day of her ENT surgery rotation with the news that her attending physician's daughter was getting married that weekend. He'd given Lauren four days off. When Avery heard the news, she'd immediately called her own supervisor and asked if she could take two vacation days. Opportunities like this didn't come around often for residents, and they might not have this much time together until they had a week of vacation next January.

So they'd spent the night before with dinner at one of their favorite restaurants, and then they'd packed their bags and had a rare late morning. Finally, they loaded up the new Lexus and headed for Garden.

"Hey, today's Thursday," Avery said.

"One of the things I love most about you," Lauren said. "Your sharp mind."

"Hardy har. *The Garden Gazette* is published on Thursday. Can you pull it up on your phone?" Avery had taken Imma's advice and purchased a subscription.

"Well, I can, but since I've just finished my trauma rotation, I'm going to insist you wait until we stop before you read it."

"That's great thinking. Or maybe you can read to me."

Lauren's head was buried in her phone. "I certainly can. Will the article about the eggs be published today?"

"That's what Imma said."

"Okay. I found it. I need your username and password."

Avery supplied the information, and a moment later Lauren had access to the online content.

"Here it is," she said, and began reading. She didn't stop until she finished, and when she did, Lauren reached over and squeezed Avery's thigh. "It's a really nice article. She said some pleasant things about your family. Not to mention that she quoted you. You're essentially famous now."

Avery smiled. She liked her quote. She sounded mature and intelligent, and she told Lauren so.

"I agree. But the article is really well written, too. I can almost picture the exhibit from reading what she wrote. I can't wait to go see it."

Avery agreed. Imma had told the story of the Russian royal family, Peter Carl Fabergé, his eggs, and the people who collected them in an artistic and informative way.

"Has your grandmother given in yet?"

Avery had told Gloria she needed to make the trip to Manhattan for the exhibit, but Gloria was dragging her feet. Her excuses were vague, and Avery suspected the situation was still very raw for her grandmother. But it had been more than twenty years, and the exhibit had done a wonderful job of celebrating her family's eggs, so Avery thought Gloria would enjoy it.

"Maybe next weekend," Lauren suggested. "We can drive down Friday night and spend the night with her, then take her back to Manhattan Saturday. Do you think you can score a VIP tour?"

Avery thought of how helpful Adrienne had been and nodded. "Yeah. I think so. It might be a photo-op for the museum."

"Let's call your grandmother. See if we can get her to commit."

"Do you think you'll be on call?" Avery asked. While she had almost no call, overnight shifts had been much of Lauren's academic schedule during residency.

"Pft." She laughed. "Uh, no. I think it's going to be an easy month."

"Good for you." Avery looked at Lauren. "Good for us."

Lauren agreed. "Let's call her."

Lauren dialed the phone, and it transferred to the car's Bluetooth. Her grandmother's name and face appeared on the screen in the dashboard, and Avery nodded to Lauren. "I'm movin' up in the world."

"It is a nice car," Lauren commented.

"Hi, sweetie," her grandmother said a few seconds later. After catching up for a few minutes, Avery explained why she'd called. "We read the article about the eggs in *The Garden Gazette*. I want to take you and Lauren next weekend. You'll really love it."

"I don't think so, Avery. I'm not up for a trip to New York."

"Gram, is it the trip to New York or seeing the eggs that you're concerned about?"

Gloria sighed. "A little of both, I suppose."

"Why don't you read the article? And the other pieces about the exhibit. I think you'll like what they did."

"I'll read it. Now what are you two up to in the middle of the day? Shouldn't you both be at work?"

Avery explained their unexpected good luck and their plan to spend the weekend in Garden. As the words left her mouth, she had a sudden guilty feeling. Maybe she should have invited Gloria to the Poconos.

Then Gloria absolved her. "I think you two will have more fun than I do this weekend. Tiffany is coming home for her high school reunion, so my weekend is going to be interesting."

"Oh, how nice. How long is she staying?"

"I'm not really sure."

"Grammy, if she's here next weekend, we have to go to the exhibit. You can hire a car. I'm sure Tiffany would love it. Or we can come home from the mountains early and go on Sunday. She has to see it. And so do you."

Gloria laughed. "You're relentless, Avery. So, okay. I'll consider it. But don't be disappointed if I don't come, sweetie. I had the pleasure of holding those eggs in my hands, and that's more than I could ever get from an exhibit."

Avery considered her grandmother's words, as well as her point of view. Maybe she was pushing her too hard. If she wanted to live with her memories, what was the harm in that? To Avery, who never got the chance to hold the eggs as her grandmother had, the exhibit had been amazing. But now she could understand how her grandmother would see it differently.

"However, I think this unscheduled trip may be fortuitous," Gloria said. "Do you think you can hike out to the cabin? I just got a letter from the insurance company about the policy on the Pocono house, and we're paying to insure the cabin against fire. I'm wondering if it's worth it. The place is probably falling down."

"Of course! I haven't been out there in years. We'll take a picnic and maybe walk over to the game lands and see the waterfalls."

"It sounds lovely, my dear. Please check in with me so I know everything's okay. On both ends," she said with a chuckle. "I may need you to call me in a prescription for Valium."

"Gram, get with the times. No one has used Valium in years. It's Xanax now."

"Whatever you say. Just make sure you answer your phone, in case it's an emergency."

"You've got it. Love you, Gram."

Avery pressed the button on her steering wheel and ended the call. "I'm so happy Tiffany's coming in. I was feeling guilty, like I should invite her on our honeymoon."

"It would have been great. She'd take a nap, and we'd take a nap."

Avery laughed. "When my grandmother starts napping, I'll start worrying."

"So what do you want to do for the next four days? Other than…"

Avery reached over and playfully slapped Lauren's arm. "Well, first we'll stop for food. What do you feel like eating?"

They discussed the menu and what they'd buy at the grocery store. Avery mentioned picnic options. The hike to the waterfalls was about five miles through the woods, but they had a backpack at the Pocono house that doubled as a cooler, which made it easy to picnic. Avery wanted to climb to the top of the mountain on their property and watch the sunrise. They'd do that the next morning, and then the next day they'd hike out to the old cabin. They'd cook out every night but maybe go out for breakfast. One day they'd drive to the outlets and shop a little. And, of course, they'd spend some time in bed.

"I love you," Avery said.

"Me, too."

Lauren pushed some buttons on the console, and in a few seconds their favorite playlist was blasting, so they sang their way across the Pennsylvania border. Avery had to admit it—she liked the car.

Before long, they were on the outskirts of Garden and stopped for lunch at a seasonal hot-dog stand. Next, they hit the local grocery store. After they finished, they headed to the house.

Rounding the curve in the driveway that brought the house into view, Avery was disappointed to see the caretaker's SUV parked in front of the garage bays. "Oh, shucks. I didn't realize Ellen would be here."

Then a man stood and waved as he recognized Avery. It was Ellen's husband, Don, who took care of the landscaping chores.

He strolled over to the car and hugged Avery as she hopped out, then greeted Lauren. "We weren't expecting you," he said. "What a nice surprise."

Avery told him about their spontaneous getaway, and he promised not to take up too much of their time. "We've been here since early this morning, so I'm sure Ellen will be finishing soon."

The sun was high in the sky as they unloaded their groceries and headed into the house. They found Ellen and exchanged pleasantries, then began unpacking their groceries. "Lauren, would you mind if I call Imma? I'd like to congratulate her on her article."

"I wouldn't mind at all. I know you talked about going there for dinner, but we have all this food and such a great view—why don't you invite them here?"

"Great idea." Avery dialed Imma's number and put the phone on the counter as she emptied the grocery bags. A few seconds later, the phone was answered.

"Imma?" Avery asked. The voice on the other end of the phone didn't sound like her new friend's.

"No. This is Mac. Is this Avery? I met you on Sunday at Imma and Jo's house."

Avery was filled with a sense of dread. Why would Mac be answering Imma's phone?

"Yes, Mac. I remember you. What's going on? Where's Imma?"

"I was hoping you could answer that question."

"Me? Why would I know where Imma is?"

"I was just hoping. She's missing."

Avery was shocked. "Missing?"

"Yeah. I took Jo fishing this morning, and when we got back, Imma wasn't here. She didn't answer her phone, so Jo pinged it. We found it in her car, parked along the river trail. But there was no sign of Imma."

"What can I do?" Avery asked.

Lauren, hearing only one side of the conversation, stopped what she was doing and came over to Avery's side. She held up both palms to ask what was going on, but Avery hushed her with her own hands and turned the phone to speaker mode.

"I'm not sure. I think we're going to organize a search party to look along the river. You're welcome to join in."

"Where are you?" Avery asked.

"At Imma and Jo's house."

"We'll be right there," Avery said.

She clicked off the phone and explained the situation to Lauren. She knew she'd spoken for her when she committed to the search, but she knew her wife, and she wouldn't want to hang out reading her book when someone might be in danger.

They were both wearing shorts and T-shirts. The day was warm but not hot. "What do you think? Should we change?"

They agreed to jeans and hiking shoes, and they packed sweatshirts, as well as the lanterns Avery's grandmother kept around the house for emergencies. A few minutes later they were out the door, on the way to Imma's house.

When they pulled into the driveway, Avery was startled by the number of cars she saw. A dozen or more vehicles crowded the driveway and the area in front of the barn.

They parked at the back of the pack and quickly walked to the house. Their knock was immediately answered, and as they entered the room, Avery saw the concerned expressions of everyone in the room. At least twenty people were there, many she'd seen a few days ago at Sunday brunch. At the front of the group, discussing the plan for this search mission, stood Mac.

Judging by her demeanor, Avery assumed Mac was in law enforcement. She was no-nonsense as she described how the groups would spread out along the path from the point where Imma's car had been found. Some would travel north, some south, and some would wade across the river and search there. Others would walk along the road in both directions.

People chimed in as Mac spoke. One woman, a school-crossing guard, said she could stop by Garden Elementary School and procure reflective vests for the people walking along the roadway.

When Mac told her that was a good idea, she excused herself to go retrieve the vests.

Someone else began collecting all their phone numbers for a group text, so they could immediately update each other on their progress. Mac had reached out to one of her police connections, and a search dog was on the way. The television stations had been notified, and they had pictures of the missing women.

Avery was confused. Women? "I'm sorry that I'm late to the meeting, but did you say women?"

Mac looked worried as she met Avery's gaze. "Yes, women. Since I spoke to you a few minutes ago, we've learned that our friend Rio is also missing."

Mac didn't need to say it. This news changed everything.

CHAPTER TWENTY-THREE

Curt drove past the parking area beside the running trail, looking for activity. At least two dozen cars were parked there, but he didn't see any of their owners.

"Fuck!" he said aloud, not for the first time since abducting the two women from the firehouse. All his life, he'd been methodical and careful, planning moves to make sure all details were covered. The times he'd been impulsive had always turned out badly. Faking his death on 9/11 had been a bad move. Killing Yvonne had been a bad move. He only hoped kidnapping Imma and Rio had not been a bad move.

But what choice did he have? Once Imma found that diamond, it was only a matter of time before she shared the information with the Garden police. And then they'd have questions. And if they started looking closer at Christopher Henry, they were bound to have even more questions, and he was likely to end up at the police station for an extended stay.

Curt only needed to buy himself some time. He didn't need weeks—just a couple of days. It was Thursday, and he was scheduled to meet Nick in Manhattan on Sunday to exchange the last egg. He needed to keep those women from talking to the police until he had time to get out of town.

This wasn't how he'd planned it. He'd decided to sell the properties to give himself more cash—a small fortune in legitimate cash. Even if he sold quickly by lowering the asking prices, he thought he'd have time to clean out the house and studio. He could spend a month—sort through personal items, donate things to Good Will. Then, he'd buy a car with his legitimate money and head someplace warm where he could start over with his new fortune.

It hadn't happened that way, though. Maybe he should have just laughed Imma off when she held out that diamond. But instead, he'd panicked.

If he left town today, he wouldn't have to deal with the mess he'd made by kidnapping the women. But he couldn't just walk out. He needed to take care of things at the house. Unfortunately, a month was no longer an option. He couldn't afford to spend his time foolishly.

During the ride to the cabin, he'd had a little time to think. First, he had to get rid of Imma's car. By leaving it near the trail, and dropping the phones next to the door, he could create a smokescreen. The authorities would begin looking there, assuming the two women wandered off. They wouldn't bother with him for a while, at least not for a few days. That was all the time he needed.

He knew where the parking areas' security cameras were located, and he had to disable one of them, the one that showed the cars coming into the lot.

After stopping a hundred feet from the car-park entrance, Curt walked slowly through the woods, his head down. He didn't want anyone to see him, but he was also looking for something: rocks, of a certain size and shape.

He picked up a half dozen, stuffing them into the pockets of his hoodie and pants. Then he looked for the cameras. One faced the river, scanning the lot and the trail beyond. The other two focused on the short road that led to the parking area—one facing in, and one out. He was interested in the former one. Coming from behind it, he was in a blind spot of all three cameras. Taking aim, he threw the first rock at the camera sitting fifteen feet off the ground.

Leave it to the nature lovers to mount it on a tall, slender pole. A tree, he could climb, but that pole was so tall and thin, it would even keep the squirrels at bay.

With a more careful aim, he hurled the second rock skyward. He missed, and it landed with a loud thump on the forest floor. He threw the next rock and missed again. The fourth hit the mark, rattling the camera but not appearing to do much damage. Curt sighed. It was a strong mount, and perhaps this effort was futile.

The next rock struck the mark again, but instead of knocking the camera free, it moved it slightly toward the left.

Okay, he thought. Maybe I can't get it down, but at least I can turn it away from the road. Then, he could pull Imma's car in unobserved.

After looking around again, he saw that he was still alone in the parking area. He reached back and threw again, missing the mark. Then he hurled the last rock. It hit and again moved the camera. It had turned only about thirty degrees, but it should be enough. From his vantage point, the lens was now pointing across the entry to the opposite side of the woods beyond. If he drove in hugging the tree line beneath the camera, he would be out of its line of focus.

Marching back through the woods, Curt planned his next move. He'd park the car, leaving both women's phones there—Rio's inside, Imma's on the ground next to the car. He'd turned them off before they left town, but he'd turn them back on. He wasn't sure how well their movements could be tracked, and some genius might be able to figure out they'd been turned off, but only if someone knew the passwords to open them. It was nearly impossible to break into an iPhone without the password.

He reached the car and climbed in, drove a hundred feet, and made a U-turn. Then he drove past his destination, using his arm to cover his face, just in case the camera's range reached the road. Then he made another U-turn and swung the car into the access road to the car park, following his plan to stay near the trees.

When the car was positioned where he wanted it, he turned on both phones and then wiped them clean. He left Rio's on the passenger seat, then opened the door. Looking around for witnesses, he saw none and dropped Imma's phone. Then he walked behind the car and broke into a slow jog. He didn't stop moving until he was in his garage.

Leaning against the wall, he watched the door drop and waited for his heart rate to come down.

What the fuck should he do now?

He'd left the women tied up, back-to-back on two kitchen chairs in the cabin. He'd used duct tape to secure them to the chairs, then taped their hands to the chair backs. He didn't need to cover their mouths— no one went anywhere near that cabin. It was tucked into the back of the Giles property and in the area of the game lands with no public parking. So he wasn't worried about someone finding them.

In fact, if he never went back, it could be years before anyone discovered their bodies.

Then he reconsidered. If someone searched for them, they might head in that direction. Not right away, though. It was miles from Imma's car, and no one would think to look there.

Curt reviewed what he had to do. If he didn't want the women to die, he'd have to go back later, to give them some food and water, allow them to use the bathroom. And that was the smart move. The police would never stop looking for him if he killed them, and even though Imma deserved it, he didn't want to make things worse for himself. They might forget about him once they found the women, if they found them alive.

Yes, that was a good idea. He'd give them something to eat tonight, then maybe skip town tomorrow.

First, he had work to do.

Trying to remain calm, Curt jogged to the first floor. From a centrally located closet, he pulled out the cleaning supplies—a mop, a bucket, towels, and an all-purpose cleaning spray. Balancing his load, he headed back to the ground floor. He'd watched television, and he knew at some point a dozen police officers would be here, searching for evidence. One of those clues would be fingerprints. Under no circumstances could he leave any for them to find. One day, when he was far away from this place, that might be the small detail that came back to bite him in the ass.

The ground floor of his house consisted of essentially three rooms—the garage, an adjacent storage area, and a large rec room taking up the entire rear of the house. It featured exercise equipment, a pool table, and a bar complete with seating for eight. It was ideal for a couple that enjoyed entertaining, and he'd always wondered what the house's former inhabitants were like. Social creatures, it appeared.

He'd once hoped they'd use this area. When they'd purchased the house, it was the one truly perfect place in it. It had never occurred to him at the time that his life would become so complicated.

They'd done no entertaining, had no company of any kind. And truly, he didn't spend much time in the basement now. Even in the cool months, except when snow was plowed high along the roads, or the temperatures were below zero, he liked to run outside. He did use the weights, but other than that, the back room was a lot of wasted space.

When Yvonne was here, it was different. They'd spread mats along the stone floor and stretch, then lift weights to stay toned and strong. He'd run on the treadmill, and she'd use the StairMaster. They'd come down from time to time to shoot pool, especially on days when they were snowed in and bored out of their minds.

But that was a long time ago, and now the space seemed barren. The bar area was sparse, with just a few dozen glasses and bottles. The rest of the room was similar. It wouldn't take him long to clean it. He started behind the bar, spraying and wiping, unconcerned about streaks, instead making sure to saturate every surface and remove all traces that he or Yvonne had ever been there. Every glass and shaker and bottle he threw into boxes, and he carried them to the yard.

It occurred to him that he could just torch the place, but that would be a mistake. As it stood, he'd already made it known that he was leaving town. A For-Sale sign was posted in front of the firehouse, and another at the end of his driveway. They'd been there since this morning, since before he'd abducted the women. There was nothing suspicious about that. If he set the house on fire, it would only draw attention to him or, at least, draw it sooner.

He couldn't believe what was happening in his life. How had it gotten to this point? Until a week ago, he was living the same quiet life he'd lived for most of his time in Garden. Then it all went to hell—all because of Imma Bruno.

Maybe he should stop what he was doing and go back to the cabin. Kill the women. It was the smart thing. If he burned the cabin, no one could prove it was him. Then he took some breaths, and his calm returned. No. He wouldn't kill them. It was better if they were alive.

While he cleaned, he retraced his moves, wondering where he might have made a mistake, something that would implicate him. Unless he'd left a random strand of DNA somewhere, he thought he was fine. The only thing linking him to the kidnappings was the victims' testimony.

Man, he'd been stupid. He should have just asked Imma to hand over the diamond and told them to get out of the firehouse. Instead, he'd created another headache for himself. But he'd panicked, and he'd screwed up. Now he had to manage that mistake.

Curt paused his cleaning and filled a glass with water. He was moving quickly, and even though it was cool in the basement, he was sweating profusely. The gloves on his hands only added to the problem.

He downed the glass and continued his task, and an hour later he felt confident the entire rec area was clean.

Next up was the storage room. Fortunately, neither he nor Yvonne was a collector, and other than the Christmas decorations, the area was empty. Curt made half a dozen trips to the backyard, and in twenty minutes, the storage area was empty, and a fire blazed in the fire pit.

Unlike with the house, Curt wasn't concerned about setting fire to its contents. Who would know? People in the mountains burned things all the time. His fire pit held lots of secrets—mostly things that had belonged to Yvonne, but mainly the remains of fallen trees. If he burned some junk there, it wouldn't necessarily raise any red flags.

His next stop was the bar. Carrying the boxes out to the fire pit, he emptied all the liquor into the pile, then put the box in his car. He'd dump it all in the trash bin at the service station by the highway later. Back at the house, he emptied all the closets and spent the next hour walking back and forth, feeding the fire with the evidence of the last twenty years of his life. Yvonne's closets had long been empty, the contents destroyed in a similar fashion years ago. As he stared at the fire, he was relieved at one less task to manage now.

It was after lunch, and Curt's growling stomach told him he should break to eat. He still had work ahead of him, and he didn't intend to stop until he was too tired to move.

After a quick bite, he went to work in his garage. Just like in the storage area, the contents were sparse—a few tools, a broom and shovel, a chest of rock salt. Curt backed his car out of the garage to give himself space, then made quick work of wiping down all the garage contents. Next, he wiped every surface, from the overhead lights to the tracks that held the garage doors in place.

When he thought he was done, he sat down, leaning against the wall. Gazing around, he looked over the garage, pleased. He hadn't missed anything.

After he gathered his cleaning supplies, he walked up the steps to the main floor to begin the process again.

This time he started in the spare bedroom. No one ever used it now, and no one had been in it before Yvonne had died, just him, when he was banished for a few days during a spat. He wiped down all the surfaces, inside and out, and finished in half an hour. He'd have to vacuum, but otherwise the spare room and downstairs rooms were done. He'd avoid them until he left, and then he would have to tidy up only a small space before he abandoned the property for good.

What next? He supposed the most practical place was the bedroom. If he took everything out of there and the attached master bathroom, he could check that part of the house off his list. He'd sleep on the couch and use the second bathroom in the hallway until it was time to make his exit.

Figuring he could finish his cleaning before dark, he went to work again. Then, after the sun set, he'd go back to the cabin and figure out what to do with Imma and Rio.

CHAPTER TWENTY-FOUR

One by one, cars pulled out of Imma and Jo's driveway and followed the lead one with Mac and Jess toward their destination.

Avery was worried, and she and Lauren said little as they drove. It was only a few miles to the parking area, and when they got there, they couldn't pull in. Police tape had been stretched across the access point, and beyond it, Avery spotted several people gathered around a car parked near the edge of the woods.

Focusing on her own vehicle, she pulled off the roadway as far as she could, and she and Lauren got out and crossed over to gather with the others who'd been at Imma and Jo's house. Another woman walked toward them, from the area beyond the police tape, looking distraught.

When they were all within earshot, Mac spoke. "They don't want anyone else to contaminate the area around Imma's car. They're waiting for the tracking dog now." She motioned with her head. "The group here will split up, and we'll walk in both directions along the river trail and along the road. I'll want one person scanning each side of the pathway. Imma was still in her pajamas this morning when Jo left the house, so we have no idea what she was wearing. You all know what she looks like, though. Rio went to work this morning in a bright-pink blouse, so that should be easy to spot."

It was the middle of the afternoon, the day warm and mostly sunny. What Mac didn't say didn't need saying to this group. They were all from Garden and knew the night-time temperatures would dip to uncomfortable levels. Even Avery, who visited the mountains only on occasion, knew better than to venture out at night without a sweater or jacket. It might not get cold enough to cause harm to young people like her and Lauren, but it would certainly stress Imma and Rio if they had to spend the night out in the woods. Both of them were in their seventies, and Avery knew that type of exposure could provoke both heart attacks and strokes.

A female officer from the Garden police department walked over and nodded to Mac before addressing the group. "I'm Officer Knox. Thank you all for coming out to help in this search. Right now, we're treating this as a missing-persons situation. We have no reason to believe otherwise. But we want to find them as soon as we can."

"Did the cameras show anything?" Ann asked.

Avery's gaze moved from Ann to the police officer as she answered. "The information from the cameras wasn't helpful. The camera that would have caught Imma's car somehow got rotated across the road, so it didn't show her drive in or what happened to her after that."

"Doesn't that seem suspicious?" Ann asked.

The detective nodded, and perhaps because she'd spent time in the courthouse with Ann as the judge, or perhaps out of respect for Mac, a fellow officer, she provided a little more information than she might have. "Here. Let me show you what I'm thinking."

They walked a few feet toward the entrance of the car park, to the spot where the stern warning on the police tape stopped them in place. "See the three cameras?" she asked, pointing. "The one above Imma's car points that way," she said, indicating the area behind them, looking out to the road and heading toward town. "It's intended to capture everyone heading into the lot and will get a fair look at the driver. As someone exits the lot, it'll show the back of the vehicle. For cars registered in Pennsylvania, that means it'll pick up their license plate. That one," she said, pointing to another camera, this one on the opposite side of the entrance, "is aimed to see cars coming in and catches a bit of the trail. So, if the women headed in that direction, we should pick them up."

"What if they were walking in the woods?" someone else asked.

The officer shrugged. "Maybe, but maybe not."

"What about the third camera?" Blanche asked.

"It's facing Garden. It will cover most of the lot and the trail heading to town. The woods are a question mark, but if the ladies left this area on the trail, going in either direction, we'll see them."

"How long until we know?" This question came from the woman who looked so worried, and Avery wondered if she might be Rio's partner.

"These are Garden PD cameras, and unfortunately, the Garden PD isn't very big. We're down one officer, who's on vacation, so that leaves four of us. We have someone at the station now, reviewing the footage. Since Jo left the house early this morning, we can't be sure exactly what time the women went missing, so we need to cover a few hours of material on the tapes."

Dominica nodded. "Jo, what time did you leave this morning?"

Avery saw her look to Mac, but Mac didn't answer for her. "Around eight o'clock."

"And you returned when?" Dominica asked.

"About eleven," Mac replied. "When we saw Imma wasn't home, we waited for her half an hour or so. But she was expecting us and indicated she'd be home, so we called her. She didn't answer, and then Jo looked for her with the tracking app. After another half hour with no response, we drove over here. The car was right where you see it now, with Rio's phone on the front seat and Imma's on the ground beside the car. We decided at that point to call the police. The whole situation just seemed odd."

Blanche spoke again, this time directing her question to the forlorn-looking woman. "Karen, when did you see Rio last? What time did she leave for work?"

Ah, Avery thought. I was right. She's Rio's partner.

Exhaling a huge breath, Karen spoke. "She was out of the house like a shot this morning. She listed both of Henry's properties on the internet yesterday, and she wanted to get the signs up. I drove past his place on my way to her office around one o'clock, and the sign was there. There's also one in front of the firehouse. And Rio's car is parked at the office."

Dominica spoke up. "If you ask me, if these two women are missing...I mean, not lost, but missing, Henry has something to do with it."

Officer Knox looked at Dominica. "Why would you say that?"

"He's not from here, and ever since he arrived in town, he's acted strange. He's a recluse. I don't trust him. And then, when we saw him in New York City last week, at the Fabergé egg exhibit, he was talking to the personal assistant to the Russian ambassador. What's a guy like Henry doing with a guy like that?"

"And he denied being there," Jo said softly.

"Really?" Jess asked.

Jo shrugged. "Imma asked him at the library, and he said it wasn't him."

Blanche stood taller. "Every one of us saw him there. It was Henry!"

"Okay, okay, everyone."

Avery could tell by her body language that Officer Knox was not impressed by the women's arguments. And Avery had heard from her grandmother about how difficult the people of Garden could be with outsiders. Gloria had told her it wasn't until she started bringing her grandchildren to Garden without Jonathon that the locals seemed to accept that she belonged there. Avery wasn't sure who this Henry guy was, but she felt a little sorry for him.

"Being a stranger doesn't make you a criminal," the officer said.

"Well, what about his missing wife? Have the police ever looked into that?"

Now, the officer's body language shifted. Cocking her head slightly, she looked at Dominica. "What missing wife?"

"Henry's. She's been missing for about five years!" Dominica's voice was climbing the scales as she spoke.

Mac raised a hand to quiet her. "C'mon, Dom. Yvonne said she was leaving. She packed up that studio all by herself. There's no reason to say something like that about Henry."

"Okay, everyone. Let's stay focused on our search. That's why we're here now. I'm going back to work, and I'll let you ladies get to it. We'll hopefully have more volunteers after the news tonight, but I'm praying we don't need them."

"Thanks," Mac said, and a murmur of thank-yous drifted up from the group.

Mac made quick work of separating them into teams and handed out assignments. Someone else distributed the reflective vests from the school. Avery and Lauren were paired up and started a slow walk along the road, heading toward Garden.

"I'm scared, Laur," Avery whispered. They were out of earshot but, still, no sense in alarming anyone.

"You should be. The car is one thing, but who leaves their phone?"

"Did you by chance check your phone?" Avery asked. "I wonder how cold it'll get tonight."

"Cold enough. It'll be about sixty. That can do some damage."

Avery expressed her worry about Imma's age. "And she's a little overweight, so I'm sure that's a strain on her heart."

"Actually, I remember from my ER rotation that a little chub can actually insulate you and hold in body heat. The ER doc said it was a shame the homeless people didn't eat better, because they'd have a buffer."

"That's harsh."

Lauren shrugged. "I don't think he meant it badly. But what about Rio? Do you remember her? Is she also a little chubby?"

Avery shook her head and frowned at Lauren. "Thin as a rail."

Lauren sighed. "We should find them." They walked slowly, just on the edge of the woods, looking into the ground cover as they moved along.

"She didn't say how far to walk, did she?"

"Why don't we go for half a mile? I'll time it on my watch. Then we can walk back up the other side of the road." The area they were in now was just a thin strip of forest near the river, a stone's throw from the walking path. But it was the middle of summer, and the vegetation was thick. Avery couldn't see anyone through the thick trees, but she could hear the search party calling out, a chorus of "Imma" and "Rio," one after the other.

"Maybe we should call out, too."

"A, if we can hear those people calling out, I'm sure Imma and Rio can as well."

Avery laughed. "You're an awful person, and I'm not sure why I married you."

"Oh, I can remind you later."

"I'm sorry about this, Lauren. It's supposed to be our honeymoon."

Lauren shook her head. "Not at all. How could we not help? This is exactly where we should be."

Avery beamed. That's why she loved Lauren. She was such a kind person, totally suited to the profession she'd chosen. The chorus grew quiet as the woods beside them grew thicker, dampening the voices of the searchers. "I think we should call now."

"Imma!" Lauren shouted.

"Rio!" Avery called.

They walked until they could no longer see the area beside the road where their cars were parked, and then Lauren checked her watch. "It's about half a mile."

They turned around and walked along the other side of the road, looking into the high grass on that side, then the forest after the clearing ended.

Before long they were back at the starting point. "There's news," Dominica told them. "Not everyone's back yet, but apparently they saw something on the security camera."

Avery and Lauren moved a little closer, and a few other women joined them as well. "Do you think the officer will tell us what they saw on the video?" Avery asked.

Dominica shook her head. "No. But she'll tell Mac, and that's as good as telling us."

Avery tried not to laugh, and she and Lauren spent the next minutes making small talk with Dominica. Of course, she knew Avery's grandfather, like most people who'd grown up in Garden. As teenagers, they'd all gone to the same camps and played the same sports and hung out at the same spots.

"Hey, everyone," Mac said a few minutes later when it appeared the entire group had re-assembled. "So we have some news from the video, and from the dog."

"Go on," someone said.

"Jo gave me Imma's pajamas. She wore them last night, so the scent on them is still fresh. The dog has her in the car, but not outside the car."

"What does that mean? Why can't the dog smell her?" Blanche asked.

Mac sighed. "Let me go on, and then the answer may be apparent. The security footage doesn't show Imma or Rio at all in this area today. It did pick up both their cars driving past, but they were too far away to get much detail. What's really interesting, though, is that Imma's car passed by here multiple times today, twice in a two-minute period at about nine o'clock this morning. Shortly after the second pass, the camera angle suddenly moved, taking the focus off the driveway here behind us and moving it to the left."

Everyone spoke at once, and Mac held up her hand to quiet them. "The police are now working on the assumption that the women aren't here, nor were they here at all today. Someone else dropped off the car."

"Where are they then?" Blanche asked.

Mac met her gaze, then met the gaze of every one of Imma and Rio's friends and family. "That's what we're going to find out."

Avery felt Lauren move a little closer, and then she took her hand.

"Does anyone know of a reason someone would want to harm our friends?" Mac asked the group.

"Mac," Dominica said. "I know you think I'm just picking on Henry, but something very odd is going on with him. I think it's worth talking to him."

Mac nodded. "The police agree. If for no other reason than Rio was at both of his properties today to put those signs up. He may have spoken to her, and he may know where she might have been heading."

"What do we do now?" Karen asked quietly.

"Whoever's up for it, we're going to keep searching. I want you all to get something to eat and change into something warmer, and bring your flashlights. The last known location for Rio was her office. We're going to start downtown."

"Let's go," Avery said.

"This is a honeymoon I'll never forget." Lauren laughed.

Avery tried to smile, but she couldn't manage to. She only hoped this honeymoon had a happy ending.

CHAPTER TWENTY-FIVE

I want you to look at the bright side, Imma," Rio said as she leaned back. Imma could feel Rio's head touching the back of hers, and the contact was comforting.

"I'd like to know the bright side. Go ahead."

"He didn't tape our mouths closed. At least we can catch up."

Imma chuckled. "Rio, what's going on? If we can figure it out, maybe it'll somehow help."

"The only thing that's going to help us is a sharp knife."

Imma looked around the room again. It was sparsely furnished, and the decor consisted entirely of dead animals hung on just about every surface. "The only thing I can think of is the fireplace. It's natural stone. There might be a rough edge that we can use to saw this tape."

"It's worth a try. Our legs aren't secure, so maybe we can walk our way over there."

"Remember when we were kids, and we'd sit back-to-back and link arms, then push ourselves up?"

"Imma, that was seventy years ago."

"Do you have a better idea?" Imma didn't want to sound snarky, but their options were limited.

"Maybe just push, and see if we can slide over there."

They were in the kitchen area of the great room, perhaps twenty feet from the fireplace Imma had mentioned. She looked down. The pine floor was shiny with wear. They might be able to slide.

Working together, they pushed sideways, and the chair slid. Just an inch, but it moved. "Wooey!" Rio said. "We've got this."

The next effort wasn't so successful. The shiny floor *was* conducive to sliding, but the chair caught on a seam between the old, uneven boards. They had to tilt the chair sideways and push, a difficult effort, given the circumstances.

After ten more such trials of sliding and tilting and heaving, Imma was drenched with sweat, and her heart pounded. Her breaths were labored. "I have to take a rest, Rio, before I code."

"I'm a little winded myself," Rio said, although Imma thought she sounded fine.

"I think we're on the Giles land," Rio said. "It borders the state land, and we parked on the access road. Then we went right, away from town. So that's the Giles property."

"Yes. I know you live on the other side of town, but I pass that way all the time. The next road from the one we turned on leads to the Giles property, but there are no signs. But I can't imagine this is the main house. Maybe it's just a man cave. Wherever we are, we're deep in the woods."

Rio sighed. "I guess he wouldn't stash us someplace easy to find. Did you see any security cameras on the road?"

"I didn't notice anything. And my car's too old for GPS."

"The phones. Imma, my office can track me on the phone."

"Rio, he shut them off. Remember?"

"Where were we when he did that?"

"I don't know. It could have been in the firehouse. He had our purses."

"Imma, that's perfect. If someone thinks to check that option, they'll know the last location of the phone. Maybe they'll question Henry."

"And I dropped my glasses in the parking lot across the street."

Rio laughed. "You what?"

"I thought it would be a clue, in case someone's looking. I thought of leaving my grandmother's ring, yet if someone found it, they might have just pocketed it. But who steals eyeglasses?"

"Maybe they'll turn them in somewhere."

"We can only hope. Are there any security cameras down there?" Imma never used the lot, so she had no reason to know. And this morning, she'd been too concerned about leaving a clue to survey the surroundings.

"I think there's a camera on that car park, but I don't think it would see the firehouse. It's not directly across the street. It's a little off-line."

"How are your palpitations? Ready to slide some more?"

"I think so." Imma sighed. "But I have a mental image of Shelley Winters in *The Poseidon Adventure*."

Rio laughed. "God, Im. Why would you think that?"

"I've put on a little weight since Jo's been sick."

"Well, if he doesn't come back soon, we'll both be a little thinner when they find us. Skeletons, maybe."

"Avery was just here last weekend, Rio. She's the only one from the Giles family that still comes up here. No one's likely to be around the property for another month."

"He'll be back."

Imma was quiet as she contemplated her situation. She'd been frightened from the moment Henry stepped through the doorway at the firehouse. She'd always sensed something wrong with him. As she drove the car, with him behind her waving a knife near Rio's neck, her fears had amplified. He was taking them into the woods to bury them. He'd slit their throats and dig their graves, and on this remote, abandoned property, no one would ever find them. She'd never known such fear, and it was only when he began to tape them to the chairs that she realized he wasn't planning to kill them. Not yet, anyway.

Her relief flooded her with such emotion that she almost cried. But then she calmed herself and began thinking. How could they escape their predicament? Who might start looking for them, and when? Henry had told them he'd be back to check on them in a little while, but how long was a little while? And he could have lied, too. He might be on his way to New York or some other far-off place, off to sell his diamonds, unconcerned about their slow deaths from dehydration or hypothermia. And what if there were rats?

Imma knew she wouldn't live forever, but she'd always hoped for heart failure. Maybe a big heart attack that she survived, with a chance to say good-bye to her friends and, of course, to Jo. What would happen to her sometimes-confused wife? That thought was worse than the prospect of her own slow, miserable death in this cabin.

She voiced her fears. "I'm worried about Jo."

Rio replied softly. "I'm not ready to give up, Imma. We're going to get across this floor to that fireplace and saw off this tape."

Imma laughed. She was usually the optimistic one, the dreamer who loved to read and imagine the sometimes fantastical things in her books. Rio was all business, a town planner and business owner who focused on money and numbers. And now she was cheering up Imma. Things must be really bad if Rio was the more positive of the two.

Another thought occurred to her as she sat quietly. Why this place? They lived in the mountains, and literally thousands of acres of forest surrounded Garden. He could have taken them someplace twenty miles away, or fifty, far from the humans who might accidentally discover their remains. Instead, he drove them five miles out of town, certainly in range of anyone searching for them.

She voiced her concerns, and Rio hesitated for a moment before answering. "I guess he's familiar with this place. His property is next to the game lands, so I'm sure he's hiked in there and explored it all. And he probably ventured onto the Giles land and discovered the cabin."

"Makes sense, I guess. But what a chance to take, breaking into someone's cabin. How would he know no one uses it?"

"Maybe he's hiked here a lot. Fished in the lake, maybe even hunted." Rio paused. "He's been in Garden for twenty years. He certainly has had time to reconnoiter."

"Rio, if he's evil enough to do this to us, I mean, let's face it. He can't let us go. We can identify him. So he has to kill us. And if he can kill us, do you think he killed Yvonne?"

Rio sighed. "Everyone knew she was leaving, Im. She probably just left."

"Yeah, but that's the perfect scenario for murdering someone. No one missed her, because everyone just thought she'd gone away on her own."

"Why would he murder her?"

Imma thought about it. Women had been murdered for much less than leaving their lovers. Dirty dishes in the sink. A sarcastic remark. Tight clothing, or talking to another man. "I think just the fact that she was leaving him was enough. But what if there was something else? The diamonds were hidden in Yvonne's freezer. Henry didn't spend much time at the firehouse. It was Yvonne's domain. What if…they were Yvonne's diamonds, and Henry murdered her for them?"

"But Yvonne's been gone for years. Why would he still be here?"

"Maybe he wanted to stay here. Maybe he likes it here. But maybe the reason he's never worked was hidden in that freezer. Yvonne went away once a month, right? The studio closed, and she left town. Maybe she went to sell a few diamonds and then brought back the money. It funded their lifestyle."

"What lifestyle? They rarely left Garden. They paid cash for the house, so he doesn't have a lot of expenses."

Imma sighed. "But he has some. How does he pay his bills?"

"Hmm. I guess I assumed he just had money. Maybe he just had diamonds. Maybe you're right. She was leaving and taking his financial security, so he got rid of her. I wish we could do an internet search and find out if she's still out there somewhere."

Imma laughed. "I already did one. And I can't find her anywhere."

Rio chuckled. "Imma, as always, you have a lot of interesting thoughts." Rio blew out a long breath. "I don't necessarily like them, but they make me think."

"I'm ready now. To scooch."

"Okay. Let's go." Once again, they pushed their feet together, causing their combined chairs to move a little. They tried again and moved farther, and kept at it a few minutes longer, until once again, Imma needed a break.

"We're making progress, Imma. I think we're going to make it."

Imma caught her breath and looked at the new scenery, and her heart sank. Indeed, they'd moved a few feet from their starting point, but now, with much of the obstruction such as the large kitchen table out of their way, Imma could see clearly toward the fireplace. Five feet away from where they now sat was a step that led to the living-room area.

They might be able to scoot their way all the way to the New York state line on smooth pine boards, but no way could they move another six feet if it involved going over that step. They'd surely topple, and one of them was bound to hit her head. Maybe that was a better option than starving to death, but she wasn't ready for suicide just yet.

"Rio, look to your left," Imma said softly.

There was a pause before she replied. "Oh, Christ," she said. "What next?"

"Plan B, I suppose."

"What's Plan B?"

"Maybe we can both think of one, since Plan A is a bust." Imma scanned the kitchen. A few appliances sat on the countertops—a toaster, and a Mr. Coffee, and an electric can opener. They were all out of reach, but even if they could figure out how to get to them, Imma wasn't sure how they could use them.

Imma mentioned the appliances to Rio, who was facing in the other direction. "Do you think we could use them somehow?"

"Maybe the blade on the can opener. But how would we reach it?"

"Yeah. That's what I was thinking."

"Our mouths aren't taped shut, Im. What can we do with our teeth?"

"It's a long way from my mouth to that tape around our bodies."

They sat in silence for a while before Rio spoke. "How long do you think we've been gone?"

"A couple of hours, I guess."

"No one even knows we're missing yet."

"Maybe they do," Imma said. Probably not, but maybe. And if they did know, what could they do anyway? Who would ever think to look for them way out here?

They were quiet again as they contemplated who was missing them.

"How about one of the drawers? Maybe we can knock one out of the cabinet."

"It's worth a try." Imma tried not to get her hopes up, but it didn't matter. Trying something, even if it exhausted her, was better than sitting there doing nothing.

They inched toward the cabinets, and Rio was able to kick off her shoe. Using her toes, she hooked one under the handle. Slowly, she pulled it open.

"Rio, it looks like utensils," Imma said as she peeked over her shoulder. "Keep going."

"Easier said than done." But she did keep on. When it was all the way at the end of the track, she kicked up with her other foot and hit the bottom of the drawer. It seemed to hop off the track on one side, for it sat at an odd angle.

"Oh. I think you moved it!"

"Let me try again," Rio said, and Imma could hear the same exhaustion in her voice she'd felt earlier.

Rio steadied her leg, then heaved it upward, and the drawer flew from the cabinet and landed with a loud thud on the floor. A variety of utensils scattered around them.

"Look, knives!" Imma shouted.

"Yes. Big ones!"

Imma stretched her leg as far as she could and was able to pull one closer to her. "I have it with my foot, Rio."

"I have one, too. But what the hell do we do with them?"

Imma sighed. Rio was right. With their hands tied behind them, they weren't very useful.

"Wait, Imma. I have an idea."

Imma turned her head to watch. "Im, Im," she said excitedly, and Imma watched as she grabbed the handle of a large knife between her big toe and its neighbor and raised it. The handle was near Rio's hand when the knife clattered to the floor.

"Shit!" they said in unison.

"It's okay," Rio said. "I can do it again."

Imma watched as she once again grabbed the knife, and this time, her fingers were waiting, and she grasped the handle.

Imma thought she'd cry with joy.

"Okay. Now, I have to saw this tape without cutting my arm off."

"It's worth the sacrifice, my friend."

"I'm so happy to have you here cheering me on."

"You've got this!"

"I can move my wrist a little," she said tentatively.

Imma squirmed in her chair to gain a better view, but she couldn't see to guide Rio.

"Shit," Rio said as the knife landed loudly on the floor again.

"It's okay. We can start again."

"I have a cramp in my hand," she said. "I need to rest."

"Okay." Imma said. She tried not to let her disappointment show in her voice. "Do you want me to try? It'll give us twice the chance."

"Sure."

Imma flipped off her sneaker, then her sock, and reached out to hook a small steak knife with her foot. Sliding it close to the chair, she grabbed it with her toes and tried to bring it to her hand. Her leg immediately cramped in the hamstring, and she dropped the knife, trying to straighten her leg to relieve the spasm, squirming in the chair to find a comfortable position. By the time the pain subsided, she was once again drenched with sweat.

"It's hot in here," she said finally, and Rio agreed.

The windows were shuttered, but Imma could see the afternoon sun through the gaps. The cabin was in a clearing, but when they had arrived, the sun was lower in the sky, and it was in shadow. Now, it seemed they had the sun's full attention.

"I wonder how cold it'll be tonight," Imma said. She'd checked the weather this morning, but she'd only looked at the high that day, not the overnight low.

"We'll be fine," Rio said. "We're inside."

They spent the afternoon trying to cut themselves free. Imma hadn't had much success, but Rio had been able to get the knife to her hand on a few occasions. Each time, she'd saw at the tape that bound her to the chair but couldn't make much progress before cramps set in.

"How long do you think we've been here?" Rio asked after a while.

Imma had been following the progress of the sun through the shutters, but the growling of her stomach told her they'd been there much of the day.

"It's about three o'clock," Imma said. "I'm starving."

"It would be nice to use the bathroom," Rio said.

"I'll bet he brings us something delicious to eat. Maybe a deli sandwich from Tori's. With a dill pickle."

"I can't even think of eating. I'm just hoping for Charmin in the bathroom."

Imma laughed. "I'm not happy you're with me, Rio. But I'm glad I'm not alone."

Imma heard Rio sigh. "I know he doesn't want to kill us, Imma. If he did, he would have already. And he's not going to ransom us off. So what's he doing with us out here?"

In between trying not to hyperventilate and planning how to escape her bondage, Imma had been asking herself the same question. "I think he just didn't want us to go to the police about the diamonds."

"If he lets us go, we'll tell the police about the diamonds."

"Maybe he plans to leave town," Imma said, "before the police can question him. And then he'll call and tell them where we are."

It wasn't likely, but Emma couldn't bear to say it out loud. "Let's try again, Rio."

This time, Rio didn't sound optimistic about her chances. "Okay," she said softly. "Let's do this."

CHAPTER TWENTY-SIX

The caravan of cars that had gathered at the car park along the trail dispersed in every direction as the volunteers went home to change and get ready to canvas downtown Garden.

Avery and Lauren were already dressed appropriately, but they had gone back to the house to eat, and they packed for what they feared would be a long night. They stuffed hoodies into backpacks and added flashlights and water and peanut-butter crackers in case they needed a little energy.

"I know this isn't great timing," Avery said before they left. "But do you think we can drop off my grandfather's car at the garage? Since we're both here, it makes sense. I won't need a ride back to the house."

So they'd gone in the other direction, and Avery left the convertible at the garage, the key stuffed into the envelope with the service order she dropped through the slot in the door.

Now they reassembled in the middle of town, near Tori's.

Both of them listened carefully as Mac and Officer Knox discussed what they'd be doing. Essentially, the group that had been there this morning, plus an additional fifty volunteers from the community, would be combing every inch of downtown, with extra focus on the area around Rio's office. While Imma's movements this morning were unclear, it was certain Rio had been downtown. Her car was still there, her computer had been turned on, and her water bottle was still on the desk.

Avery was amazed at the conclusions the police officers reached, based on such sparse evidence. For instance, they didn't think Rio had been at her desk for very long before she was called away, because her water bottle was still nearly full. Wherever she went, they decided she didn't plan to go far, or for very long, because she left her computer on when she left.

"It's so fascinating," Avery whispered to Lauren. "I should have become a detective."

"You did, sweetheart. You're a pathologist."

Avery nodded. "You're right. I guess I made a good choice."

Mac began handing out assignments. Basically, they were supposed to check all the shops and offices in town, looking for anyone who might have seen Imma or Rio that morning. They were to inquire if anyone had security footage that the police might review. They were to hang missing-person flyers. And finally, they were to inquire if anyone had seen anything at all out of the ordinary.

Mac handed everyone photocopied pictures of Imma and Rio, as well as one of Imma's car, and she instructed the volunteers to hang them on every surface: telephone poles and windows, under windshield wipers and on mailboxes.

Avery and Lauren were assigned to the end of Main Street, and they set out on their task in late afternoon, hopeful they'd catch the business owners before they left for the day. They stopped first at an insurance agency. Both the owner and the receptionist had been at the office by eight o'clock that morning, had stepped out for lunch, and hadn't seen either Imma or Rio. The owner, a woman, gave permission to hang as many fliers as they wanted from her window and doors.

Next up was a store that specialized in women's handbags, and the owner had already heard about the missing women when the ladies entered. Although she was anxious for news, and wondered if she should be worried for her own safety, she had no information. She did grant permission to hang more fliers, so Avery and Lauren taped them to her windows before moving on to the next storefront.

They found themselves at a consignment shop. The owner wasn't there, but the teenager behind the counter thought she'd seen Imma that morning when she was on her way to the office. She recognized not only Imma, but her car as well.

Avery felt optimistic. The young lady stated that the woman she'd seen was "an old lady," who drove "really slow," and she'd been behind her "for miles" on the way into town. The woman had parked in the lot at the trailhead, next to the nail salon. When the girl got out of her car near the consignment shop, she'd looked up and saw the two missing women meet on the sidewalk and walk back toward the end of town.

Avery took out her phone and called Mac on the newly programmed number.

"Mac here," she answered.

Avery introduced herself and told Mac what she'd learned. Mac took the shop's address and instructed Avery to keep on with their mission, and to let the young employee know she'd be there in a few minutes to talk to her.

Avery asked if she could post the fliers, and the girl gave her blessing. They hung one on each exterior window of the shop before moving on.

"That sounds promising, huh?" Avery asked.

"Yeah. It doesn't look like there's much of anything at the end of town except the old firehouse. Where do you think they were going?"

"I have no idea. I think there used to be a gym there or something, but it closed years ago. So who knows?"

They stopped at the next door to find a sign that said "Closed" and posted some fliers before moving on to the next. That office, belonging to a dentist, was also closed. They adorned his windows as well. Next was a pet-supply store. "Oh. Homemade doggie treats," Avery said. "I'm going to pick some up for Daisy."

"Your grandmother's dog is one lucky puppy," Lauren said.

Avery agreed. She'd never had her own dog, but since her grandfather's death, her grandmother had kept one. Since Avery spent so much time there, she felt like Daisy was her own, and she loved spoiling her.

They went into the shop and inquired about Imma and Rio, but unfortunately, the clerk had only come on duty that afternoon. Avery quickly made her purchase, and they again taped fliers to the door and windows before moving on to the nail salon next door.

Unlike the shops they'd already visited, which were empty, the nail salon was hopping. All six chairs were full, and techs sat before each one, trimming and buffing and applying polish to their customers' nails. Avery looked down to her own feet and promised herself she'd come back before the weekend was over. No one was at the checkout counter, so Avery approached the women at the last chair and told them her mission. Neither of them had seen the missing women, but they promised to keep an eye out for them. Avery proceeded down the line of chairs, and Lauren went to the other end, and they asked their questions and showed their pictures. They both shook their heads when they met in the middle. No one at the nail salon had seen Imma and Rio.

Once again they posted their fliers and looked around the street. The nail salon was the last storefront on Main Street, but the parking area lay beyond it. The girl from the consignment shop had seen Imma turn into the lot.

"Should we check it out?" Lauren asked.

"Can't hurt," Avery replied.

They walked along the sidewalk and into the parking area. Half a dozen cars were in the lot, and the two of them walked between them, searching the ground for anything unusual. They were near the center of the lot when Lauren stopped and bent down. Avery stopped beside her and looked closely at the object she held in her hand.

"Do you think they're Imma's?" Avery asked.

"Let's look," Lauren said as she handed Avery the eyeglasses and pulled out the flier.

Avery inspected the rectangular-shaped wire frames and compared them to the glasses Imma wore in the photo. "I think it's a match. What do you think?"

"You should call Mac."

Once again, Avery dialed Mac's number.

"Mac here," she said again.

Avery introduced herself and told her about the eyeglasses.

"Well, the young lady here was quite positive about the car, and pretty sure about the women she saw walking along the road. I think finding the glasses in that lot confirms her story. That was Imma, and Rio by association."

"So what should we do now?"

"Stay there. Detective Knox and I are on our way. Don't touch anything in the area, and don't touch the glasses any more than you have already."

Lauren and Avery rested against the wooden fence that bordered the lot while they waited. "Why would she leave her glasses?" Avery asked.

"Did she always wear them?"

"I don't think so. She definitely had them on when we met at the coffee shop. But I don't recall her wearing them at her house the next day."

"So, maybe they were for driving."

"Well, how did they end up on the ground?"

"Maybe she took them off before she got out of the car. She put them in the door, and they fell out?"

"Wouldn't she put them in a case when she took them off?"

"Maybe she was in a hurry."

Avery pursed her lips as she considered Lauren's idea. Another thought occurred to her. "What if she left them there on purpose. As, like, a clue."

"That's a really interesting idea," Mac said.

Avery turned and nodded to Mac and Officer Knox.

"Why would you think that?" Mac asked.

Suddenly Avery felt apprehensive, thinking back to how Mac had questioned her earlier that day when she called to talk to Imma. "You don't think I have anything to do with their disappearance, do you?"

Mac shook her head. "No. But you're sort of removed from the situation, since you're not from Garden. You're a little more objective than the rest of us."

"And besides, we need some good ideas about now," Officer Knox said with a nod. "Go on."

"Well, let's assume the women were abducted. That's why the security camera was moved and why Imma's car was parked in the road instead of the lot. Maybe they were abducted here, in this lot. And she left her glasses as a clue."

Mac nodded. "I've known Imma a long time, and I'd say there's no way she'd go down without a fight. So you're probably right."

Avery held out her hand. "Here you go."

Officer Knox took Imma's glasses.

"Show us where you found them," the officer said.

They walked a few feet to the spot. The lot wasn't paved, but there was gravel over the dirt below and nothing but rocks all around the area. "Not even a gum wrapper," Mac said as she toed the rocks and sent some scattering.

Avery felt her frustration. "So the girl from the shop said Imma crossed the street and met Rio, and they kept walking. Did anyone check the shops on that side?"

"Working on it. But it's that place that interests me," Mac said as she pointed at the firehouse.

"Let's go have a look," Officer Knox suggested.

They crossed where they were, rather than walking the fifty feet to the crosswalk, and headed straight up the paved area in front of the large garage door. Spaces for four cars were available in front of the building, and Avery saw space on the side for additional cars.

The large garage door had been painted with a floral pattern that resembled graffiti, as had a standard-size entry door to the left. In a small patch of grass beside the building, a *For Sale* sign had been planted. They spent a moment looking around the ground but saw nothing to suggest the missing women had been there.

Mac tried the doorknob with no luck. "Let's walk around back," she suggested. There was a beat-up sidewalk, and grass took advantage of cracks to sneak through in thin streaks. Single file, they headed toward the back of the firehouse, following the walkway as it made a left turn near the rear of the property. They found no windows at ground level to peek through, and the metal door had none either.

"Holy shit," Officer Knox exclaimed, and they all looked at her. She was staring at the door. Protruding from the doorknob was a key, with a paper tab on a wire hook attached.

The officer leaned down and pulled a pen from her pocket, then used it to lift the paper tag. "It says 'The Firehouse.'"

Avery felt a rush of adrenaline. "Do you think it's Rio's key?" she asked.

"We can check her typical key tag, to see if it's the same. And I'm sure we can check it for fingerprints."

"What does it mean?" Avery asked.

Officer Knox spoke. "Rio was listing the building. For some reason, she came over, expecting to be here just a minute. She left her computer on, right? She met Imma. Probably that was a pre-arranged meeting, since there was a call from Imma's phone to Rio's this morning. That was the only call Imma made, by the way. Rio made about a dozen, but it was a work morning for her. Anyway, they met on the street, and Imma accompanied Rio to this spot. Then, someone came along and changed the plan."

A lump formed in Avery's throat, and she swallowed before speaking. "Do you think…they might be in there? Should we go inside?"

"We have two missing women, and we know they were here today. I think that's reason enough to enter."

The officer unsnapped the tab that held her firearm in its holster, but she didn't remove it. "You stay here," she said, and then she turned the key in the lock, opened the door, and entered the building. Even from a few feet away, Avery heard the alarm begin to beep, a gentle reminder to enter the security code.

"Well, now we'll have everyone's attention," Mac said with a chuckle.

They kept their eyes trained on the door, and the rhythmic "beep, beep, beep" was the only sound coming from the building.

"Can we assume Rio had the alarm code?" she asked suddenly. "I mean, if she has a key, she needs the code, right?"

"That makes sense," Mac said.

Avery's pulse raced as she tried to put the pieces of this puzzle together. "So, Rio opens the door and turns off the alarm, then resets it before she leaves, but doesn't take her key."

"She could have been in a hurry on the way in and just overlooked it on the way out," Lauren said.

"Especially if someone had a gun in her back," Mac suggested.

"What if it's another clue?" Avery asked.

Mac tried not to smile. "Once again, I wouldn't be surprised."

Mac had hardly finished her sentence when the alarm's timer expired, and the gentle beeping turned into an angry, constant wail.

"It's loud enough," Mac said.

They all stared at the door as they waited for something to happen.

"Should we go in?" Avery asked. She could tell Mac wanted to. She looked tense, ready to strike. And though she hadn't drawn a weapon, her right hand seemed ready to pull at the soft bulge in the back of her shirt.

Just then, Officer Knox returned. "No one here," she said.

Mac bit her lip. "You want to talk to Curt Henry," she said. "I think, in about five minutes, you'll get your chance."

CHAPTER TWENTY-SEVEN

Curt stood in the middle of the hallway on the main floor of his house. The downstairs was finished, completely clean, and this floor was as good as he could get it for now. His bedroom was empty, much of the contents burned in the backyard. Likewise for the master bathroom and the spare bedroom.

All that remained was the kitchen/dining area and the living room. He planned to save those areas for last. He had to stay somewhere in the house, and this was the most practical area.

Curt had moved his toiletries to the bathroom in the hallway, and he walked in that direction. He hadn't showered since the day before. He'd gone to the firehouse that morning to pack the last of Yvonne's things and was there when he heard the women talking in the kitchen. He'd jogged there, with the idea that he'd throw the contents into the trashcan at the trail-head parking lot. Once he cleaned the place out, he would have no need to go back.

But then, once again, Imma Fucking Bruno had shown up and caused problems. He should have known when she saw the ice cubes in the firehouse sink that she'd figure out about the diamonds. But why? Why did she have to keep poking her nose around in his life? What had he ever done to her? He'd minded his business. He wasn't friendly and inviting, but he wasn't downright rude, either. He simply wanted to live in peace. She'd fought him since day one.

Now he had such a headache to deal with.

A million thoughts had gone through his head while he'd been cleaning, and the best one involved going straight back to New York as soon as he finished the job. If he simply let the women go, it wouldn't be a big deal, would it? The authorities wouldn't pursue him too aggressively for holding them for a day or two, would they? He'd cut them free of their tape, and by the time they found their way down the driveway, he'd have crossed two state lines and be lost in the city. He'd leave his car double-parked on the street with the four-way flashers on, and someone would steal it in about fifteen seconds. Most likely, no one would ever see it again.

Curt hopped into the shower and washed off the sweat and the smoke and the anxiety, then toweled off. He was famished, and he needed to take the women some food and water. He sliced turkey off a breast in the fridge and put together four sandwiches. Then he poured himself a glass of milk and glanced at the clock.

The local news would be on soon. Should he stick around to watch it? There would surely be a commotion in town, because both women were local. Through her job at the library, Imma probably knew everyone in Garden. And Rio worked on Main Street and was involved in all kinds of community-service projects. By now, someone must have figured out they were missing. What was happening? Were they searching? Had they found the car yet?

He shook his head. Why hadn't he thought to look earlier?

He grabbed his phone, typed in his password, and pulled up the local news. An article had been written at three o'clock, only two hours ago, and already updated once. He scanned it. Imma's car had been found almost immediately. Police were treating her disappearance as a missing-person's case, assuming the two women had gone hiking on the trail and lost their way. Perhaps one of them had been hurt.

The update told him the police were now treating the disappearance as a possible abduction.

Fuck! Why? He'd left their phones and the car. Surely they'd just wandered away. What made them think the women had been abducted? Had he made some sort of mistake? Were the police already looking for him? After running to his bedroom, he willed himself to calm down.

The bedroom faced the front of the house and had a view of the driveway and the property all the way to the main road. It was wooded, with only about two acres of the land cleared for the house and the barn. He cautiously moved the blind, certain he'd see police vehicles in his driveway.

He sighed loudly in relief. Still, he hesitated to show himself, searching the woods along the front of the property from the shadows of his room. For a full minute he scanned and saw no movement.

He ran to the back of the house and looked there as well, finding nothing out of the ordinary.

"Calm down, Curt!" he said aloud.

If only it was so easy. He'd been nothing but nerves since his meeting with Nick, when he'd seen those women from Garden on the street in New York. It seemed nothing had gone right since then.

What next? What could possibly go wrong next?

An abduction meant an abductee was at large. Would they suspect him? The police were bound to ask him about Rio. He'd talked to her just yesterday and met with her to give her keys to both properties. And she'd posted *For Sale* signs. They'd want to know when he'd seen her last. As long as no one had spotted them leaving the firehouse, he'd be safe.

But how did the police know it was an abduction? They must have figured out what he'd done to the camera. But they didn't know it was him, right? He'd turned his phone off at the same time he'd turned off the women's and hadn't powered it up again until just now. They couldn't possibly track him.

Could they?

Fuck!

He'd lost his appetite but forced himself to take a few bites of his sandwich. Then he cleaned up his mess and packed the sandwiches into his backpack. He threw in a flashlight as well, just in case he was delayed. The last thing he needed was to break an ankle in the woods at night.

Okay, he said. All set. He threw his car fob and phone into the backpack's pocket and headed down the stairs. He was backing his car out of the garage when a shrill noise came through his phone, alerting him that one of his alarm systems had been breached.

Curt quickly looked around and hopped out of the car. Had he accidentally triggered the house alarm? Jogging into the garage, he checked out the alarm panel. Everything in the house was okay. That left the firehouse.

Curt ran back to the car and pulled his phone from his backpack. A second later the screen was unlocked, and he confirmed the problem.

He was pulling up the live camera feed when the phone rang in his hand. It was the security monitoring company.

Fuck! The Wi-Fi wasn't working, so he couldn't see the cameras at the firehouse.

He answered the call and told the rep his code, and that he didn't have any idea why the alarm had triggered. Yes. He thought the police should be notified.

He hadn't even disconnected the call before he raced down the driveway. What the fuck? Why would someone break into the firehouse? If Imma Bruno wasn't duct-taped to a chair in the cabin, she would have done it. But why would someone else be poking around? He was sure nothing incriminating had been there when he gave Rio the alarm code, so he wasn't worried the intruder would find anything. But why were they looking in the first place?

Turning right at the end of his drive, he raced down the road into town and pulled into the firehouse parking lot a few minutes later. A police car was parked in front of the door, two women standing next to it.

Swallowing hard, he opened the car door and got out, and the sound of the alarm blaring assaulted his senses. He walked quickly in the direction of the women. Holding out his hand to the police officer, he introduced himself as the owner of the building.

"Dee Knox, Garden Police Department."

"What's going on?" he asked. The alarm continued to scream, and he asked if it was okay to disarm it.

Officer Knox walked with him, along the side of the building and into the open back door. A few seconds later he punched in the code, and the alarm fell silent.

He breathed out a sigh of relief. "That's better," he said with a smile. It was forced, but better to be nice to law enforcement than to piss her off.

"Much," she said.

"So what's going on?" he asked.

She quickly explained about the missing women being spotted near the firehouse and how she'd found the key still in the closed back door.

Curt could have screamed. He'd never thought to look. He'd come in that way but exited through the front, with Rio and Imma.

"It was necessary to enter the building to ascertain whether the women were inside," she said. "They are not."

"I'm sorry to hear about all of this," he said. "Rio Barrett is my realtor. I'm sure that's her key in the lock, and she has a code for the alarm system as well. So she may have been here today. I have no way of knowing."

"No notifications on your phone?" she asked.

"No," he said. "I don't have that feature."

"How about the cameras? I noticed you have quite a few of them."

"Yeah, when my wife—ex-wife—worked here, we thought it a good idea for her safety. But since she closed the business, they're really only for show. It's expensive to have security, and it's just an empty building."

"When was the last time you were here?" she asked.

Curt thought. Did anyone see him this morning? Probably best not to lie. "This morning. I usually go for my morning run and come by to check on the place."

"Even though it's just an empty building?" Officer Knox asked.

Hmm. Game on. Good thing he was thinking this all through, because apparently she was listening to every word he said. "It's cheaper than paying someone else to keep an eye on the place."

She nodded. "And when you were here this morning, did you see Ms. Barrett? Or Ms. Bruno?"

Curt shook his head.

"Did you see Imma's car in the lot? You did come through the lot from the trail, right?"

He didn't see her car because she'd arrived after him. It was probably safe to say that. Then it occurred to him that he probably shouldn't know what kind of car she drove.

"I'm not sure what she drives, but nothing stood out."

"And you left the same way, through the back door and then across the street to the trail? No stroll up Main Street for your morning coffee?"

"No. I went home."

"And did you notice anything unusual? Anything at all?"

He shook his head again. Curt wanted to be helpful, or at least to give that appearance. But he was afraid to say too much around this woman.

"Was the alarm set when you came in? Did you have to deactivate it?"

"Yes." Curt cleared his throat, then made a show of coughing a few times so he didn't seem nervous. He was so fucking nervous.

"And did you come in through the front door or the back?"

"The back."

"Why is that?" she asked.

Curt was starting to feel a little defensive, but he tried to sound casual. Helpful. "Just habit. There's a parking area on the other side of the building, and my…Yvonne and I usually parked there. It was closer to come around the back. Plus, that's the entrance into the office area, and that's where we'd leave our coats and shoes."

"Would be safer to come in through the front door."

He looked her in the eye. "I suppose so. I have an alarm at that door, too, so there's no reason I can't. But as you know, I'm selling the building, so I won't have to think about it for much longer."

She smiled. "No. I guess not. But you're sure Ms. Barrett's key was not in the lock when you arrived?"

"No. It wasn't in the lock when I came in. I didn't check when I left."

Curt stood silently, wondering what he should do next. What should he say? If he hadn't kidnapped two women, he probably would have told her to buzz off, but he had, so he was trying his hardest to be polite. She saved him from further contemplation.

"Did you leave through the front door or the back door?" Fuck, Curt thought. What was the best answer?

"Mr. Henry?"

"Sorry. I was thinking," he said with a smile. "I usually go out through the front door, so I'd say I left that way." It was a lie, but what was one more? Besides, it didn't matter. If someone saw him leaving through the front door, they would have seen Rio and Imma, too, and he'd already be under arrest.

"But you don't remember?"

Curt offered a half-smile, and a truth. "I was sad this morning. Thinking it might be the last time I'm here. I just sort of wandered around for a few minutes, remembering." He shrugged, and the officer nodded.

"Where are you going?"

"Hmm?" What?

"Selling your house, selling the firehouse. Where are you going?"

Fuck. Why all the questions? "New York. City. That's where I grew up, and I think it's time to go home. It gets a little lonely here." He hadn't realized how true that statement was until he made it, but he was filled with a sudden sense of sadness. "What do you think happened to those women?" he asked, partly because he thought he should, and so she wouldn't ask more about his plans. And maybe he could turn this around and find out what she was thinking about the investigation.

"Someone took them, I'm afraid. And I think they took them from this building."

Curt was genuinely surprised. How could she know that? He wasn't aware of any nearby security cameras except one in the lot at the trail-head, and it was pointing away from the firehouse. "Really?"

The officer nodded but didn't offer any further explanation. She simply looked around Yvonne's office as if expecting the women to jump out from under the desk.

"What makes you say that?"

"An eyewitness saw them walking this way. Where else would they be heading? And they can't get far past the building, because of the stream there. Plus, Rio's key was in the lock. It's very suggestive."

Curt nodded. An eyewitness. He supposed he shouldn't have been surprised. It was daylight, and though many of the businesses weren't yet open when he'd taken the women, some obviously were.

"Well, I hope you find them soon, Officer Knox." He was trying to end the conversation, politely, but she didn't appear to notice.

"Does your alarm have that feature where you can tell who comes and goes? What time the alarm was set and disarmed?"

"I have no idea," he said.

"I'd like to check with the alarm company. Can we give them a call?" she asked.

"I'm not sure what you want me to ask them," he said, buying time, trying to think. He'd disarmed the system when he entered the building this morning and hadn't reset it. So when Rio and Imma came in, they wouldn't have had to enter the code. And he'd set it from the front door when he left. Okay, there was probably nothing there to get him into trouble. One code in, one out. Just what he wanted her to think.

"Simple. I want you to ask them what time the alarm was deactivated this morning, and when it was set again. Whether it was disarmed more than once."

She stared at him. Then, almost as an afterthought, she smiled.

"Okay, sure," he said. Scrolling through his contact list, he dialed the number for the alarm company. To his dismay, the officer began walking around the office. She stopped and knelt, touched the floor. Pulling her finger up to her eyes, she rubbed it with her thumb.

"Home security," a friendly woman on the line said. "Please hold."

"I'm on hold," Curt said. "Did you find something?"

"Just dirt. But if it's okay with you, we'll do a more thorough search."

"That's fine," he said. Of course she'd want to do a more thorough fucking search. He could only hope there wasn't another diamond on the loose somewhere.

He watched her walk out the back door and stifled a scream. He hadn't been back here to clean the place up after he kidnapped the women. Why had he spent the entire fucking day cleaning his house, where two kidnapped women *hadn't* been leaving their DNA all over? Why hadn't he come here and found that fucking key in the lock, and whatever other clues they'd managed to leave?

He walked toward the countertop, where Imma and Rio had been standing when he walked into the room. As casually as possible, he glanced around, searching. If Imma had found one, there could be another diamond. He took a paper towel from the holder and got a bottle of vinegar, then began wiping down the surface.

"What are you doing?"

Officer Knox practically flew across the room. Curt stood back defensively. "I'm wiping the counter," he said. "What's the problem?"

"The problem is, this could be a crime scene. And you're destroying evidence."

"There's dust," he said. "That's all."

He looked over her shoulder.

"Home security," a voice on the line said. He took a breath, dropped the paper towel into the bin, and asked about the alarm history. He had to answer a few security questions and give account information, but finally the woman on the other end of the line said she would check the account. She told him to hold.

"She's looking at the account. You think these days they could do voice recognition or something," he said, trying to restore their prior camaraderie. He smiled at the officer, then at another woman, who had just arrived.

Officer Knox gave him a small smile in return.

"Do you want me to put it on speaker?" he asked.

"That would be great."

"Mr. Henry," a voice asked a few seconds later.

"Yes. I'm still here."

"I have the information you're looking for. Do you want to write this down?"

Looking around, he moved to Yvonne's desk and opened the drawer. "Hold on. I'm getting a pen."

When he was ready, he told her. The officer, he noticed, had also taken out a notebook and pen and stood poised to write. "Okay, the alarm was deactivated this morning at 7:46, then reset at 8:32." He'd known what she was going to say before he'd dialed the phone, but he was still relieved to hear her words.

"That's it?" he asked.

"There was a breach of the system at 5:20 this afternoon. Just a few minutes ago. The police were called, and there's a note that we spoke to you."

"Yes. That's correct. No other activity today?" he asked, trying to be helpful.

"That's all."

"Hold on, please," he said to the tech.

"Anything else?" he asked the officer in a whisper.

She shook her head.

"Okay. Thank you for your help."

"Thank you for choosing Home Security."

Feeling elated, Henry disconnected the call.

"Would it be all right with you if we have a look around?" Officer Knox asked.

Curt shrugged. "Sure, but why? Obviously the women weren't in the building this morning."

"Yeah, it would appear not. But your sidewalk was the last place they were seen." She opened her notebook and flipped through several pages, then looked at him. "And according to the girl who saw our missing women, they were here at the exact same time you were."

CHAPTER TWENTY-EIGHT

C'mon," Curt growled as the traffic in front of him crawled out of town. He tried to keep a respectful distance between his car and the one in front of him. The last thing he needed was more attention from the Garden police.

When he reached his driveway, he turned and gassed his car. As soon as the house came into view, he activated the remote and watched the garage door open.

He parked in front of the garage, hopped out, and ran inside. After meeting with Officer Knox, he'd abandoned the idea of cleaning out his house. Images of the FBI surrounding the place flashed through his mind as he threw some essentials into a bag. Toothbrush, deodorant, diamonds, Fabergé egg. That was all he needed.

It wasn't ideal that he was leaving so much evidence. His DNA, his fingerprints, the house contents. But at the same time, that evidence would lead nowhere. When they found his fingerprints in the house, they would be unable to link them to anyone. Curtis Hutchins had no record, and neither did Chris Henry. Likewise with his DNA. He'd just have to be careful and never put himself in a position where anyone would check him in the future.

He wasn't sure how much time he had, but it couldn't be long. The police officer had questioned him relentlessly, and Curt felt certain he'd said something suspicious. She was probably at the police station right now, poring over her notes, looking for something incriminating he'd said. He didn't plan to stick around to learn what it was.

He should just take off and get out of Garden right now. He could head to the bus station and board an east-bound bus, then melt into the crowd at the Port Authority bus terminal. He could disappear in New York City until he could vanish for good. But the police might check the bus stations, and he'd be a sitting duck on a bus if the police were after him. It was equally risky to drive. If the police started looking, the corridors between Garden and New York would be too dangerous.

However, Jonathon's convertible was still in working order and parked a few miles away, on the Giles property. Avery drove it every time she visited the mountains. Curt had been to the house and investigated, and she left the key on the seat. It was perfectly safe, in the garage they'd added to the house. He could break into that as well, using the side door with the combination lock.

Standing in the center of the home he'd known for more than twenty years, Curt was surprised at how little he felt. He might have once been sad, but the sadness had passed in the past few years. Sadness that he'd made such poor choices in women, and in life. Sadness that Yvonne had betrayed him and that he'd had to kill her. Sadness that his life had amounted to so little.

He used to think of what he could buy with all his stolen money, but it had occurred to him years ago that he'd bought nothing but grief.

He didn't feel fear, either. The police would surely be here soon, if for nothing else than to question him again. But eventually someone would realize how short Chris Henry's resumé really was. No one could link him to Curtis Hutchins—not yet, anyway, but they were bound to figure out he wasn't really Chris Henry. They could arrest him for identity theft and, eventually, kidnapping, but it didn't seem to matter anymore.

He slowly spun around the main floor of his house, taking it all in—the wall of glass, the floor-to-ceiling stone fireplace, the comfy leather furniture. Carefully chosen sculptures and art. He wouldn't miss any of it. Then he saw it, and his pulse slowed as he walked toward the one masterpiece that was truly his.

"Fuck," he said aloud. "Fuck, fuck, fuck!"

He'd been able to scan Avery's picture and had it printed, and now it hung on the wall between the kitchen and breakfast nook, a 24×36-inch canvas print of a drawing in crayon. Perhaps because of this picture, which he saw every day of his life, Curt remembered that day so well. The sky was so clear and blue, and Avery had asked if he could pick her up so she could touch a cloud. In the picture, the clouds were laying lower than he and Avery were atop the South Tower. They'd seen a pigeon that day, and in response she'd drawn an entire flock of colorful birds resting atop the building and flying above it. Across from them, workers sat at tiny desks in the North Tower. He'd pointed out the spot where the MGT offices were, and she'd drawn her grandfather in the picture, waving up at her from his kingdom. And, of course, the Statue of Liberty sat in the middle of the harbor, larger than both towers combined.

If his departure from Garden had gone as planned, Curt would have taken the canvas with him. Now, with the hike he had planned, it wasn't practical. And in his haste to clean out the safe, he'd kept the egg and the diamonds, but he'd thrown the original copy of Avery's drawing into the fire. The computer he'd used to scan it had been trashed long ago.

"Fuck!" he screamed. The only remaining copy of this treasure was the one staring back at him from the wall. Impractical or not, he had to take it with him.

Pulling it from the wall, Curt slipped it into a clear plastic trash bag and knotted the top closed. It wasn't ideal. He'd have to carry it through the uneven floor of the forest, giving him only one hand to catch himself and prevent a fall. At least it was light.

Gazing once again around the circle of the house's main floor, he decided that this time he hadn't forgotten anything. Slipping the backpack over his shoulder, he grabbed Avery's picture by the knot in the plastic bag, then headed downstairs. He didn't bother to turn off the lights. Maybe it would deter the police for a while if they thought he was barricaded inside.

His car was parked outside where he'd left it. He piled everything inside and drove away. He planned to leave it at the car park near the bus stop. The authorities would probably think he'd hopped a bus, and that would buy him some time while he disappeared in Jonathon's car.

The only problem was the car park's location, and as he passed the driveway to the Giles estate, he lamented his walk back. He could hardly jog along the road wearing a backpack and carrying a large canvas. Not if he wanted to be inconspicuous. The car's location was supposed to point out of Garden, not back toward town.

His best chance of avoiding detection was walking away from Garden, toward the interstate, then back beneath the underpass, up a grassy slope, and into the woods on the opposite side. Hopefully, he wouldn't encounter a tractor trailer on the highway. After all he'd been through, that wouldn't be a proper ending to his story.

Hitting the trip timer, he watched as each tenth of a mile ticked off on the car's odometer. He figured it was about three miles from the Giles driveway to the car park. Unfortunately, the cabin was on the other side of the property, nearer to the game lands and his house. But once he reached the Giles driveway, the walk would be easy. It was paved most of the way, and with no eyes following him, he could run. He only had to make it as far as the main house. That's where the convertible was parked, and he could drive it to the cabin before making his escape.

At this point, he was tempted to drop a letter in the mail and let authorities know where the women were. But he had to go to the cabin anyway. He might as well give them something to eat and free one of their hands. By the time they pulled off all that tape and were free, then walked to the highway, he'd be lost in New York City. They'd never find him there.

At the car park, he was relieved to find twenty cars already there. His would be just one more. He hopped out and left it unlocked, the key on the seat. It would be great if someone came along and stole it. It would confuse the police even more.

After gathering his things, he began walking. Other than the canvas, he looked just like any other hiker out for the day. Although it was late, he could have been about to climb to one of the local lookout spots known for great sunsets. Maybe if someone saw him, they'd think he was an artist, climbing to the top to paint the sunset.

At the entrance to the interstate, he scrambled down the embankment, doubled back, and climbed the hill to the forest behind the service plaza. A few tractor trailers were already parked for the night, and they hid him from view. As he'd anticipated, the walk was a rough one. Following the road to Garden, which he could see from his position fifty feet from the forest's edge, he picked his way along.

But Curt was worried. The sun was nearing the point where it would disappear behind the mountain, and already shadow blinded his view into the forest. He paused and looked at his watch. It was six thirty. He had three miles to walk and hoped he could cover that distance in the two remaining hours of daylight.

Picking his way slowly through the forest, he found the darkness came more quickly than he'd thought it would. Curt paused and gulped water from his pack, then turned on the light. He could no longer see the road, so he didn't fear someone there would see him. But he was forced to slow his pace, make shorter steps as the uneven forest floor became harder to see in the waning light.

Finally, his light broke through the trees, and the Giles driveway came into view. He wanted to cry with relief. Instead, he stopped again and finished the first bottle of water. Then he re-seated his backpack and slowly jogged toward the main house, Avery's picture bobbing along in his left hand, while his flashlight pointed the way from his right.

He covered the mile in good time, not stopping until he reached the garage attached to the house. After punching in the code, he opened the door.

"No fucking way," he said as he stared into the empty space where the convertible should have been. Then he screamed.

He took a few steps in and set down the painting, then held his head with both hands.

Where was the fucking car?

How could this happen? Leaning against the garage wall, he closed his eyes and willed himself to breathe. After a minute, he felt calmer. Calm enough to think.

It didn't matter where the car was. He needed a new plan. Getting out of Garden had suddenly gotten a lot more difficult.

He supposed he should abandon the idea of feeding the women. Fatigue hadn't yet set in—the walk was hard, but he was used to that sort of activity, and the jog had been easy. If he simply turned around and returned to his car, he could take off for New York. He could put a note on the door of the vet's office next to the bus terminal, explaining where the women were. By the time they opened in the morning, he'd be lost in New York.

Sighing, he considered his other options. Did people still hitchhike? Maybe, but that would just provide another witness. Could he steal a car? That might alert the police even faster.

Were the police already after him? He pulled out his phone. Great. At least he had service. He typed in the information for the news site.

Police Identify Person of Interest in Garden Disappearance. He didn't need to click to know who they were interested in, but he did anyway. A picture of him, downloaded from his driver's license, popped up. Next, they showed live footage from his house, with multiple state and local police cars sitting in front of it. Officer Knox from Garden told people to be on the lookout for Curt and to consider him armed and dangerous.

"This is just fucking great!" he said. He sighed and spotted the gun safe against the wall. It was a post-9/11 purchase, one as big as the safe Jonathon had kept in the North Tower to hold his eggs and financial papers. This one was for his guns. Curt knew because, just like her husband, Gloria had kept the combination on a sticky note.

Standing before it, he spun the large, decorative dial, left and right and left, then pulled the handle. Relief filled him when it opened, and he reached in to pull out his favorite gun.

He'd tried them all, replacing the ammunition to defray suspicion, but there was one he preferred. It was a shotgun, which was great for killing small nuisance animals like groundhogs, but it mostly just scared them. It would kill a human, though, if he aimed at their chest instead of their feet, and he wouldn't hesitate to aim where he needed to.

This recent turn of events told him he should take this gun, along with Jonathon's pearl-handled pistol. Dumping a box of ammunition for each weapon into his bag, he closed the door and spun the lock to secure it.

Now what? He leaned against the safe and slugged more water, then hit the restroom. If he left everything except the pistol, he could use the road and run back to his car quickly. Then he'd drive here, empty the safe, then hit the highway. To avoid detection, he'd head northeast, toward Boston, then double back toward New York City. He might even catch a bus, leave the car parked in a large commuter lot where it wouldn't be easily noticed.

Yes. That was a good plan.

He wasn't at risk of anyone finding the stuff here, but the bag did contain about thirty million dollars in jewels. He wouldn't get that much for it, but it was still a fortune, one that needed protection.

Once again, he opened the safe and stashed his bag and the long gun, and Avery's picture. He loaded the pistol and tucked it into the waistband of his jeans, then turned on his flashlight and jogged from the garage.

CHAPTER TWENTY-NINE

D o you think the bleeding's stopped?" Imma asked.

Rio's most recent effort with the knife had elicited a sharp wail, followed by a few choice words, and Rio had shared that she'd nicked her hand with the blade.

"I think so. But I can't feel my fingers anymore."

She'd been able to apply pressure, she told Imma, but it had taken a while for results. "Damn aspirin," she said.

"At least you won't bleed to death. But I guess our adventure with the knives is over."

"At least until I can feel my fingers again."

"I don't know if I'll ever move my shoulder again."

"I hear you."

They were both beyond hungry, and thirsty as well, and the aches and pains Imma felt from sitting in one position in the hard, wooden chair reminded her of her age.

"Thank you for turning on the light, Rio. At least we're not in the dark." If there was any moon out tonight, they couldn't see it through the cracks in the shutters.

"Are you cold?" she asked Rio. Imma wasn't warm, but the sturdy old cabin did seem to be well insulated, and it wasn't cold, either.

"I'm okay," Rio said.

"What about the front door?" Imma asked.

"Huh?"

"I'm just thinking about how to get out of here. Maybe if we can get to the door, we can open it."

Rio seemed perturbed. "Imma, are you out of your mind? If we leave this cabin, we'll be eaten by coyotes. And all this blood on my hands will just be an invitation to dinner."

Imma felt awful that she'd dragged Rio into this mess and told her so. But instead of a reassuring denial that would have eased Imma's guilt, Rio just remained silent. That she'd endangered her friend was heartbreaking,

"Rio, we can't quit. I've been thinking that maybe we can get down that step."

"How? Without toppling over and cracking open our coconuts?"

"Our feet are free. If we can reach the edge, and I go first, I'll inch my feet along, then support my weight with my legs. When the chair reaches the edge, it won't even fall, because my feet will be on the ground ahead of it."

"Imma, these are heavy chairs. We could fall right over. And then we'd really be in trouble. At least now we're somewhat safe. Both of us are breathing and warm. But if we fall…"

"Rio, I don't think he's coming back. It's possible the police will find us before we starve to death, but it's also possible we're going to die right in these seats. I'd rather go down trying."

Rio was quiet, and Imma wasn't sure she had the will to talk her into this. She was tired. It had been an emotionally exhausting experience, not to mention the physical effort they'd put into their escape plans. And the adrenaline had officially worn off, leaving Imma drained.

"Okay, Imma. Tell me what to do."

After moving toward the light switch earlier, they were now about ten feet from the drop, with the chairs turned so Imma had almost a straight shot to the edge. Imma gave Rio the cue, and they pushed with their feet, moving several inches for their efforts.

"I think we're getting the hang of this. Again!"

Each successive effort pushed them closer to their goal, but when they were only about a third of the way, Imma needed to rest again. This time, instead of enjoying their banter, Imma was filled with dread. She really didn't think this would work. Their arms would never reach the rocks. They were too securely fastened, and since they were back-to-back, they couldn't get close enough. But it felt good to do something. She would have tried just about anything at that point.

After a bit of rest, she told Rio she was ready to continue. This time, her adrenaline kicked in. Her heart was pounding, not just from the effort, but from her determination. Imma refused to give up and rot to death in this old cabin. Maybe she'd die of a broken neck or a fractured skull, but she'd die with dignity.

"Do you need a break?" Rio asked after a few minutes.

"Nope. I'm good. How about you?"

"I'm good, too. Never better."

Imma laughed. "Concentrate."

They pushed and heaved, and in another few minutes Imma told Rio to stop. "I'm going to see how close I can get if I dangle my toes." Straining against the tape that held much of her torso in check,

Imma reached her foot out. Nothing but air.

The ledge that separated the kitchen from the sunken living room was about eight inches high. Feeling with her toes, Imma estimated that about two or three inches of floor separated the chair leg from the abyss on the left, and a little more on the right. Moving much farther probably wouldn't improve her chances of a safe landing.

"Okay. Here's what we'll do. You're going to push up and back, and hopefully you push me far enough forward that we go over the edge. And then my feet will catch us, and I'll slide you over and down."

"Okay. Tell me when."

"I'll lean forward as much as I can." There really wasn't much wiggle room in her torso, but a human head was heavy enough to tip the balance. She put hers forward. If she landed on it, either of the awful outcomes she'd thought about were real possibilities.

"On three, Rio. One, two, three."

Rio pushed, but instead of the chair falling forward, it slid. The left leg, going off the edge slightly before the right one, caused them to topple in that direction. Imma had no chance to get her feet underneath and catch them, no opportunity to guide their landing.

Falling hard, she did her best to pull her head back. A split second later, she heard a deafening explosion as she struck the floor with such intensity she saw white, and a second later, she was unconscious.

CHAPTER THIRTY

A very felt fortunate for the old coffee pot at the Pocono house, because it gave her something to do. She needed to feel useful, helpful. They'd learned quite a bit since they'd last gathered here. Mulling it all over, she watched the first drops of coffee begin pouring into the large pot.

While Rio had made many calls that morning, the only one from Imma's phone had been to Rio, so the police were assuming their meeting had been planned. The security camera caught Imma pulling into the lot and leaving alone, with no sign of Rio. But perhaps the most interesting thing they saw on the video was Henry. Only one time. The camera clearly showed him coming from the trail into town, but it didn't show him leaving. He'd obviously left in Imma's car.

Now he was missing, too.

"Coffee's ready," Avery announced.

Someone from the neighborhood had baked a cake, and Tori had sent over a tray of sandwiches for the group. Avery couldn't help thinking how much the gathering felt like a funeral. She tried to push the thought from her mind.

"How long should we stick around?" Lauren whispered in her ear.

Avery shrugged. Her mood had shifted as the darkness approached. She'd been scared but optimistic when they'd met here earlier in the day, when she'd thought Imma had just gotten lost while out walking. Then there were two missing women, which was more serious. And then they were abducted, and that had changed everything. Avery couldn't help thinking how futile their efforts were, when in all likelihood the women were far away from Garden at this point. Far away, or close but dead.

"Do you think we should call it a night?" Avery asked. It was nearly nine o'clock, and she knew they could only wait, and support Jo, who looked so lost. Even though Avery would have done it, many more people in the room knew Jo much better, and she would probably feel more comfortable having one of them at her house.

"Maybe we should. Let's find out the plan for tomorrow morning," Lauren suggested.

Mac was engrossed in her phone when Avery approached. "Just checking the forecast," she said.

"How's it look?"

"High fifties tonight."

"I sure as hell hope they're inside somewhere."

"Yeah. So, you heading out?"

"Yes. Can we do anything else? Any supplies we need?"

Mac smiled. "I think we're good," she said as her phone rang in her hand. "It's Dee."

"Mac here," she said, and Avery watched her closely, listening as well, hoping to catch the other side of the conversation.

When she finished the call, Mac spoke briefly to Jo and Karen and then turned to everyone.

"Dee Knox is at Henry's place. He didn't answer their knock, but the lights were on there, and the officers were concerned for his welfare, so they entered the residence. It looks like it's been cleaned out, and there was a fresh fire in the pit out back. No sign of Imma or Rio."

"Should we start searching again?"

Mac sighed as she looked around the room. "I know we'd all like to do that. But a search at night would be extraordinarily difficult. Perhaps even dangerous. And if we're out looking, we won't have fresh eyes and fresh legs in the morning, when we'll be able to see something. But we can have a mental search party. Think of your own properties— say anything within a two- or three-hour walk from here. Do you have an old barn, an unused rental cottage, an abandoned hunting cabin? Anywhere he could have taken them and been back within about an hour, when the camera suddenly changed direction down by the trail. At this point we can assume Henry's gone. We just have to worry about finding our friends."

"We have quite a few buildings in the game lands," Blanche said. "Maintenance sheds where they keep materials and tools."

"That's good. That's just the kind of ideas we need. This will give us a list of places to search at first light."

"Do you think we should all head home, then?" Blanche asked.

"That's exactly what we should do. The sun will be up tomorrow at six o'clock, so plan to be out by seven. That gives us less than ten hours to recharge our batteries before we're back at it. Pack just as you did today—maybe some peanut-butter-and-jelly sandwiches so you won't starve if you're off in the woods without access to Tori's fine sandwich platter."

Mac looked around at all the faces. They were all tired and scared, and she seemed to notice that fact. "We're going to find them. So go rest, think of places he might hide them, and let's meet back here at 6:45. I want to be on the road by seven o'clock."

One by one and two by two, people began to hug Jo and Karen, then head to their various homes. Avery and Lauren fell silently into the line, gave good wishes, and then walked to Gloria's Lexus. Neither of them spoke until they were in the car.

"I can't be of much help," Lauren said. "The only places I know of are on your property."

"That's true. But we have a few, don't we? The old barn, the boathouse, the cabin. Maybe we should check them all out in the morning before we head in," Avery said.

"It's a good idea. We can rule them out, at least."

"And don't forget that my grandmother wants me to look at the cabin for the insurance. We'll accomplish two goals."

"Perfect."

"My grandfather once kept loaded guns there. Can you imagine?"

"It was a different world."

"They're all in the house now. A solid dozen, I'd guess. But at least we have a gun safe."

"Oh, yeah? Where?"

"In the garage, behind his car. The safe's so damn big, it was the only place in the house it fit. But maybe...with all this going on, I should open that safe, Lauren. Get one of the guns out."

Avery could feel Lauren staring at her. "Whoa," she said softly. "I never really thought you were a gun person."

"I've never held one and wouldn't know how to shoot it, or load it. But if we were threatened—I mean if we stumble upon Mr. Henry in the morning, he wouldn't know that, would he?"

Turning left from the road, Avery pulled into the long driveway leading to the main house, then around to the back, where the garage had been added to the house. The road took them around the left side of the structure, closest to the garage, and made a gentle loop through tall trees that sheltered the house from approaching cars. When the house finally came into sight, it was visible in all its magnificent, three-story splendor.

The garage was at ground level, and for aesthetics, they'd made the new addition match—a two-story sunroom that was a haven for plants. As they rounded the corner, Avery pressed the remote to open the door. It was the third button on her grandmother's console, a fact she'd learned just that day. Though she'd expected to see the main building's marvelous stone and the tall timber holding up the roof, she stared at the new addition. Beneath the great walls of glass, on the ground floor, the door was wide open.

Avery stopped the car. "Lauren, look." She nodded toward the house, but with all the lights, triggered by timers as darkness fell, the garage door wasn't so obvious. It was only when Avery pointed it out that Lauren gasped. "Maybe Ellen and Don left it open."

"What should we do?"

"Let's call Mac."

Avery reached for her phone and dialed. "I have service," she said as the phone rang.

"Mac here," the now-familiar voice said a moment later.

"Mac, it's Avery," she said, then explained the situation.

"Stay where you are. Don't go in the house. I'll be there in ten minutes."

Avery disconnected the call and looked at Lauren again. "Do you think we should get a gun?"

Lauren turned in the seat. "Why don't we just meet Mac down by the main road? I'm sure we'll be safe there, and we won't risk blowing off any of our fingers."

Avery wanted to joke about fingers being important to surgeons, but she couldn't make her mouth form the words. Instead, she just nodded and did as Lauren suggested. As she drove in silence, the dark road seemed endless, but four minutes later, she parked at the end of the driveway, where it met the main road from Garden.

"Should we call Ellen and Don? Lauren asked.

Avery felt stupid, but of course everyone was on edge in Garden today. "We should," she said as she scrolled for their number. "But Laur—when we went back to the house to eat, they were gone. And I don't think the door was open then."

"It could've been open a crack, and the wind blew it."

The call went to voice mail, and Lauren asked Ellen to call her about an urgent matter. "I just don't know," she said as she sat back in the car's plush seat.

Multiple cars passed, which was surprising, as it was almost ten, and the locals should be home by now. Then she saw flashing lights, and a police car pulled into the driveway, while another car stopped behind it.

Officer Knox rolled down her window and nodded at Avery. "So, you had a break-in?" she asked.

"I'm not sure. Lauren just reminded me that the caretakers were here today, and they may have left the door open. I have a call in to them now."

Dee nodded. "Okay, but under the circumstances, we should have a look. Is that all right with you?"

"Absolutely," Avery said.

"Follow me," but before Dee pulled away, Avery commented, "When the driveway splits, stay to the left. Then follow it all the way around to the house."

"Got it."

As the car began to move up the driveway, the second car, which had been sitting on the road, turned in. It was a large Jeep, with Jess at the wheel. Mac leaned over from the passenger seat. "I thought it best to get Dee involved."

"Great idea," Avery said. "I'll follow you."

Avery pulled onto the road, then backed up before entering the driveway. Both Dee and Jess were waiting for her, and she followed them. At the fork, Dee turned to the left, as Avery had instructed her, and drove around the house to the back. Jess pulled up abreast of the other two cars, and everyone got out.

"So this garage door was open when you got here?" Dee asked.

Shaking her head, Avery explained that she'd opened the garage door reflexively as she'd made the turn. It was the pedestrian door that had raised her suspicions about an intruder.

"You mentioned a caretaker?" Dee asked.

"I did. She and her husband were both here today, and they come and go through the garage. So it could have been them. They're not answering."

"Let's check the place out."

"You want backup?" Mac asked.

Dee nodded, and both of them drew their weapons, then announced themselves. Avery thought it was a bit much, since she'd already been at the house fifteen minutes earlier. Only a deaf, blind intruder would still be there after the notice she'd given. Yet she stood there, in the parking area, silently watching the house, Lauren doing the same beside her.

No one seemed to be in the mood to talk, but Avery decided to ask Jess about the topic that had been on her mind tonight.

"I have guns in the safe, Jess. Do you think I should take one out?"

"Do you know how to use it?"

Avery frowned as she shook her head.

"It's probably not a good idea. But maybe I should spend the night here. Mac's heading back to Imma and Jo's place, and I feel comfortable with weapons. My handgun's locked in the car, and I can use any long gun you have, as well."

"You're a doctor, right?" Lauren asked.

Avery sucked in her breath, worried about where her wife was going with this query. Lauren was not a fan of guns. But she was gentle, and Avery appreciated her restraint.

"You don't mind guns, considering the trauma they do to the human body?"

"I grew up here," Jess said, "so guns have been part of my life since childhood. Back then, we didn't have the kind of violence we have today. But I share your concerns, and I'd like to see a lengthier process involved for purchasing guns—affidavits from a physician about medication use, for instance. Mental-health screening. Perhaps urine/drug screening. And there's no reason for assault weapons. We just need to meet in the middle politically to have better stewardship of weapons, to keep them in safe hands without falling into the wrong hands."

Avery smiled. "Well said."

Lauren nodded as well. "I'd like to nominate you for office, Doctor."

Jess laughed. "One day, maybe, after I've climbed Mount Everest."

Avery turned. "Really?"

"No," Jess said, and they all laughed.

Just then Dee and Mac emerged from the house, traversed the length of the garage, and came back outside.

"No one's there. Avery, I'd like you to have a look around to see if anything seems out of place or missing. It might be hard, though, right? If the housekeeper was here today."

Avery wasn't optimistic, but she agreed.

Nothing was amiss on the first floor, and on the second, Avery found their luggage just inside the master-bedroom door. She'd been sleeping in that room when she was here alone, because it had a television and a fireplace. Other than that, she saw no sign anyone had been there.

"Is there alcohol in the house?" Dee asked. "Sometimes teenagers will break into these vacation homes and rob the liquor cabinets."

"Let's check," Avery said, and they all followed her to the first floor, where a large bar took up a wall in the great room. Walking behind it, Avery took stock. "I don't really drink much of this stuff, but if anything is missing, it's only a bottle or two. Not so much that I'd notice."

"Can you try the housekeeper again?"

Avery called, and this time Ellen answered. She admitted to using the garage door to exit, and though she thought she'd locked it behind her, she supposed it was possible that she hadn't closed the door all the way.

Everyone seemed to sigh in relief. "I suppose that answers that question," Avery said.

Dee and Mac nodded, but Avery wasn't sure they were convinced. "It's hard to buy coincidences when you're in the middle of an investigation," Mac said.

"Page eighteen of the detectives' handbook," Dee said, and Mac smiled.

Jess repeated her offer to stay the night.

Avery looked at Lauren, and they both nodded. "Sure. That would be great, as long as Mac doesn't mind."

"You'd be doing me a favor, really. I won't have to worry about Jess being alone."

Dee offered to drive Mac back to town, and after Jess retrieved her handgun from her car, they watched as the police SUV disappeared.

"You want to get the other guns out, just to be safe?" Jess asked.

Avery walked over to the safe and sighed. "Damn! I thought the combination was right here."

"Is it something you can remember, like a birthday?" Lauren asked.

Shaking her head, Avery frowned at the other two. "No. It's just the way it came. Pre-programmed or whatever."

"Do you know where the paperwork is?" Jess asked.

Avery shrugged and laughed. "No clue. But maybe I can call my gram. Or Ellen again."

Jess waved her off. "We're fine. If someone was here, they're gone now, so I don't think we have anything to worry about. Let's just get tucked in for the night so we can get up in the morning and start searching for our friends."

Jess ran a hand through her hair, obviously exhausted. The disappearance of Imma and Rio would have a tremendous impact on many people if they didn't find them in time.

Getting a good night's rest, so they could start fresh in the morning, was a great idea. "Sounds like a plan."

CHAPTER THIRTY-ONE

Imma! Imma! Please answer me!" Rio's voice sounded far away and thick, and as Imma opened her eyes, she tried to focus all her sensations at once. Rio's voice, the floor a few inches in front of her, and the burning, searing pain from her left ear to her shoulder.

"I think my shoulder's broken." Imma was stuttering.

"Did you hit your head? Anything else hurt?"

It was hard to take stock with such an all-consuming sensation, but she wiggled her toes and ankles, moved her legs. Her right arm seemed okay, as did her back. It was a little hard to breathe, but that might have had more to do with her position than an injury.

"My head hurts. But not as bad as my shoulder." Trying to reposition herself to take pressure off her left side, Imma felt a little give to the chair.

"Rio, I don't want to get your hopes up, but I may be able to move a little."

Imma felt Rio begin rocking, a motion that intensified the pain. She bit her lip in response.

"I noticed that, too. When you were unconscious. I think the backs of the chairs broke when we hit the floor. I can feel some splinters of wood."

The chairs were rounded at the top, old-fashioned spindles connecting a top plate to the base. At most half or three-quarters of an inch thick, perhaps seven or eight spindles spanned the base in a semicircle.

"Does it hurt your arm when I move?" Rio asked.

"No." Imma was lying, but she didn't want to discourage Rio's efforts. Her neck hurt too, and her head was getting worse.

In response, she felt Rio moving beside her, pushing up with her back and down with her hips, cracking wood audible over the sound of her own heavy breathing.

"Imma, I think my chair back is completely broken off the base. Let me see if I can feel anything."

Imma felt Rio's fingers moving, touching hers, probing the chair for cracks. Every movement seared her, caused daggers of pain in her shoulder and arm and upper back. She squinted back silent tears and squeezed the fingers of her uninjured right arm until she thought her palm would bleed.

Then Rio stopped, and Imma was left with only the baseline agony of lying on what she was sure was a broken shoulder.

"Imma, kick. See if you can break the chair bottom free."

As much as she wanted to, Imma didn't think she could move. The pain was just too much, the effort beyond the willpower she'd had just a few minutes ago.

"I can't."

Rio continued to struggle behind her, thrashing her legs and her hands, and then suddenly, she stopped. "Did you hear that?"

A sense of dread filled Imma. Had Henry come back to finish them off?

"What?"

"Listen."

Imma felt Rio's hands moving behind her and heard the unmistakable sound of fabric tearing.

"The tape is tearing, Imma. I must have cut it with the edge of the chair. Or maybe it was the knife."

Rio grunted, then arched and twisted her arms, and Imma found herself holding her breath, listening for the sound. She heard it. Again, and again, little rips, and a second later a whoop as Rio announced her hands were finally free.

Now, Imma allowed herself the luxury of tears.

"I can't really move my arms. They're stuck to the tape." Imma could feel Rio moving behind her, and suddenly her own adrenaline kicked in. "You can do it. Wiggle those arms."

"I can't move them. But wait a minute." Imma felt Rio's hand again, this time working on the chair spikes, wriggling back and forth.

"Ha-ha! I got the spoke out."

The end pieces were taped, but those in the middle weren't, and one by one, Rio wiggled them free. Even the ends came loose, and by rotating her shoulders, she freed them of the board that had stabilized the top part of the chair. "Now, I have some wiggle room."

Imma felt more moving and tugging, and Rio let out another triumphant howl as she announced she'd gotten her right hand free.

Imma knew she should feel happy, but as Rio's voice faded, she felt nothing but the pain, and then nothing at all.

CHAPTER THIRTY-TWO

What the fuck?" Curt said aloud as he saw the car parked in the Giles driveway. Instead of turning as he'd intended, he slowed just a little but kept driving right past it. It was impossible to tell on the dark road, but it looked like an SUV. Was it the police, just sitting there waiting for speeding traffic? Or taking a break on patrol? He'd turn around in the service road ahead and have another look.

Then, in the distance, he saw flashing lights. Instinctively, he slowed the car and watched a police SUV barrel pass, another car just behind it.

"Please, no. Please. No! No! No! NOOOOO!"

He pulled into the service entrance and turned around, dreading the return trip. The way his day had gone, the police car was heading to the Giles estate.

On the dark country road, he saw the flashing lights ahead. He slowed again. They appeared to have stopped. Was there an accident? But he'd just driven that way—he would have seen it.

Then the lights moved, not farther from him, but to the left. The police car was heading to the Giles house.

How could they have found the women so quickly? Dread made his heart pound wildly—his backpack was in the garage safe.

The car that had been sitting at the bottom of the Giles driveway pulled onto the road, turned, and followed the other two cars, and Curt saw only the glow of their lights as he drove past.

Surely the cavalry was on its way, and he'd be apprehended soon. No doubt, Imma and Rio had identified him. They were probably already looking for his car. Now he needed to decide how he wanted to live the rest of his life—behind bars or fighting.

Hadn't enough people in his life died already? He should just surrender peacefully, even if it meant prison.

Who was he kidding? He'd spent the last thirty years living with all the comforts money could buy. He'd rather die than go to jail. He felt the pistol, still in his right pocket. He'd swallow Jonathon's gun and be done with this miserable life.

He approached the plaza near the highway, where he'd parked the car earlier. Had that really been only four hours ago? Turning on his blinker, he pulled into the car park, found a spot facing the road, and killed the ignition. Even though it was nearly ten o'clock, and much of Garden was asleep, the truck stop was still busy. A dozen trucks had pulled in for the night, and several cars were nestled next to the gas pumps.

One of them was a state-police car. A uniformed officer stood beside it, watching the action near the trucks. Another officer exited the service plaza and handed his partner what appeared to be a cup of coffee.

What are they doing? Why aren't they heading over to investigate the scene at the cabin, or at least offer backup to the Garden cops? Curt continued watching, and a few minutes later, the officers climbed back into their SUV and made a left, away from Garden. He watched their lights disappear on the interstate entrance ramp.

What the fuck?

Abandoning his plan to eat his gun, once again he started the car and headed toward Garden, speeding until he reached the Giles property, then slowing as he drove past. He didn't see anything. On this strip of road, the darkness was uninterrupted.

He drove a quarter of a mile and did a K-turn, then pulled to the side of the road. This was a long, straight stretch, and if he saw someone coming, he'd move. He killed his lights and sat quietly for a moment, and then his nervous energy took over, and he reached for his phone. How long had it been? Ten minutes? Not much more. He turned on the lights and pulled onto the road, driving slowly again as he approached the driveway. No sign of life.

Driving a quarter-mile past, he once again turned the car and pulled over, watching.

"Fuck!" he said aloud as headlights suddenly appeared in his mirrors, but the car merely drove along the center line when the driver saw his car. Still, it was dangerous to just sit here along a dark country road. He checked the phone again. It had been seven minutes since he'd last checked it. They'd been there seventeen minutes, give or take.

How long should he wait? He didn't dare drive onto the Giles property, not with the police there. But maybe this was the time to act, while it was still dark. If he walked through the woods, it was probably less than a mile to the house. About two hundred feet of cleared land surrounded it, but some large landscaping rocks nearby would help conceal him if the police were at the main house. He could easily get in and out of the garage in a few minutes, and then he'd get the hell out of Garden for good.

But what were the police doing there?

If they'd found Imma and Rio, wouldn't there be a parade of police vehicles, not to mention a couple of ambulances?

He pulled back onto the road, heading toward Garden. Unlike the cabin, the main house had an alarm. Could there have been a breach? With no one at the house, of course the police would investigate.

He drove past the driveway once again and repeated his ritual. K-turn. Lights off. Check phone. Twenty minutes.

How long did it take to check out an alarm call?

Another set of headlights announced the approach of a car, but this time Curt didn't move. Apparently, cars pulled over on the shoulder of the road didn't concern the citizens of Garden.

His anxiety grew as he sat there, and he decided he needed to move. Was this a good place to leave the car? The Giles driveway curved to the left, and that's where he was positioned. If he walked across that road and into the woods, he'd run right into the house. The accent and security lights would make it an easy target in the woods, as long as he wasn't too far off his mark. He searched the night sky for light, but the trees beside the road were tall, and he couldn't even see their tops.

"Okay," he said. "A few more minutes."

He turned on the headlights, pulled into the road, and made another pass. *Maybe I missed them when I was at the car park.* But could the police have come and gone so quickly? It seemed unlikely. He turned again and pulled off the road. His phone told him twenty-eight minutes had passed.

He waited another five, then drove slowly toward Garden. He'd made up his mind. He'd park the car and hike to the house. He had his flashlight, and the burner phone surely had a compass to guide him. Would it be better to park on this side of the road, nearer the house, or turn around and face back toward the interstate?

He decided to turn around and face out of town, and as he made his turn, he saw headlights in the distance. A series of headlights. He started driving and passed one car, then another, then saw the last car wasn't on the road at all. It was in the Giles's driveway. He watched it pull out and head toward the interstate.

It was the police vehicle he'd seen earlier!

Was it safe now? Maybe he could drive all the way to the house— it would save him time, and he wouldn't risk breaking a leg in the woods.

He decided to make a few more passes on the road, just to be sure it was clear. Then he'd get his jewels and go.

CHAPTER THIRTY-THREE

Avery knew she needed sleep. It had been a long, emotional day, and she wanted to be up first thing in the morning to help search for Imma and Rio. As Mac had pointed out, they wanted to be well-rested for what might be a long day.

Yet she couldn't relax. Beside her, Lauren was already asleep, but she thought she heard Jess wandering around a floor below.

Easing quietly from the bed, Avery padded to the door and slipped from the room, then headed down the stairs. Just as she'd suspected, Jess sat on the couch, one of her grandmother's hard-covers nestled in her lap.

"Hey," Avery said.

"Can't sleep?" Jess asked.

Suddenly, Avery's emotions bubbled out, and she choked on her tears. "It's just so awful, Jess. Why would Henry do this?"

"We can't be sure it's him. Sometimes people just freak out and do stupid things. Henry's a really private person, and all this attention could have pushed him over the edge. But I agree with you—he does look guilty."

"What does Mac think? Why Imma and Rio?"

"They're looking into his background to see if they can find something. Apparently, he had an interesting past."

"How so?"

"I guess he's incredibly wealthy. Did you know he was at the Fabergé egg exhibit?" Jess asked.

"Really?" Avery found that surprising. From what she knew, high art didn't seem to be his style.

"Yes. We saw him with this guy who works for the former Russian ambassador."

"Bichefsky?" Avery asked.

"Yes. That sounds right."

That was odd. "Is that why Imma was looking into Bichefsky? To learn his connection to Henry?"

"Avery, with Imma, you never know. She's constantly questioning. She's just incredibly bright and a few steps ahead of everyone else, making associations and forming conclusions that leave us spinning."

Avery laughed. "I could tell, and I don't even know her that well." Avery thought about what Jess had said. Why did a guy like Henry, friends with the ambassador, end up in Garden? Not that it was a bad place. It was just a quiet place. Not the sort of place for, well, the high-art society members.

"Maybe that's the motive, Jess. Imma was trying to figure out something about Henry's past, and he would rather keep it hidden."

"There's something else. Did you hear about the diamonds?"

Avery shook her head. "What diamonds?"

"A woman exercising her dog found a small fortune in diamonds on the walking trail outside of Garden. Like maybe $300,000 worth of them. Near where they found Imma's car. The police think they were hidden in ice, and someone accidentally dropped them."

"How is that connected to Henry?"

"No one knows. But it's really odd. All of a sudden, so many strange things are happening around him. The Fabergé eggs exhibit. He denied he was at the exhibit, even though we all saw him. He tried to steal the fax you sent about the insurance investigation into your family's eggs. He put his properties up for sale, after refusing offers for years. And now, the woman who writes the article about the eggs turns up missing, and the last place she's seen is at Henry's firehouse. It makes you wonder if the diamonds are connected to him, too."

"Wait. My head is spinning," Avery said. "Why would he want to steal the insurance report?"

"Who knows? That's why Imma was so interested. She was trying to find the connection among all these strange occurrences."

Avery stood, walked to the window, and looked out. A big moon was shining over the lake in the distance, but even so, it was dark. What were Chris Henry's motives?

"I wonder if it was him today. In the garage. Maybe he knows we have guns."

"It wouldn't surprise me if he knows Don. He worked at the garden center for years. But I don't think Don would talk about your family guns. It would almost be an invitation to rob you. Could Henry know about them some other way?"

Avery thought of all the times she'd been at this house, and at the lake, and felt like someone was watching her. She'd always considered it more of a mystical presence, the ghost of her father. Maybe it was Henry. She told Jess about the feeling she'd had. "Do you think he's a stalker?"

Jess sighed. "I don't know. Did he ever try to contact you?"

Avery was sure he hadn't. But then she thought of something else. "I almost drowned when I was little. The babysitter wasn't paying attention, and I went under. My brother saved me. But the weird thing is, someone told my grandmother to keep an eye on our babysitter. We always thought it was a neighbor. Maybe it was Henry. Maybe he was watching us that day."

"So he's a good stalker?"

"Not if he kidnapped Imma and Rio. But I guess that's a crazy idea. I'm sorry I mentioned it."

"Do you want to try to get some sleep?"

"I don't know if I can," Avery said. "Should we check the safe? I know Dee and Mac looked through the house, but maybe we should see if the safe was tampered with. Then we'd know if he was here."

"Would it make you feel better?"

Avery shrugged. "Maybe."

Jess stood and slid her handgun into the pocket of the sweatpants Avery had lent her. "Let's go."

Avery led the way from the great room to the alcove near the kitchen. Flipping a light, she cautiously descended the narrow staircase to the ground floor. Jess was a step behind her as she opened the door that led to the garage.

Standing in front of the safe, with a gun pointed toward them, was Chris Henry.

She gasped when she saw him, but for some reason, he was the one who looked shocked.

CHAPTER THIRTY-FOUR

Once again Rio's voice coaxed Imma back to consciousness. She was lying on her back, Rio hovering over her.

"You're going to be okay, Im. We're free. Now we just have to get out of here. Are you with me?"

"I must have passed out."

"Yeah. For like ten minutes. I'm worried. We should get you to the hospital."

"I think it was just the pain."

"Can you sit up? I'll help you."

Imma blinked her eyes into focus. "Can you find something to splint my shoulder?"

Rio pursed her lips. "I bet I can still make a sling. Let me see if I can find a towel."

Imma did a little survey while she waited for Rio, and nothing hurt except her shoulder. That was good. Her heart was pounding, but she would have been more worried if it weren't beating extra fast.

"Okay, Imma. Be strong," she said aloud, then planted her feet on the floor and slid herself back toward the kitchen. When her head was almost hitting the step, she used her good arm to push herself up. While sliding had been painful, getting up was excruciating. Still, she managed to make it to a sitting position, and that's where she was when Rio came back.

"Hey. Wait for me," Rio said. "I have a sheet, but I need to cut it up a little."

"Just tear it."

"Good idea."

Rio returned to her side and carefully created a cradle for her arm, then looped the excess material around Imma's neck. "I want it to be snug, but not too tight."

"I think it's good."

"Now can you push yourself up and sit on the step? I can probably get you to stand from there."

"No sweat," she said.

Imma closed her eyes and focused all her energy on her right side as she pushed with both her leg and her arm. Pulling her right knee in, with Rio's help she positioned the left beside it. Then Rio offered an arm, and Imma pulled herself up.

"Water. I just want water," she said. "And then the bathroom."

Rio helped her to the sink and filled two glasses with water from the tap, and then they both used the restroom.

"We have a long walk now. But it doesn't matter how much time it takes. We're okay. We're going to survive."

Imma smiled. "Thanks to you. You'll have to share the details about what happened after you knocked me out."

Rio began opening cabinet doors. "If you were a flashlight, where would you be?"

"I don't know when this cabin was last used. If there is a flashlight, it's probably dead. Maybe we should use the oil lamp." Imma pointed to one sitting near the hearth.

"I think those are matches sitting on the wood pile."

Imma watched as Rio retrieved the lamp and shook it. "It feels full." Rio knelt and struck a match, then lit the wick of the lamp and adjusted the flame. "This should keep us from falling into a ditch," she said with a chuckle.

Imma smiled and started walking across the kitchen toward the door. Rio cut across the living room and met her there. "Ready? We'll take it slow."

Rio held the lantern in her right hand, and Imma clutched her left one as they descended the steps and walked along a moss-covered stone path that led to the driveway. "Where does this lead?" Imma asked.

"I've never actually been on the property, but I've seen it on Google maps. This driveway goes to the house, but it continues all the way to the main road."

"How far?"

"I'd say two miles. Not more."

"On the treadmill, I walk two miles an hour."

"There you go."

"I think I'll be a little slower today."

"If we're tired, or it's too much, we can just stop at the house. If we break in, it'll trigger the alarm. And if there's no alarm, we can use the phone. All these old houses have land lines because the Wi-Fi is so wonky."

"That sounds good, Rio. I don't know if I can do two miles."

"Do you want to stop? I can leave you and come back with help."

"In all the horror films, they split up, and the killer finds them. I think it's best if we stay together."

Rio laughed. "That's a good point."

They walked in silence, concentrating on moving their feet and remaining upright. The lantern provided enough glow for them to stay on track. But it was heavy, and soon Rio asked if Imma thought she could walk without her, so she could switch the lantern to the other arm.

"I'll try."

It was harder to balance without Rio's support, but Imma thought she'd be okay. They just walked slowly, mindful of each step. Imma's pain was much improved with the sling Rio had fastened, though it still felt awful, especially when she put weight on her left leg. The shoulder was broken, or maybe dislocated, or maybe both. Whatever was wrong, it was the most painful experience she'd ever had. Still, even if the doctor had to amputate her arm, it would have been worth it. That fall on her shoulder had broken the chair that had ultimately led to their freedom.

"So what happened while I was knocked out?"

"I thought you were dead, but I knew I couldn't do anything to help you until I got us free. Without the chair backs behind us, I had extra room, so I wiggled until I got my arms above my head. Then I actually slipped out of my shirt. After that, I found scissors and cut you free. That's it."

"Amazing, Rio. But I'm happy I was out. I don't think all that wiggling you did would have felt good on my side of the chair."

"Probably not. Hey, look," Rio said. "There's the house."

Imma looked and could see lights glowing in the distance. The finish line was still a good distance away, but she was elated to see it.

They walked in silence. Imma could only imagine what Rio was feeling, but she was relieved. Once she was home in her bed, she'd need a week's sleep to recover from her mental and physical exhaustion.

As they approached the house, Imma marveled at it. A massive old stone structure set in a clearing, it had a half-dozen intersecting roof lines, all A-shaped to shed the mountain snow. The largest of these, in the center, extended over a porch that faced the lake. To the rear, it covered another porch facing the woods. A smaller porch sheltered the side entrance. The entire place glowed with landscaping lights that followed the gentle break of the land toward the water. As she surveyed the house, Imma realized lights were on inside as well.

Suddenly, she was nervous. Was Henry hiding out at the Giles's house? She stopped and whispered. "Rio, someone's there. What if it's Henry? Should we keep walking and just go to the main road?"

"Let's take a look. But be careful. And quiet."

The driveway curved, and they followed the path that would take them to the side entrance. They were slightly above the garage level and could see clearly through the window.

Henry was standing there, holding a gun.

CHAPTER THIRTY-FIVE

"Avery," Curt said. He caught himself and took a step back, trying to distance himself from her. He'd seen the cars in the driveway but never imagined one of them was hers.

Behind her, the emergency doctor, Jess somebody, pointed a handgun at him. "Drop the gun, Henry."

"Who are you?" Avery asked, ignoring her.

Curt couldn't point a gun at his daughter. What if it went off by accident? He lowered it slightly and looked at her, as if for the first time. She so closely resembled Morgan, but he could see himself in her, and he smiled. He lowered it to his side.

"Who are you?" Avery shouted.

"Bend down and put the gun on the floor," the doctor commanded.

Keeping his eyes on Avery, he answered Jess. "You put your gun down. Then no one will get hurt."

"If I put this gun down, you'll shoot us."

"I can shoot you anyway. If I wanted to, you'd already be dead. I'm not interested in killing anyone. I just want to get my stuff out of the safe, and then I'll be out of here. Avery, I need you to open the safe."

Avery looked at him, and he sensed she was in shock. "Avery, please open the safe, honey."

"I don't know the combination," she whimpered, and he thought she might cry.

"It's okay, A. I'm not going to hurt you. I would never hurt you. Now go ahead," he said softly. "I'll tell you the numbers."

As Avery moved toward the safe, the doctor stayed where she was, her gun aimed at his heart. He lifted his own arm and chuckled. "This is like a showdown, Doctor."

"You're not getting out of here, Henry."

Curt sighed, a long, slow exhale. "I have nothing to lose by trying. Avery, turn the dial three times to the left."

He waited silently, unwilling to take his eyes off the doctor's gun. How long would it take the police to get here once they called them? All he needed was the keys to one of the cars in the driveway. His escape would be quick, but would the police be faster?

He could collect their cell phones, but he knew the house had a landline. He had no idea how to disable it, other than searching through the place for every phone. Even then, he might miss one in an obscure place, and they could use it to call the authorities.

Fuck. He might have to take them with him, at least halfway down the driveway.

"Okay," Avery said. Her voice seemed stronger. Good. She wasn't in shock.

Curt gave her the first number of the combination, then the next two. A click told him the door was open.

"I need you to get me the backpack."

"Okay," she said, and he reached his left arm under his right and took it from her, then held his arm in the air until it settled onto his shoulder.

"There's a canvas in a plastic bag. I need that next."

He ventured a peek in Avery's direction. She was still, staring at her picture in its plastic shroud.

"How did you get this?" she asked. Out of the corner of his eye, he saw her moving toward him. He backed away, but she grabbed his arm. "How did you get this picture?" she asked again, louder.

Henry pulled away from her and switched the gun to his left hand, away from her. He needed to leave, fast.

Avery grabbed at him. "This is my drawing. I drew this! It has my name on it."

He started backing up, but she pulled at him. He whirled, trying to break free. "Avery, please. Back off."

"How do you know my name? How did you get this picture? I drew it for my father!"

Curt looked at her, saw the fear in her eyes. He could only imagine what she was thinking, that some stalker was following her. A madman, with a collection of Avery artifacts lining his bedroom walls and shelves.

He needed to go. He needed to go now. But he couldn't leave her with those thoughts. "My name is Curt Hutchins. I'm your father."

Avery's mouth flew open, and she stepped in front of him, between the doctor and her gun.

"Avery, move out of the way," the doctor commanded, but she either didn't hear or didn't care.

"My father is dead! He died on September eleventh!"

"I didn't die. I was in the lobby when the plane hit."

"Why didn't you come home? All these years…"

"It's hard to explain, honey."

"Why would you do something so cruel? We thought you were dead!"

"It would take a long time to tell you everything. More time than I have. But if you'd like, I'll call you and tell you the whole story."

"Do you know my phone number?" She no longer seemed scared, but fascinated.

"Yes," he said. "I know almost everything about you. I've been watching you all these years."

"It was you, wasn't it? You told Gram about the babysitter!"

"She wasn't responsible. She couldn't be trusted with you."

"Is Pop-pop alive, too?" she asked, her eyes wide open in wonder.

"I don't think so. Avery, I have to go."

"Don't move!" the doctor said as she slid around Avery, trying to shield her.

"You're not going to shoot me. You're a doctor."

"But I will. I'm a cop."

Curt spun around and couldn't believe his eyes. Officer Knox and another Garden police officer had their guns trained on him. The two women he'd kidnapped and Avery's wife were hovering at the edge of the garage door. As he shifted his gaze back and forth, two more police cars pulled into the driveway, their lights flashing.

"Drop the gun," Officer Knox commanded.

Curt looked at her gun. It was big, much bigger than the little pistol in his hands. The other cop's gun was just as big. If he moved his right arm, even a little, they'd shoot him. They wouldn't miss. He would never have to go to jail. He would never have to face the consequences of his actions.

But what would that do to Avery, seeing him bleed to death in front of her? He knew he was a stranger, that his death shouldn't affect her, yet how could it not? He'd been so selfish when he'd run away from Morgan and his children, concerned only for his own needs. He'd been selfish with Yvonne, too.

"Drop. The. Gun."

Curt knelt and gently placed the gun on the garage floor.

CHAPTER THIRTY-SIX

Imma sat back in her comfortable chair, enjoying the sunshine and the buzz from her pain medication. Jess had warned her about the high some patients got from the opioids, and Imma now understood why people became addicted to them. Her pain was nearly gone, and if she sat still—which was hard for her—her arm was comfortable. Better than that, though, was the feeling of peace. In spite of everything that had happened, she felt mellow and relaxed, and even a little happy. It was a great feeling, but she wasn't high enough to think it would last.

"Im," Jo whispered softly in her right ear. "You awake?"

"Hmm," Imma replied without opening her eyes.

"You have company. Avery and Lauren are here."

Poor Avery, Imma thought. Was it worse that your father was killed by terrorists or that he'd pretended to be? "Please tell them to come in."

Imma rubbed her eyes and yawned, then tried to sit up a little in her chair. Wincing, she stopped and decided to stay put.

"Avery! Lauren!" Imma said. "How nice to see you."

Both of them knelt in front of her, resting hands on both of her knees, mindful of her injured wing.

"How are you feeling?" Avery asked.

"High," Imma said. "Can you believe I'm seventy-five years old and have never taken a pain pill before?"

"That's probably why you're still going strong," Lauren said.

"Does it help your pain?" Avery asked.

"It really does." She reached out her good arm and placed her hand atop Avery's. "I wish I could do something for yours."

Jo walked in with folding chairs and opened them, and their visitors sat. Jo stood protectively behind Imma's good arm.

Avery stared from Imma's face to the forest beyond the sunroom and back again. "I don't think they make anything for this kind of pain."

Imma squeezed. "They do. It's called therapy, and it'll probably help a great deal."

"They think he killed his wife. Yvonne."

"Did he say that?"

"No, but the police grilled him for half the day yesterday, and apparently they had a lot of questions about her."

Imma didn't have the heart to share her own suspicions. What good would it do? "Avery, I don't know about that. He seemed crazy about her. She just got sick, and I think she was tired of pretending and left."

"The police can't find her."

"Who knows? Maybe she did what your dad did—you know, changed her name."

"I'm just glad you're okay."

"The wonders of modern medicine. A couple of nails and screws, and I'm good as new."

"How about your mental state? It must have been terrifying."

Again, Imma decided a little lie was best. "You know, Avery, he was never rough with us. I believe he intended to come back to set us free. And he didn't even cover our mouths, so Rio and I could talk."

"He had sandwiches for you in his backpack."

"See?"

Imma couldn't believe she was defending Henry, but she thought it was best for Avery. "Did you get a chance to talk to him?"

Avery nodded. "Last night. I was with him for about two hours, and he told me his whole story."

Imma didn't know what to say. Of course, she wanted to know the whole story herself, but it was rude to ask. Fortunately, Avery volunteered the information. "He said he was unhappy with my mom, unhappy with his job, and he took advantage of the circumstances and just walked away. He started a new life, and he chose Garden because he knew my brother and I would spend time here. He thought he'd get to see us once in a while."

Again, Imma remained silent, not pointing out that he'd bought the property with Yvonne before the attacks on the World Trade Center.

"He said it seemed like a good idea, but by the time he realized how stupid he'd been, it was too late."

"Where did he get the diamonds? And the Fabergé egg?"

Avery sighed. "He won't talk about the diamonds. And he said my grandfather gave him the egg. He decided to sell it after all these years because he saw an opportunity with the exhibit in New York. He'd met the ambassador at a gala, and he knew he collected eggs."

Imma didn't ask Avery if she believed him. What did it matter?

"I'm not sure I believe him," she said, and Imma almost chuckled at Avery's mind-reading. "But there really isn't anyone alive who can refute his statements."

"What happens next?"

"Can you believe it isn't illegal to fake your own death? So there's no consequences to him. The only charge they have is kidnapping you."

Imma wondered how long a sentence kidnapping would give him. Not long enough. And without a body, she was sure they couldn't arrest him in connection to Yvonne's disappearance.

"The police are having the egg authenticated. It's already in New York." Avery sighed. "I think the Garden police didn't want to be responsible for it."

"Wouldn't that be a miracle, if it's real? Your family must be thrilled."

"I haven't told them yet. We're leaving Garden now and heading to my grandmother's house. My aunt is there as well, so I can talk to them both. My grandmother will probably have to re-pay the insurance company, but I think she'd love to have the egg back."

"I imagine she would."

Finally, Avery smiled. "I'm just happy you're okay, Imma."

Imma squeezed her hand. "Me, too." Imma looked at Lauren. "I'm glad you're here for Avery." Imma didn't thank her for the night before, when Lauren had responded to the sound of breaking glass in the Giles living room and promptly called Mac's cell phone. Fortunately, Mac and Denise had been at the truck stop, just a few miles away, when the call came.

"I'll text you next time I'm in Garden." Both young women stood and kissed her on her right cheek. She didn't turn but listened as their footsteps faded across the house.

Just then, Jo returned to the sunroom. "I was thinking."

"Oh?" Imma said to Jo as she once again succumbed to the power of the pain pills, floating lazily in her chair.

"Since you can't drive for a while, it's the perfect chance for me to start again."

Her biggest worry when she'd been tied to that chair was Jo. Who would care for her? But Jo seemed fine, and Jess had told her that many people with mild Alzheimer's still lived independent lives. Jo might not have much time left. But neither might she. She knew that too well after her recent misadventure. Imma wasn't going to smother Jo to death.

"I think that's a great idea," Imma said as Jo softly kissed her temple.

"Rest," Jo said.

Imma closed her eyes again, but instead of letting herself drift off, she was thinking. *If I were Henry, where would I hide a body?*

About the Author

Jaime Maddox is the author of nine novels with Bold Strokes Books and was awarded the Alice B. Lavender Certificate for her debut novel, *Agnes*. She has co-authored a book on bullying with her son, Jamison, and written an unpublished children's book about her kids' uncanny ability to knock out their teeth. A native of Northeastern Pennsylvania, she still lives there with her partner and twin sons. Her best times are spent with them, hanging out, baking cookies, and rebounding baskets in the driveway. When her back allows it, she hits golf balls, and when it doesn't, she does yoga. On her best days, she writes fiction.

Books Available from Bold Strokes Books

Language Lessons by Sage Donnell. Grace and Lenka never expected to fall in love. Is home really where the heart is if it means giving up your dreams? (978-1-63679-725-0)

New Horizons by Shia Woods. When Quinn Collins meets Alex Anders, Horizon Theater's enigmatic managing director, a passionate connection ignites, but amidst the complex backdrop of theater politics, their budding romance faces a formidable challenge. (978-1-63679-683-3)

Scrambled: A Tuesday Night Book Club Mystery by Jaime Maddox. Avery Hutchins makes a discovery about her father's death that will force her to face an impossible choice between doing what is right and finally finding a way to regain a part of herself she had lost. (978-1-63679-703-8)

Stolen Hearts by Michele Castleman. Finding the thief who stole a precious heirloom will become Ella's first move in a dangerous game of wits that exposes family secrets and could lead to her family's financial ruin. (978-1-63679-733-5)

Synchronicity by J.J. Hale. Dance, destiny, and undeniable passion collide at a summer camp as Haley and Cal navigate a love story that intertwines past scars with present desires. (978-1-63679-677-2)

The First Kiss by Patricia Evans. As the intrigue surrounding her latest case spins dangerously out of control, military police detective Parker Haven must choose between her career and the woman she's falling in love with. (978-1-63679-775-5)

Wild Fire by Radclyffe & Julie Cannon. When Olivia returns to the Red Sky Ranch, Riley's carefully crafted safe world goes up in flames. Can they take a risk and cross the fire line to find love? (978-1-63679-727-4)

Writ of Love by Cassidy Crane. Kelly and Jillian struggle to navigate the ruthless battleground of Big Law, grappling with desire, ambition, and the thin line between success and surrender. (978-1-63679-738-0)

Back to Belfast by Emma L. McGeown. Two colleagues are asked to trade jobs. Claire moves to Vancouver and Stacie moves to Belfast, and though they've never met in person, they can't seem to escape a growing attraction from afar. (978-1-63679-731-1)

Exposure by Nicole Disney and Kimberly Cooper Griffin. For photographer Jax Bailey and delivery driver Trace Logan, keeping it casual is a matter of perspective. (978-1-63679-697-0)

Hunt of Her Own by Elena Abbott. Finding forever won't be easy, but together Danaan's and Ashly's paths lead back to the supernatural sanctuary of Terabend. (978-1-63679-685-7)

Perfect by Kris Bryant. They say opposites attract, but Alix and Marianna have totally different dreams. No Hollywood love story is perfect, right? (978-1-63679-601-7)

Royal Expectations by Jenny Frame. When childhood sweethearts Princess Teddy Buckingham and Summer Fisher reunite, their feelings resurface and so does the public scrutiny that tore them apart. (978-1-63679-591-1)

Shadow Rider by Gina L. Dartt. In the Shadows, one can easily find death, but can Shay and Keagan find love as they fight to save the Five Nations? (978-1-63679-691-8)

The Breakdown by Ronica Black. Vaughn and Natalie have chemistry, but the outside world keeps knocking at the door, threatening more trouble, making the love and the life they want together impossible. (978-1-63679-675-8)

Tribute by L.M. Rose. To save her people, Fiona will be the tribute in a treaty marriage to the Tipruii princess, Simaala, and spend the rest of her days on the other side of the wall between their races. (978-1-63679-693-2)

Wild Wales by Patricia Evans. When Finn and Aisling fall in love, they must decide whether to return to the safety of the lives they had, or take a chance on wild love in windswept Wales. (978-1-63679-771-7)

Can't Buy Me Love by Georgia Beers. London and Kayla are perfect for one another, but if London reveals she's in a fake relationship with Kayla's ex, she risks not only the opportunity of her career, but Kayla's trust as well. (978-1-63679-665-9)

Chance Encounter by Renee Roman. Little did Sky Roberts know when she bought the raffle ticket for charity that she would also be taking a chance on love with the egotistical Drew Mitchell. (978-1-63679-619-2)

Comes in Waves by Ana Hartnett. For Tanya Brees, love in small-town Coral Bay comes in waves, but can she make it stay for good this time? (978-1-63679-597-3)

Dancing With Dahlia by Julia Underwood. How is Piper Fernley supposed to survive six weeks with the most controlling, uptight boss on earth? Because sometimes when you stop looking, your heart finds exactly what it needs. (978-1-63679-663-5)

Skyscraper by Gun Brooke. Attempting to save the life of an injured boy brings Rayne and Kaelyn together. As they strive for justice against corrupt Celestial authorities, they're unable to foresee how intertwined their fates will become. (978-1-63679-657-4)

The Curse by Alexandra Riley. Can Diana Dillon and her daughter, Ryder, survive the cursed farm with the help of Deputy Mel Defoe? Or will the land choose them to be the next victims? (978-1-63679-611-6)

The Heart Wants by Krystina Rivers. Fifteen years after they first meet, Army Major Reagan Jennings realizes she has one last chance to win the heart of the woman she's always loved. If only she can make Sydney see she's worth risking everything for. (978-1-63679-595-9)

Untethered by Shelley Thrasher. Helen Rogers, in her eighties, meets much-younger Grace on a lengthy cruise to Bali, and their intense relationship yields surprising insights and unexpected growth. (978-1-63679-636-9)

You Can't Go Home Again by Jeanette Bears. After their military career ends abruptly, Raegan Holcolm is forced back to their hometown to confront their past and discover where the road to recovery will lead them, or if it already led them home. (978-1-636790644-4)

A Wolf in Stone by Jane Fletcher. Though Cassilania is an experienced player in the dirty, dangerous game of imperial Kavillian politics, even she is caught out when a murderer raises the stakes. (978-1-63679-640-6)

One Last Summer by Kristin Keppler. Emerson Fields didn't think anything could keep her from her dream of interning at Bardot Design Studio in Paris, until an unexpected choice at a North Carolina beach has her questioning what it is she really wants. (978-1-63679-638-3)

StreamLine by Lauren Melissa Ellzey. When Lune crosses paths with the legendary girl gamer Nocht, she may have found the key that will boost her to the upper echelon of streamers and unravel all Lune thought she knew about gaming, friendship, and love. (978-1-63679-655-0)

The Devil You Know by Ali Vali. As threats come at the Casey family from both the feds and enemies set to destroy them, Cain Casey does whatever is necessary with Emma at her side to bury every single one. (978-1-63679-471-6)

The Meaning of Liberty by Sage Donnell. When TJ and Bailey get caught in the political crossfire of the ultraconservative Crusade of the Redeemer Church, escape is the only plan. On the run and fighting for their lives is not the time to be falling for each other. (978-1-63679-624-6)

Undercurrent by Patricia Evans. Can Tala and Wilder catch a serial killer in Salem before another body washes up on the shore? (978-1-636790669-7)